2011

To my darling sister.
Hope you enjoy.
Bob

Y0-DNK-878

MILE HIGH MURDER

A Benjamin Roan Mystery-Thriller

Robert L. Hecker

Published by World Audience, Inc.

(www.worldaudience.org)

303 Park Avenue South, Suite 1440

New York, NY 10010-3657

Phone (646) 620-7406; Fax (646) 620-7406

info@worldaudience.org

ISBN 978-1-935444-74-9

©2011, Robert L. Hecker

This book is dedicated to all those who have a deep affection for old warbirds and dream of helping them live again in the wild blue.

CHAPTER ONE

To me, one of the greatest, most soul-satisfying manifestations of pure freedom is to cavort through blue skies in an old Stearman biplane. Spinning, diving, rolling and doing proverbial hand-springs through pristine skies always sets my heart pounding and my spirits soaring in the joy of pure freedom.

But flying, I also discovered, has its dark side---dark as death.

Death, especially murder, was the last thing on my mind when I parked my old Corvette near Jack Blucher's hanger that California morning. It was a great day for flying: brilliant sunshine, with just enough breeze from the distant Pacific Ocean to keep the temperature below boiling and to pin a thin layer of smog against the distant San Gabriel mountains.

Walking toward the old hanger that had Jack's "Angel's Flying School" sign painted over big double doors, I was stopped cold by a sound that sent a chill up my spine. I knew what it was without looking: a WWII P-51 fighter. A Mustang. Only the pulse-surging, deep-throated roar of a 1,600 horsepower 12-cylinder Merlin engine could make that sound, an arrogant roar that made your heart pump and your blood flow faster. I turned and watched the sun glint off a silver Mustang as it lifted off from a touch-and-go landing with the grace of a condor and the deep, magnificent thunder that could only come from such propeller-driven perfection.

The beautiful plane climbed and banked around for another approach while I walked over to where Jack was standing beside one of his two Stearmans. He'd just come down off an aluminum stepladder next to one of the Stearman's rotary engine and stood watching the P-51. Like all fliers he couldn't help himself. When one of the magnificent old warbirds was in the air, everything on the ground came to a halt.

"Ever get the urge to fly one of those?"

He answered without turning. "Been there, done that."

I wasn't surprised. In fact, I wasn't surprised at just about anything Jack told me about himself. There wasn't much he didn't know or hadn't done that had to do with the military, including how to kill a man with his bare hands if there wasn't anything else handy like a pencil or an AK-47.

"You like it better than a Stearman?"

"Not better. Different. Like the difference between making love to a big blonde and a nubile little brunette."

I gave a nod toward the Stearman. "And you chose the brunette."

He made a small shrug. "Blondes are expensive. You know how much it costs just to fuel up one of those monsters at six dollars a gallon? And they burn a gallon a minute, if you're careful. One nick on the prop, fifty thousand. Change an engine—if you can find one—and it's close to half a million. I'd have a heart attack every time some wild-blue-yonder yahoo climbed in the cockpit."

I watched the silver Mustang touch down and bounce twice before it settled to three points and coasted down the long runway.

"I see what you mean," I said. "If that were my plane, about now I'd be having a heart attack."

Jack spat on the asphalt. "At least he's on the runway. Last week he was all over the place. Damned near took out the entire flight line."

"Who owns that one? Some billionaire?"

"Not hardly." He gestured toward someone wearing white coveralls standing beyond the flight line in front of the hanger next to his. "That's her over there."

Her? He was right. Only a well-constructed woman could make flight coveralls look like a page out of Glamour Magazine. And while some men might have such a mass of black, curly hair, they couldn't possibly make it look like something you'd like to see splayed across a white pillow on a drowsy morning. She was too far away to be certain, but I sensed that her eyes, under heavy brows, were as dark and limpid as wet velvet.

Even though she was wearing pilot's coveralls, I couldn't believe any woman with those curves could handle a plane as powerful and demanding as a WWII fighter.

"She flies it?"

"Gives lessons. Name's Sharon Daadian."

Daadian? It sounded Middle Eastern. When tied in with her dark, sultry looks I would guess Armenian or Lebanese or maybe Israeli.

Jack jerked his head toward the hanger next to his. "That's her hanger."

Like Jack's, there was a sign over the hanger's big double doors, only this one read "Warbird Flying School."

"How does she give lessons? Mustangs are single-seaters."

"That one is. Some people yank out the radio and the behind-the-seat fuel tank to make room for a passenger behind the pilot."

"Must be a pretty tight fit."

He snorted. "Always was. In the big war, after a six hour mission some of those guys had to be helped out of the cockpit."

"But hers is a single-seater. You don't just climb into one of those off the street."

"No way. She starts her students in a Stearman. Then an AT-6. Then, if they're good, in the Mustang."

"Yeah, but those old warbird are irreplaceable. I don't see how she can bring herself to allow some student to even start the engine."

"The way I hear it, she needs the money."

"But if they wipe out her plane, she loses everything."

"Tell me about it."

The touch of worry in his voice surprised me. When he had sold his paintball range, I'd assumed he came away pretty well fixed. But I suppose buying and maintaining his two Stearmens and renting the big hanger soaked up a chunk of money. Thinking about it, I realized he didn't have that many students. I know he was letting me fly well below his usual fee. I'd allowed him to charge me less because I thought he didn't need the money. I'd have to talk to him about that.

Sunlight glinted off the distant P-51 as it circled to make another approach. I could still hear the sound of its engine, and I thought of the pilots in World War II taking off at dawn for combat in the chill, deadly skies over Germany not knowing whether they would ever return. And if their luck held out, doing it again the next day, and the next, and the next until ...

I shook my head. "I was born about fifty years too late."

Jack looked at me. "Too late for what?"

"To fly one of those."

"Not if you've got the money."

"I mean in combat. You know. Dogfights."

Jack was silent a moment, and I knew he was thinking the same thing. He might have flown modern jets in combat——it wouldn't surprise me if he had somewhere in the world——but modern aerial combat is conducted with long range missiles. You might never even see the enemy pilot who killed you, a far cry from the dogfights of World Wars I or II or even Korea.

"Yeah," he said. "Those days are gone forever."

"I'd still like to fly one someday."

"If you can afford it, why not now?"

At the thought my pulse began to throb. "You think I'm good enough?"

"Hell yes. During the war some of those kids had way less time in the air than you have. Come on, I'll introduce you."

Walking beside Jack toward the woman, a million reasons why I shouldn't to it churned through my mind: it would be too expensive, too dangerous. What if I crashed? What would happen to Roan Security? On the other hand, I could almost feel myself in the cockpit of the fighter, diving, rolling, dogfighting a phantom Messerschmitt or a Focke-Wulf, or hedge-hoping just above the trees to strafe make-believe ground targets. It was definitely something to think about.

When we were close enough to the woman for me to get a good look at her, my mind switched off all thoughts that did not involve soft lights and sexy music. She didn't wear a hat. Her dark curly hair was pulled back and loosely fastened so it tumbled down her back like a sunlit waterfall. Her face was a little too angular to be beautiful, more like handsome, with a small cleft in the chin. She was shading her eyes with her left hand which gave me a chance to check for a wedding ring. Beautiful hands, long, slender fingers, but no ring. If that meant anything. Some married people didn't like to wear a ring, as though it somehow gave the wrong message about their precious independence. I hoped she wasn't one of them.

"How's he doing?" Jack said.

She answered without taking her eyes off her million dollar investment, "I don't think he'll ever have the feel."

She meant that the guy flying the Mustang lacked a feel for his plane. Some people just couldn't become as one with a machine. You could sense it even in the way they drove a car. Riding with them kept you clutching the seat and trying not to suck air through your teeth at every curve and corner. Riding with someone who had a feel for his machine you could take a nap, confident you'd arrive safely at your destination.

Still, every pilot, just like every driver, wasn't a natural. But somehow they got the job done. The guy in the Mustang was obviously one of those who just got the job done--barely. I was glad it wasn't my plane he was horsing around like he was driving a garbage truck.

"He's better than he was last week." Jack said.

"And I'm ten years older."

We watched in silence for a moment, listening to the deep drone of the P-51's engine.

"You got time for another paddlefoot?"

Paddlefoot? Why had he said that? I was a long way from being a paddlefoot, whatever that was.

She took her hand down from shading her eyes and turned her deep, dark eyes on me. I noticed that the black pupils were surrounded by a ring of amber. From a distance I'd thought of her eyes as limpid, filled with the pain of unrequited romance. But up close I was not thrilled to discover that they could be as hard and impersonal as obsidian. Beneath dark eyebrows and impossible eyelashes, her eyes—at least when they looked at me—had the look of a woman wary of being approached by men.

I gave her my guaranteed heart-warming smile. "Hi."

It wasn't working. Those incredible eyes were like lasers, stripping away all my pretensions, leaving me feeling like a fifteen-year-old trying to lie to his mother.

"What do you fly?" she said.

Well, at least she had a warm, husky voice that took some of the chill out of her gaze. "Jack's Stearmans," I said.

When she sighed and her eyes kind of rolled back, Jack quickly said, "He's pretty good. Almost as good as me."

Her sensuous lips lifted in a tiny smile, "That good, huh?"
Dimples? I couldn't believe it. When she smiled her slightly hollow cheeks pulled into dimples that erased all evidence of steely strength. Who ever heard of a predatory hawk with dimples?

Jack grinned. His teeth weren't nearly as beautiful as hers, but his smile told me he liked her and wasn't offended by her jib. And if Jack liked someone, they had to be genuine. "It'll take a lot of work," he said. "You can make a fortune."

"In that case..." She held out her hand. "When do we start?"

Her hand was cool and slender, but with a strong grip, the kind you needed to control a powerful Mustang, whether a horse or an airplane.

"How about tomorrow?"

"Eight a.m."

"Right. Eight a.m."

The P-51 had landed and taxied off the runway. Even on the ground it looked beautiful but all business, like its owner. If you didn't handle either of them to their satisfaction, they could give you a lot of hurt. But when it comes to gorgeous women and beautiful airplanes, like most men, I was a willing fool.

"Don't be late." She went to meet the P-51 that was taxiing toward the flight line.

Watching the way her hips moved in the coveralls as she strode away I was certain I wouldn't be late. In fact, I might even wait here all night.

"Keep your mind on your work," Jack said. "She can't afford to lose that Mustang."

"You know me," I said. "When it comes to flying, I'm all business."

"Yeah, well, don't try mixing business with pleasure. You do and that plane will kill you."

I whacked him on the back to show I got the message and headed for the small airfield's locker room to change into my flying clothes. He was right, of course. Even flying a 250 horsepower Stearman that only cruised at a 100 miles an hour required concentration. I could imagine what it would take to control more than 1,600 horses at about 400 miles an hour. The real test in flying, however, the one that separated the men from the boys, was in landing. A lot of really good pilots never mastered the art of making their plane stop flying at the exact instant the wheels touched the earth, especially if there was any wind. It was tough enough touching down at fifty miles an hour in a Stearman. Landing a 6,000 pound package of dynamite at more than 100 miles an hour would require a small miracle, even for a born flyer like I am. And, unlike the Stearman, in a Mustang it would be hard to walk away from a mistake.

The locker room was not constructed for the country club set. Squeezed between the two corrugated steel hangers with doors so pilots could enter from either hanger or from the front, it looked as though it had been built as an afterthought. It reminded me of a school locker room with rows of lockers secured by combination padlocks and with long benches between the rows. The benches were bare wood on top of ugly linoleum that had curling edges. There was a lavatory in the back and four shower stalls. The tile shower floor was always wet, and the sagging tarpaper-covered roof leaked if there was even a hint of moisture in the air. Light came from grimy windows set high up at each end and from incandescent, 40-watt ceiling bulbs enclosed in thick, protective glass.

The place reeked of oil and gasoline. The smell was augmented by the pungent aroma of sweaty clothing, the result, no doubt, of fright-induced perspiration generated by student pilots during landing attempts.

On the walls framed photographs of famous aviators standing beside their vintage airplanes gave a hint of the room's age: The newest of the group were faded black and white images of Charles Lindberg, Amelia Earhart, Wily Post and Bob Hoover.

I wondered if Sharon had her own locker room or whether she was one of those lady jocks who believed in unisex facilities. With my luck I didn't think so.

There weren't many student pilots in the middle of a weekday so the room was deserted, the only sound the distant drum of an aircraft engine being worked on by mechanics in one of the nearby shops.

I'd opened my locker and was taking out my flight coveralls when I heard the side door leading to Sharon's warbird hanger open and close followed by the sound of steps.

There was a row of lockers between us so I couldn't see them, but it sounded like more than two people. They were talking--arguing actually—in some language I didn't understand. It was one of those languages that always seemed to be spoken as though the recipient was slightly deaf. My guess was eastern European: Bulgarian or Romanian. Or maybe Middle Eastern, like Farsi or Egyptian or Armenian.

Whatever it was, it sounded as though two men were berating a third, who was giving back as good as he got. They stopped out of my sight on the other side of the row of lockers, and I heard one of the locker doors being yanked opened without a break in their angry conversation.

Abruptly one of the two attackers called the third some kind of name. The word was quickly followed by the sound of a blow, and the row of lockers shook as somebody banged into it. I figured it was none of my business until the lockers shuddered again with such a heavy blow I thought they might come crashing down.

Even then my brain told me to keep out of it, but my curiosity forced me to walk around the row of lockers. I expected to see a group of burly, stubble-bearded grease monkeys who I hoped would respond kindly to a jovial smile.

Instead, like the click of a camera's shutter, my eyes locked on the picture of two tall, thin men wearing black business suits with white shirts and skinny, black neckties standing over the figure of a man wearing pilot's coveralls who was lying on the floor between the bench and the lockers. The two guys in suits had short black beards and long, thin noses. What brought me to a quick standstill was the sight of an automatic pistol in the hand of one of them. It was pointing at the man on the floor until its owner saw me, then the round, black eye in the end of the muzzle swung around to stare at me.

With the instincts of a scared cat, I dived for cover beneath the long bench, expecting the last thing I'd ever hear would be the explosion of the gun. Instead of my life flashing before my eyes, my brain was occupied with the search for a hole to crawl into. But the guy who seemed to be in charge pushed the gun's impersonal eye aside and snapped something to the gunman in a hard, tough voice, and the guy put the gun back in a shoulder holster. The head suit stared at me out of eyes that had the same friendly look as the gun's muzzle. He gave another sharp command, and the two of them walked out the front door, leaving it open.

The man on the floor sat up with one hand holding the top of his head like he was afraid it would fall off. He had the same thick, black hair and dead black eyes as the two suits, but he was clean shaven. I scrambled to my feet and went to help him, but he pushed me away and, using the bench for leverage, got to his feet and without a word, staggered out the side door leading to Sharon's hanger.

I sank down on the bench, feeling weak, struck by the thought that my life could have ended less than a minute ago. I was not prepared for death. Looking back, it seemed like an awfully short life, a life that I would very much like to continue for another few decades. By some standards it might not have been the most exciting or successful life in the world, but it was the only one I had, and I was very attached to it. Would anyone miss me if the gun had ended my life? Off hand, I couldn't think of anyone who would be affected for more than a few hours. I was an orphan, raised for the most part in foster homes. Because I had been a difficult charge--today they would say I had suffered from Hyper Active/Attention Deficient Disability--I had been shuffled from one home to another until I was sixteen and had turned my back on the system and tried not to look back. Maybe it was habit, but I did not make friends easily. Actually, I didn't try. I was pretty much self-contained, having learned early not to depend upon anyone. Maybe being something of a loner came from a long habit of self protection. I had lots of acquaintances, but—except for Jack—no really deep friends. Over the years there had been bright spots of affection from girls who had whirled in and out of my life. But the only ones who mattered had either died or wanted more from me than I was prepared to give.

Staring into the barrel of the gun had been a poignant reminder to mind my own business. If I were destined to die, I preferred it would be doing something of my own choosing, or—more likely—my own stupidity, such as taking a curve too fast in my Corvette or riding a spinning Stearman into the ground.

Which I came very close to doing a short time later.

CHAPTER TWO

My favorite wish from the time I was a little kid was to fly like a bird, which I guess was not particularly unique. Who hasn't watched a big hawk or eagle, its wings outstretched to heaven, floating effortlessly, riding the waves of an unseen ocean, high above all cares and worldly worries, and not wished they could fly. And who has not watched with envy as a sparrow or swallow swooped and darted in carefree aerial acrobatics, seemingly delirious with the fun of it.

I tried skydiving, but it wasn't the same; it wasn't really flying. The thrill was there, of course, the thrill of death sitting on your shoulders while a terminal velocity tornado tore at your sanity. And there was that heart-stopping eternity between the time you pulled the ripcord and you felt the shock of the chute opening. There is no thrill like it unless maybe its losing your footing when rock climbing without a rope, or when bullets are zinging past your head. But those heart-stopping thrills last only an instant (unless your parachute failed to open, then the thrill could, I'm sure, get increasingly intense until terminated abruptly). By adding wing-like cloth inserts between my legs and to my arms, I found it possible to glide and turn like a flying squirrel, but there was no feeling of majestic soaring. no real sense of flying.

So I'd had a fling at hang gliding and parasailing. I learned to ride the mountain-lifted up-drafts, to spiral heavenward on summer thermals, to soar like an eagle, to bank and turn majestically with nothing between me and the earth, making it as close to being a bird as humanly possible.

But humans had one great advantage over the birds that I missed. Power. With prodigious effort some birds can fly more than a hundred miles per hour. And some can plummet like a kamikaze. Others can dart, and twist, and turn with unbelievable agility. And some can even hover if they beat at the air like berserk fan-dancers.

But they couldn't thrill to the sense of raw, soul-churning horsepower. And no bird ever experienced 6gs of gravity trying to pull their brains into their stomach. And no bird ever looped, rolled, spun and stalled or pulled out of an inadvertent spin with a sickening sense of relief.

Actually, I got to be pretty good at aerobatics in a Stearman. When Jack Blutcher had opened his flying school at Stead Field, a small, private airport located in an area of gently rolling hills inland from my office in Newport Beach, California, it was the perfect excuse for me to learn what real flying was like, to have wings with a powerful engine and a propeller.

The first time Jack took me up in one of his two bright-red and brilliant-yellow 1941 Boeing Stearman biplanes and the 220 horses in the Continental engine lifted us off the earth with a surge of power that pressed me back into the seat with the wind in my face and roar of the engine in my ears, I knew this was the answer.

I'd flown before, of course. Commercial airlines, skydiver's lift planes, and passenger helicopters. But this was not the same. Sitting in the rear cockpit of the old Stearman PT-16, wearing goggles and a WW-I aviator helmet buckled under my chin, with the vibration of the powerful engine and the blur of the spinning prop bringing joy to my body, looking over the side of the open cockpit with the wind whipping my face, banking and rolling with nothing between me and the earth far below....this was Rickenbacker and the Red Baron, this was Frank Luke shooting down observation balloons and Snoopy flying his dog house, this was flying.

Fortunately, my company, Roan Security, in Newport Beach had grown to the point where my staff was able to run the operation with a minimum of my interference, so I was able to get away for the necessary hours each week to pursue my new hobby.

It had taken more than a year before I was able to dance around the sky in one of Jack's Stearmans with what I hoped was the grace of a ballet dancer, and when Jack and I relived WW-I dogfights (sans guns, of course), twisting and turning in mock battles, I was hooked for life.

Usually, Jack won the dogfights. Strange how realizing that if it were a real fight you would be plummeting toward the earth in flames, could produce heart-stopping moments of terror. At least I had a parachute. I could only imagine the hopeless fear a WW-I pilot, a mile above the earth with no parachute, must have felt when an enemy fighter bored in for the kill. But I was getting better.

Today I planned on shooting Jack down with a maneuver called a yo-yo I'd read about in a book about aerial combat.

By 10:00 A.M. I was up in the blue in one of Jack's Stearman biplanes practicing the maneuver. A warm wind was in my face and the sun was at my back, and tearing up the sky with loops, rolls, stalls and spins had driven away all thoughts of the incident in the locker room. Three thousand feet below me, the hills, still mostly green from spring rains, gently rose to the 6,000 foot crests of the San Joaquin range. Way off to the west I could just make out the blue of the Pacific. The Stearman's engine was throbbing perfectly, and cavorting in a clear blue sky, I felt like the cross between a darting sparrow and a soaring eagle I had always dreamed of.

The old Stearman took it upon itself to remind me that if I didn't keep my mind on what I was doing, I could die just as quickly in the air as on the ground. In a fit of joyous euphoria, I put the Stearman through a series of rolls. But, like a fool, I failed to concentrate, allowing the plane's nose to get too far below the horizon and it fell out in a spin. I regained control, telling myself to keep my stupid mind on what I was doing, and began climbing back to my mile high practice altitude.

I never made it.

Something huge shot past about ten feet over my head with a deafening sound. A blast of turbulence flipped the Stearman over on its back in a flat, inverted spin so quick I thought I had been hit by a 747. I fought to get the nose down, afraid to look back at the empennage because it might not be there. "Bail out!" my brain screamed. "Bail out!"

But if I tried it while in the spin, I'd probably be hit by a flailing wing or the whipping empennage, if the plane still had an empennage.

Oh, that beautiful Stearman. It responded to my frantic hands and feet and put its nose down. Then, as though to make up for the mistake, it tried to kill me by refusing to stop spinning. But with the nose down, I had it. Using the stick and rudder, I brought it out of the spin without tearing the wings off with less than a thousand feet to spare. Climbing again I looked around for the big jet that had just missed me.

It wasn't a jet. I caught sight of the tapered, square-tipped wings and long nose of a silver P-51 as it banked in a forty-five degree turn. What the hell was wrong with that idiot? He'd almost hit me. If he had, it would surely have killed me and maybe him.

I watched him sweep around, hoping to catch a glance of his I.D. number and markings so I could report him to the FAA after I'd beat him about the head a few times.

I didn't get the chance. He came around in his turn and I found myself looking at the P-51's huge propeller as it bored in toward me.

It took me about one nanosecond to realize that the first pass hadn't been an accident. Charging toward me at about three hundred mile an hour, he was going to do it again. And this time if the turbulence created by a near miss at 300 mph flipped the Stearman into a spin, I wouldn't have enough altitude to recover. They'd have to dig me out of a smoking hole in a California hill, chalking it up to another stupid pilot who'd made one mistake too many.

As the silver disc of the P-51's steel propeller closed in on the fragile Stearman, I had the terrifying sensation a mouse must feel watching the outstretched talons of a diving hawk.

But I had one advantage: the Stearman could maneuver quicker than the P-51. With my nerves screaming at me to do something, I waited until the last second, then whipped the agile Stearman into a diving right turn and the P-51 rushed by so close I could have counted its rivets.

For an instant, as the Stearman bounced and bucked in the P-51's turbulent wake, I thought I'd cut it too close. I fought to keep the Stearman from going over on its back, using all my strength and skill to work the stick and rudders. When the old plane finally steadied and I pulled it out in a shallow turn, the sweat of fear and exertion was stinging my eyes and making my hands slippery.

Frantically, I searched the sky for the Mustang.

There it was, high and to the right, circling in a tight turn to come in behind me for another pass.

Could I do it again? Slip aside at the last second? Maybe once or twice, but sooner or later he would catch on to the maneuver and chew me up like a berserk weed eater.

Desperately, my brain searched for another maneuver. I was down to about five hundred feet so I didn't have a lot of sky to work with. A Luffberry circle? I could turn inside him all day. But all he had to do was climb and pounce, and he could do that all day. Except that it would probably only take a couple of pounces and I would be gopher food.

What could I do?

Playing cat and mouse was definitely not the answer. Eventually the cat would win, unless I could find a hole to crawl into.

That was it! Get out of the sky! The sky was his domain. Find a hole he couldn't enter. And find it quick because he was already lunging in for the kill.

It took all my will power to tear my eyes away from the charging P-51 and frantically search the ground. Hills, hills, damn, damn hills. And trees. Bushes. Damn California. If this were Kansas or Oklahoma, I'd have a whole prairie for a landing field.

I yanked my gaze back to the Mustang. He was coming. Lower. Anticipating a diving turn. Boring in behind the killer propeller.

Now! It had to be now! Field or no field. Better to smash into a hill or a tree than to be chewed up by a shark.

I yanked back on the throttle, shoved the stick forward and dived for the ground.

The Mustang dived with me.

There! A meadow the size of a Persian carpet, rimmed with trees. Could I come in over the trees? Not enough room! Dive between them. Oh God. Was there enough clearance? Tilt the wings a little. Flash through the opening, leaves slapping, branches flying, the P-51 arrowing overhead. Straighten, straighten! Fight the turbulence. Hit the hard ground, dry, dead grass flying off the landing gear. Bounce. Roll, roll. Bouncing like a ship in a gale. Working hard to keep the wing tips off the unyielding ground. Trees on the other end of the field charging forward. Stop, damn it, stop!.

I whipped the rudder hard over and there was just enough headway to whip the plane's tail around and the plane came to a lopsided stop in the shade of the trees, the tips of the prop trying to harvest the dry grass.

I sat for a second in stupefied disbelief. Impossible. I couldn't be alive. Not after that.

Automatically, I cut the engine. I should be yelling for joy, waving my arms in victory. But I couldn't move. I was consumed by wonder, breathing fast and deep, basking in a vast surge of relief.

It was sound that brought me back to reality; the heart pounding sound of a diving Mustang. My head jerked around. It was him, coming in at treetop level, already almost on top of me.

Why? He couldn't land. He had no guns, no bombs. What the hell was he trying to do? I decided not to stick around to find out.

But I only had time to get one leg out of the cockpit when he flashed past. He had his cockpit canopy open and one arm sticking out. As he whipped past, small gouts of dirt jumped from the ground near the Stearman, and I heard the unmistakable whine of ricocheting bullets.

The son-of-a-bitch was shooting at me!

Even as the realization struck me, he was gone, climbing into the blue, the deep roar of the big engine fading like a dream.

He wouldn't be back. What would be the point? I could hide under the trees where he couldn't find me. And there wasn't a field nearby where he could land the Mustang.

Suddenly, the adrenaline that had kept me charged with fear-driven energy seemed to drain from my body leaving me weak and shaky. Climbing out of the cockpit was one of the hardest tasks I'd ever faced. Finally I was able to lean against the Stearman's wing. My feet were blessedly flat on the earth, but my brain was locked on the image of the P-51 pilot, staring at me over his pistol as he flashed past. Despite his helmet, I recognized him. It was Sharon's student pilot, the same guy I'd tried to help in the locker room.

CHAPTER THREE

It took almost two hours after I called Jack on my cell phone for a flat-bed truck to arrive with a winch and two burly men. Jack did a walk-around check of the Stearman, pulling broken branches and tree leaves from the wings' wire braces and the undercarriage. He looked at the space between the two trees where I'd angled in to land and shook his head. "How the hell did you do that? Those trees are closer together than the wing span."

Staring at the small space between the trees, even I couldn't believe it. "I tilted the wings. Just made it."

He stared at the place where the plane's tire tracks began a bare thirty feet from the trees. "Okay. But how the shit could you get back level before you touched down? You couldn't have had more than a couple of seconds."

"Stark fear," I said. "I guess it speeds up your reflexes."

Jack nodded as though he knew what I was talking about. "It do have that effect." He stared at the plane's tracks where they'd mashed down the brush and weeds, and at the weeds whose tops had been chewed off by the Stearman's propeller. "Fear and a shit pot of luck."

Looking at the tracks and where the Stearman sat just short of the trees on the other side of the small field, I had to reevaluate my ideas about luck. I'd never considered myself lucky. If anything, I'd always thought lady luck had turned her back on me. It had begun early. I had been left on the steps of an orphanage as a baby. I'd grown up, rebellious, bitter about my bad luck,

I guess you could say that somewhere along the way my luck had changed because today I was more than six feet tall, in great physical shape, reasonably good looking, and the owner of a successful business.

But except for the good looks, luck had little or nothing to do with it. I'd labored at dozens of dirty jobs, put myself through school and college, started a business specializing in industrial security. My good health came from being strict about my diet, plus hard physical workouts, including a daily swim around the Newport Beach pier. And I sure wasn't lucky in love. I'd always had to worked hard to get a date with a pretty girl. Well, maybe that had changed after I grew taller and put on a little weight and learned that a smile and a compliment worked better than a scowl and a growl.

Still, I hadn't consider myself lucky—until now. I'd been almost killed by a maniac in a plane and had barely escaped a fusillade of bullets. All things considered, it might be a good time to take a vacation in Las Vegas or at some Indian-owned casino.

With the help of the winch we were able to muscle the Stearman up a ramp onto the bed of the truck. We had to trim a few lower branches from couple of scrub oaks to haul the plane out of the small field. It would have been virtually impossible to truck the plane through the narrow mountain roads then through traffic all the way to the airport, but there was a dirt road a couple of miles from the field where we found a stretch straight enough and long enough to act as a runway. After stationing guys at each end to halt any cars, and with me sulking in the passenger's seat because Jack thought I might be too nervous to fly, Jack took off and flew the plane back to the airfield.

Maybe it was best that I didn't have to concentrate on flying. My mind was churning with a mixture of anger because that idiot had tried to kill me and wonder about why. I'd never met the guy, never seen him in my life until that incident in the locker room. I'd even tried to help him. So why did he want me dead?

After analyzing all the facts and coming up with no answer, I decided the best solution would be to ask him.

Coming in to land, I saw the Mustang parked in front of Sharon Daadian's hanger, but no sign of the pilot.

Immediately after we'd landed and rolled the Stearman into Jack's hanger where he could give it a good inspection, I told him I was going to look for the bad guy.

"He's probably long gone by this time," he said.

"That girl, Sharon. She'll know where to find him."

"She won't tell you."

I'd started for the big hanger doors, but Jack's words stopped me. "Why not?"

"She won't believe you for one thing. And for the second, she'll think you're a nut case."

I stood staring at him. He was right. I hadn't a shred of proof. It would be my word against his, unless I could beat the truth out of him. And to do that I first had to find him.

"Yeah, well, we'll see how much of a nut I am when I bring her that guy's balls on a platter."

"If you need any help, I'll be here."

"Yeah, Okay."

I was confident I could handle the guy. When I'd seen him in the locker room he hadn't looked like a jock. Also, Jack had spent a lot time teaching me how to defend myself. Jack knew every trick in the book. He'd been with Special Forces in the U.S. Army and for a time with the French Foreign Legion as well as fought as a mercenary in many parts of the world. As a result he knew more ways to kill or maim with his bare hands than the worst jock on those no-holds-barred television shows. He'd taught me enough so I was confidence I could handle anyone as skinny as the guy I'd seen.

Walking past the P-51 in front of Sharon's hanger, I could feel heat from the engine. There was no mistake. This was the plane that had tried to kill me. It was hard to believe that such a beautiful piece of machinery had been developed to kill people and break things. In the air it was as elegant as a dolphin in water, effortlessly skimming the azure currents. Even resting on the ground it looked graceful. Graceful but deadly. I couldn't believe I'd survived aerial combat with it. No, not with it——with its pilot. But now he was on my turf.

Inside Sharon's spacious hanger there was a plane I recognized as an AT-6 World War II trainer. Like the P-51, it had Sharon's flying school logo painted on the side of the fuselage.

Sharon had walled in a section in the rear of her hanger to form a large office cubicle. I opened the door and walked in without knocking. I hoped I would surprise the guy I was looking for. But the man I surprised was a stranger wearing a tan suit with a crisp white shirt and no necktie. He had a large head crowned with precisely cut dark brown hair. His face was round with smallish dark-brown eyes. His teeth were so white they dominated his face. He sat in a high backed wooden chair leaning forward as he talked to Sharon across a big oak desk that looked as thought it had been purchased in a yard sale that specialized in beat up Civil War relics. I had interrupted the guy in the middle of a sentence which seemed to annoy him because he sat up straight and glared at me.

But his glare paled in comparison to Sharon's. "Yes?" she said. There was so much ice on the word it froze me in my tracks.

"Uh, I was looking for that guy, your student pilot."

"Jorge?" She gave it the Spanish pronunciation: hor-hey. "What for?"

Jorge? The Spanish name explained his black hair and dark complexion. "Where is he?" I said. "I'd like to talk to him."

"Why?"

It was the guy who'd asked, immediately telling me he knew the guy. I considered ignoring him, then decided that a little shock effect might produce an impulsive answer. "To find out why he tried to kill me."

It worked, sort of. The guy stood up with the swift reflexes of an athlete and took a step toward me. It was a reaction I hadn't expected, and I backed a step. "What the fuck do you mean?" His voice was quiet, but it had a deadly quality like the sound a rattlesnake would make if it could talk.

His move and his voice were so belligerent I half expected an attack, and I turned a little so I could kick if necessary. "Just who are you?" I said.

He gave me another surprise. His eyes crinkled with humor, changing his attitude so quickly he was like a different person. He smiled with his beautiful white teeth and held out his hand. "Morris Harlen," he said.

I shook his hand, fighting bewilderment at his chameleon-like change. "Benjamin Roan."

"Roan? Anything to do with Roan Security?"

Another surprise. He'd heard of my company. "That's me," I admitted.

"Proud to know you. I've heard good things about your company. Might be over to see you one day."

"Any time." The subservience in my voice irritated me. He'd taken over the situation with the overpowering bonhomie of a talk show host.

"You know Miss Daadian, of course."

I glanced at her. "We've met."

"What's this about Jorge?" she asked.

I turned toward her, working on my own attitude to get the ball back in my court. "I was up in the Stearman. That S.O.B. tried to ram me."

"Tried to? You mean an accident?"

"The first time I thought it might be an accident. He came so close I spun out."

Harlen said, "First time?"

"He came at me again. This time I was ready. Just did get out of his way. But when he came around again..."

Sharon stood up. "I don't believe it. Why would he do that?"

"That's what I'd like to know. Where is the bastard?"

Harlen said. "He was in the Mustang and you were in a Stearman?"

"That's right. He—"

"If that were true, you'd be dead."

"Yeah? Well, it is true and I'm not."

"He's my best pilot. You wouldn't have a chance."

"Your pilot? He works for you?"

"Part of my team. That's why—"

I interrupted him: "You're gonna have to get another player. When I finish with the S.O.B. he'll be flying a kite."

"I don't believe this," Sharon said. "When I see him we'll get this whole thing straightened out."

"Where is he? We'll do it right now."

"I have no idea. He left almost an hour ago."

Was she covering for him? After all, he was one of her student pilots. Could their relationship go beyond that? I remember he was pretty good looking if you liked the Darth Vader type.

"I don't suppose you'd give me his address."

"That's right. I wouldn't."

The anger building inside of me was beginning to effect my ability to think clearly, and I took a deep breath, fighting to get my rising blood pressure under control. There was no reason why she should give Jorge's home address to a stranger just because he'd come in with some wild story she didn't believe anyway. It might even be better if I didn't square off with the bastard until I had my attitude a little more under control. As Jack had told me time after time: 'Don't get stupid angry; get smart angry. Use it. Don't let it use you.' When I saw Jorge, or whatever his name was, I wanted answers, not blood. Well, answers first, then blood.

I sucked in a long, slow breath before I asked, "When is he coming back?"

"Tomorrow. Eight a.m."

"I'll be here."

I moved to the door.

"Bring some proof," Harlen said.

I lost a step, then went out and closed the door. Proof? I had no proof. As far as I knew there were no witnesses. No real damage to the Stearman and certainly not to the Mustang. The fact that I'd made an emergency landing in a field was not proof I'd been forced down. Damn. Why couldn't the bastard have been a better shot. A couple of bullet holes in the Stearman would be proof enough.

In the deserted locker room I was still fuming as I changed my clothes, trying to think of something that would prove my story. In the odd chance someone on the ground had seen the P-51 trying to bring down the Stearman, they would probably think it was a couple of nuts playing combat. And how would I locate a witness anyway? Place an add in a newspaper? The Internet? I was as likely to turn up a friendly witness as Senator Kennedy had been at Chappaquiddick.

The sticking point that was hard for me to believe was motive. What was the guy's beef with me? Except for that brief encounter in the locker room I'd never seen the guy in my life. So it had to go back to that.

I tried to remember the details of the event, searching for some clue, however minute. Jorge. That was a Latino name, Spanish for George. I'd heard him quarreling with the other two guys, who, now that I thought of it, also looked kind of Latino. But their language sure hadn't been Spanish.

His locker. When they'd knocked Jorge down, I think he'd been trying to get into his locker. Maybe there was something important inside, even his home address. With his address I could pay him a visit. I would get the story straight from the horse's mouth, one way or the other.

I walked around the row of lockers to the other side where I'd seen him. If the lock on his locker's door was a cheap padlock like mine, I was quite sure I could open it.

I never got the chance to find out.

I recognizing him instantly. He was slumped on the floor, his back against the far wall, his head leaning back, his eyes open, staring. I didn't have to check his pulse to know he was dead. He was wearing his flight coveralls, and the front over his chest was covered with blood, some of it still wet, glistening. Bullet wounds wouldn't produce that much blood. As near as I could tell without a close examination, he'd been stabbed several times. And judging by the number of flies circling like miniature buzzards it had happened some time ago.

Moving carefully so I wouldn't contaminate the crime scene, I backed up, then went back into Sharon Daadian's hanger and to her

27

office. This time I knocked on the door before I pushed it open. She was alone behind her desk, shuffling through papers. The expectant look on her face turned to a scowl when she recognized me.

"I told you he isn't here," she said.

"I know where he is," I told her. "You'd better call the police."

"The police...?"

"And you can cancel his lesson for tomorrow. In fact, you can cancel all of them."

CHAPTER FOUR

It was the time of death that saved me. When the coroner's preliminary examination established the time of death as approximately an hour ago, I had plenty of witnesses to prove I'd been miles away helping put the Stearman on the flatbed truck.

Answering questions from the investigating detectives dragged on for almost two hours. It shouldn't have taken that long; I told them all I knew in the first fifteen minutes. But they had me repeat my story two more times. I wasn't sure if it was because they were slow thinkers, or because they hoped I'd make a mistake. After the third time I began to suspect it was the former. Maybe they wouldn't have been so thorough, but Sharon—or someone—had told them my story about being shot at by somebody flying the P-51, and I thought it had been the dead guy, which, if true, made me a prime suspect with a revenge motive. There were also numerous questions about why Jorge could have wanted me dead, questions for which I had no answers.

When they asked me about it and I'd explained how he'd tried to kill me and I'd managed to survive, they looked as skeptical as had Harlen and Sharon. They looked even more skeptical when I told them how Jorge, when he'd failed to force me to crash, had tried to shoot me. They did, however, send and officer out to search the Mustang for a gun. Naturally, he didn't find one.

I assumed that after killing him, the killer—or killers—had taken the gun, but it left me wondering why Jorge hadn't been able to defend himself if he had the gun with him.

The detectives kept asking me about the other two men I'd seen fighting with Jorge. As of now, they were the prime suspects in his death, and I was the only person who could identify them, which, they said, could be the reason why Jorge had tried to kill me—if, in fact, he had tried. I described them as well I could. By the time the detectives finished asking me a million questions about them, I wasn't sure myself what they looked like.

When the detectives finally left I was so drained I wasn't even sure of my own name. The only thing of which I was at all certain was that now I'd never learn Jorge's motive for trying to kill me.

But, whatever it was, it was over. I was out of it.

"Maybe not," Jack told me a little later. We were in the rear of his hanger where he had shoved together a desk, a few chairs and filing cabinets to form a cluttered office. "If those two guys are so worried about you being able to identify them that they sent Jorge to kill you, now they've got another reason."

"Jorge's murder?"

"Assuming they killed him, you're the only one who could tie them to the murder."

Something along the same lines had occurred to me, but I'd tried to dismiss it. Subconsciously it had been giving me chills since I'd found Jorge's body; now Jack's words increased the chill. I said, "You think they'll try again?"

"Maybe not," Jack said as though he didn't really mean it. "By now they're probably on a plane to wherever they came from."

"And if they're not?"

Jack's grin was about as reassuring as that of a cannibal looking at a missionary. "Then I wouldn't go in any dark alleys for awhile."

A hot tide of resentment drove away some of the chill. The thought of two men looking to do me great bodily harm was going to haunt my life for days, perhaps weeks, forcing me to shy at ominous shadows, to treat every stranger as a potential killer, and to lose a lot of peaceful sleep.

Then another thought struck me, one that seemed to make little sense. "I understand why they might want to kill me," I said, "but why Jorge? He was on their side."

"They had a fight with him. That leads me to believe they were unhappy with him."

"A fight is one thing, murder is another."

30

"Assuming it was the same guys."

I wished he hadn't said that. I'd assumed I only had to worry about two potential killers. Could there be more? "Maybe those two guys were mad at him for failing to kill me."

Jack nodded. "Yeah. Since he didn't break the connection by taking you out, they did it by taking him out."

As much as I disliked the idea of anyone being murdered, I found myself smiling. "Right. Without him, there's no way of finding them, so I'm off the hook."

"Looks like it. You can get on with your exciting life."

Now that hurt. I guess that next to Jack's sybaritic life style, mine did seem pretty boring, but, hey, I liked it. Besides, since he'd given up freelance soldiering, his own life wasn't all bullets and wild women.

My scathing reply was interrupted by sunlight reflecting from the hanger's painted concrete floor as the small personnel door in the base of the big hanger doors opened, followed by the echoing sound of footsteps as someone approached through the hanger. An instant of panic made me tense for flight. Could it be the killers coming for me?

I jerked my head around. Damn the shadows. Because of the late afternoon gloom inside the hanger, all I could make out was the figure of a tall, slender man striding toward me, his arms swinging. That was good. He wasn't carrying a rifle, nor, as far as I could see, a pistol.

I relaxed. With Jack's help, I was confident I could take care of myself against anyone who wasn't armed with a gun, or a knife, or a club. Still, I was not unhappy when the steps got close enough for me to see that the guy making them was Morris Harlen, the guy I'd met earlier in Sharon Daadian's hanger.

"Mr. Roan," he said as he approached. "I was hoping to catch you before you left."

"You just make it. I'm heading back to my office."

He stopped and held out his hand across Jack's desk. "You must be the famous Jack Blutcher."

Jack stood up, "The Blutcher part's right." He stared at Harlen for an instant with his eyes kind of hooded. I knew that look. He was put off by Harlen's air of bonhomie that didn't quite seem to fit him. Then he took Harlen's hand. "And you're Morris Harlen."

"You've heard of me?" Harlen seemed delighted that Jack knew who he was. But I could sort of understand why. Jack might not be a famous movie star, but during the few months he'd lived in the area his combat exploits had become common knowledge, due as much as anything to his love for telling stories about himself, most of which I knew were true, although they might be somewhat embellished for his audience.

"Everybody knows about Harlen Waste Management," Jack said. "What can I do for you?"

Without waiting for an invitation, Harlen sat in one of Jack's chairs. "Did Mr. Roan tell you Jorge Mendez was working for me?"

Jack shook his head, and I sat up straighter. Did Harlen's visit have something to do with the murder?

"Had no idea," Jack said. He did not ask the question that was burning a hole in my brain: what did waste management have to do with pilot training? But Jack sat quietly, waiting.

As though he read my mind, Harlen said, "Advertising. I'm putting together a team to perform at air shows."

"Air shows?" I couldn't keep quiet any longer. "For waste management?"

"Why not? Air shows have a larger attendance than all your sport programs combined. They're all over the world. Four hundred a year in the U.S. alone. You can't beat that for advertising."

"This 'team' of yours," Jack said. "One pilot?"

Harlen brushed his hand across his face in disgust. "Now, one pilot. Jorge was the second."

"The second?" I said. "Who's the first. Does he train here too?"

"In a way. It's Daadian."

"Sharon Daadian?" Jack's voice said he didn't believe it.

32

"That's right."

"She's going to fly her Mustang to advertise your company?"

"Well, it isn't exactly her Mustang. Not yet."

Jack slowly nodded. "So that clears that up."

"Clears up what?" I said.

"How she could afford to fly that gas-eating monster that makes millionaires out of mechanics and gas stations." He looked at Harlen. "I suppose you pay for the maintenance and ground crew."

Harlen smiled. "Part of my team."

"That's only one Mustang," I pointed out. "What was Jorge going to fly? Or were you going to alternate?"

"I've got my eye on another Mustang."

"And now?" Jack asked.

Harlen's smile was rueful. "With the unfortunate...uh... thing that happened to Jorge, I'm short a pilot." He looked at Jack. "I understand you've flown Mustangs. How would you like to be part of my team?"

For the first time since I'd known him, Jack's eyes got a misty look of old memories, and they brought a thin smile to his craggy face. Just as quickly his eyes hardened and his face assumed its usual expressionless mask. He shook his head. "Too damned old," he said. "I can handle a Stearman, but pulling six or seven gs would kill me."

"Not with a g-suit. You could handle up to ten gs."

My mouth was hanging open, but I couldn't help it. Jack was a terrific pilot, but he might be right. Putting on an exhibition at an air show would require at least some aerobatics at high g forces. Jack had flown high performance planes enough to know that he probably couldn't handle the physical beating over a prolonged period.

"Maybe," Jack said. "You willing to risk a million dollar plane to find out?"

Harlen's laugh had more than a touch of insincerity. "I might be willing to take a chance on the million dollars, but those planes are hard to replace."

Jack's voice was as dry as Mohave dust when he said, "Not as hard as my life."

"Point taken." Harlen hesitated before he stood up. "Well, if you think of anyone, let me know."

He'd taken a couple of steps toward the hanger doors when Jack said, "How about Ben here? He's a hell of a pilot."

I stared at Jack, wondering if he'd lost his mind. It was not only the first compliment I'd ever heard from him, but performing aerobatics in a 140 horsepower Stearman was a far cry from risking life and limb in a 1,600 horsepower warbird.

Harlen's slow turn toward me and his long stare gave him time to give the idea some thought. I was sure it also gave him enough time for a good laugh. Instead he said, "I didn't realize you were checked out in a Mustang."

For a fraction of a second I considered lying. The idea of careening around the sky in one of the big warbirds was vastly appealing. How difficult could it be? A plane was a plane, wasn't it? And if Jack thought I could do it...

Then reason took over and I spread my hands. "Never flew one in my life."

Harlen's eyes swiveled to look at Jack, who quickly said, "How soon is your first show?"

"I was hoping to make Acapulco in July."

"Two months. He could be ready by then."

The idea, incredulous as it was, set my heart pounding. I could almost feel myself flying one of the big P-51s, zooming around the wild blue at 20,000 feet, sweeping down to hedge-hop across the landscape at 400 miles per hour. Then reality kicked in. "You've got to be kidding."

"Shit," Jack said. "In world war two they had kids who'd never been in a plane flying combat in six months."

"Government planes," Harlen said. "Nobody gave a damn if they smashed them all to hell."

"The difference is that he's already a good pilot. I think he

34

could do it."

Harlen used one hand to scratch at the back of his neck. "Aerobatics in a Stearman is one thing, precision flying in a Mustang is another."

"I saw your guy Jorge fly. He didn't have it."

"Maybe. But I need a pilot who can put on a good show."

"It doesn't need to be fancy. They've got aerobatic planes for that. You just need somebody to make a few passes. Just seeing and hearing a couple of Mustangs doing a flyby at about fifty feet would be enough."

Harlen was silent, his forehead furrowed with doubt.

Jack gave him a verbal nudge: "You won't get another pilot this late in the season."

Harlen kept me on pins and needles another few seconds before he said to Jack, "Will you work with him?

Jack lifted his hands. "Don't have a plane."

"All right." Harlen stepped close to me, staring into my eyes, which I was sure were bulging out like two marbles. "You work with Sharon and Jack. You qualify with the FAA, I pick up the tab: lessons, fuel, maintenance, everything. But if you quit after I put out all that money, you pay for it."

The desire to fly one of the big warbirds clouded my sense of reality--and mortality—and I started to agree. Then what he had said about paying if I quit began to register and my finely honed sense of self preservation kicked in. "I..uh..I don't see how I can make that kind of promise. I..."

"Why not?" Jack said. "I thought you wanted to fly one of those monsters."

"I do. But"—My ego wouldn't let me tell him it was about the money.—"we're not talking a couple of hours a week. It'll have to be a full time job. I've got a business to run."

Harlen gave me the same kind of cold stare a Beverly Hills haberdasher would give a bum off the street. "I'll give you twenty-four hours," he said. "You want the deal, give me a call."

He walked toward the hanger door, the sound of his hard footsteps impinging upon my brain like rife bullets, each with the same message: "Stop, stop. Tell him to stop."

But I said nothing, and when the hanger's personnel door slammed shut behind him, I had to sit down in one of Jack's battered office chairs, knowing I might have missed the opportunity of a lifetime.

"Business," Jack kind of snarled. "You'd give up a chance like that for business?"

I lifted my head out of my hands. "I worked a lot of years for what I've got. I'm not about to let it slip away for a few months of thrills."

Jack was silent, trying to comprehend my thinking. In his entire life he'd probably never put the future ahead of present desire. His philosophy had always been 'Do what you want to do now, and let the future take care of itself.' Anyone who thought otherwise was beyond his understanding.

I, on the other hand, always considered the effect of my actions on tomorrow. Maybe it was because my years in and out of orphanages and foster homes had made the present so painful, so ephemeral, I had been forced to focus on the future, always looking for some form of security.

As the years had passed and I had achieved increasing forms of future security, I had been able to relax a little, to find some enjoyment in activities that did not overly threaten my hard-won security. I was definitely the have-and-hold type.

Thus far, aerobatic flying in a nice safe Stearman was about as far as I had allowed myself to push the envelope. Was I ready? Was I willing to put my entire future on the line for the next phase? I wanted to. The thought of flying one of the big warbirds was a powerful aphrodisiac.

What was it Harlen had said: "I'll pick up the tab: lessons, fuel, maintenance, everything. You quit, you pay." That could run into hundreds of thousands of dollars. Was it worth taking a chance on losing Roan Security, or even my life? My intellect told me no.

"Sorry, Jack," I forced myself to say. "I can't take the chance."

"Well, give it some thought. He said twenty-four hours."

"Okay. But I don't think it'll do any good. Twenty-four hours won't change anything.

How could I have been so wrong?

CHAPTER FIVE

My secretary, Judy Wong, was waiting for me when I got back to my office in Newport Beach. This surprised me because, except for the night operator, Larry Wright, at the security computer console, everyone had left for the day. She explained with her usual efficiency, "You've got a visitor. He won't leave, and I didn't want to leave him here with just Larry. I thought I'd better stick around."

A niggling alarm in my head sounded a warning. Could the guy be here to accomplish what Jorge had failed? "Do we know him?"

"No. He's government. DEA. That's why I didn't throw him out."

Drug Enforcement Administration? The worrisome alarm eased but did not go away. It simply changed from a fear of bodily harm to apprehension about the company. Was one of my guards or other employees mixed up in drugs? Many of our contracts were with government agencies or companies with government contracts. The government, and many of these customers, required that we maintain high level security clearances. Any taint of elicit drugs among our employees could have a negative impact not only upon Roan Security's reputation but worse, upon our security clearances.

"How long has he been here?"

"Almost an hour."

An hour? That didn't make sense. If he were here because of some security breech, he wouldn't have come at five o'clock in the afternoon. He would have arrived during regular business hours. And he sure as hell wouldn't have hung around for an hour. More likely he would have called and asked me to come to the DEA's regional headquarters in Santa Ana.

But maybe it wasn't a dope problem. The man's timing and his unusual behavior made me wonder if his visit had anything to do with the murder of Jorge. It didn't seem likely. Where would the DEA fit in that scenario?

A new thought intensified my apprehension. "Did he show his identification?"

Judy hesitated, and my heart started pushing the blood through my veins so hard and fast it sounded like waves beating against rocks in a storm. He could be a killer who said he was DEA to get me alone with him.

"He showed me an I.D.," she said. "It looked authentic."

I gave her a forgiving smile. It wouldn't be good for employee moral for the boss to display fear.

"Okay, thanks."

When I walked into my office I was still holding the smile, but I was ready to either dive for cover or hold out my hand.

He was sitting in my visitor's leather chair with his hands in plain sight holding the copy of Forbes Magazine I kept on my desk to impress potential clients. He made no sudden moves such as whipping out a gun or knife and my heart responded gratefully by slowing to a respectable pounding.

My office's big picture window provided a splendid view of Newport Bay with its yacht slips and waters-edge shops and apartments. It also flooded the office with bright light from the low evening sun, so that sitting with the window behind him put the man's face in shadow. Not that it would have made much difference if I had a good look at his face. I didn't know any one with the DEA and hired killers did not always look like Boris Karloff. And he did wear dark glasses and a dark suit and red necktie, which somewhat allayed my trepidations. Hit men always dressed like ordinary people, and natives in yacht-crazy Newport Beach did not wear dark wool suits during the day——ever.

"Hello," I said in a strong, clear, unworried voice. "Hope I didn't keep you waiting too long."

He stood up and I tensed. This was the critical time. If he meant harm, it would come now. He held out his right hand, empty, with his left hand holding the magazine. That was good.

"Supervising agent David Bremm," he said. "DEA."

I shook his hand, keeping a wary eye on the hand holding the magazine, my legs braced for a karate move.

"Benjamin Roan," I answered.

He let go of my hand and reached for the breast pocket of his suit jacket, and my heart responded nicely. When his hand came out of the pocket it held an ID folder that he flipped open just long enough for me to see a badge. He quickly flipped it shut, but before he could return it to his pocket I held out my hand.

"Mind if I check that?"

He grinned, and handed me the folder. It was a DEA ID with his badge and picture. I compared the picture to what I could see of his face. I guessed him to be in his forties. His face was lean, with a good nose and lines beginning to form beside his nose to the corners of his mouth. I couldn't tell the color of his eyes because of the shadows and the glasses, but they had a hard, direct look that seemed to shoot right through the dark lenses like a laser beam. His hair looked to be dark brown, but flecked with grey, especially at his temples. Reading his name on the ID triggered a memory. David Bremm. Of course. Now I remembered: Bremm was agent in charge of the DEA's Orange County district with offices in Santa Ana.

I was breathing much easier when I closed the folder and handed it back to him and sat on a leather couch near my desk. "What can I do for you, Mr. Bremm?"

When he sat down and returned the folder to his jacket pocket I caught a glimpse of a gun butt in a shoulder holster. If I'd seen the gun before I'd checked his ID, my hair might now have more grey in it than his.

"You can tell me about the altercation between you and Jorge Mendez."

My chin came up. "You know about that already?"

"Ordinarily we wouldn't, but we've been...ah...interested in Jorge and his employer for some time."

"By 'we' you mean the DEA?"

40

"That's correct."

"His employer? Who would that be?"

"Morris Harlen."

Ah. So the DEA also knew about that. I wondered why. So I asked, "Why are you 'interested' in him?"

He stared at me a moment before answering, his eyes invisible behind the dark glasses. "Tell me about the altercation with Mendez. You claim he tried to kill you."

Until now he had been fairly jovial, but the way his voice had hardened it was obvious he wanted to regain control of the questioning. So I told him about Jorge's fight with the two men and how he'd tried to kill me.

He listened without interrupting, and I had the impression it wasn't the first time he'd heard the story. It was obvious the DEA was working closely with the Orange County Sheriff's Department, at least where it concerned the murder of Jorge Mendez.

"The two men...," Bremm said. "What was your impression of them and their relationship with Mendez?"

"My guess is they were working together on something and Jorge screwed up."

"And you'd never seen Mendez until that time?"

"That's right."

"Why do you suppose he wanted to kill you?"

"Like I told the detectives, I don't know."

He leaned forward and the light from the big window glinted off his glasses. "My guess is because you could identify the two men."

"That occurred to me. But I only got a glimpse of them. I'm not sure I could ID them in a lineup."

"But they don't know that."

"So? Would they risk another murder for that?"

"They probably wouldn't. But Mendez apparently took it upon himself to make sure. If he could cause you to crash and burn, it would look like an accident. But when he failed... Well he brought a lot of attention on himself, and by association, on them."

I got the picture. Jorge had screwed up, first by making a big deal out of something I probably would have forgotten in a couple of days, then his failure to kill me had brought their association with him to the attention of the law. Jorge had to be silenced before he could be questioned about why he had tried to kill me.

Another thought sent a chill through me. "Those two guys probably killed Jorge. If they change their mind about me, they might try to..uh, you know, take me out."

"It's possible. It's more likely they're already out of the country."

The lack of concern in his voice irritated me. "Likely, but not positively."

"Well, of course we can't be positive. But your death now would only bring more attention to them. I doubt that they—or their organization—would want that."

"Organization?"

He stood up and moved to stare out the window. But I doubted that he was concentrating on a couple of big yachts that were easing up the bay heading for their slips before the sun set because he said, "What I'm about to tell you is classified. Will that be a problem for you?"

"Well, no. Roan Security is cleared through top secret. So am I."

He turned his back to the window. "Very well. But this is for your information only. Not for any of your staff."

What the devil was he getting at? And what did the murder of Jorge Mendez have to do with the DEA? Now I really was curious. "I understand," I said.

"Good." He hesitated, as though making his mind up about something, then said, "The murder of Jorge Mendez leaves us with a dilemma."

"Us?" I didn't like the sound of that. "You mean the DEA."

"Yes, of course." He stood silently looking at me for so long I began to have a bad feeling that his next words where not going to be happy ones. "Jorge Mendez was training to be part of Harlen's aerial team."

"I heard that."

Why was he telling this to me? As far as I was concerned, our interrogation was over and he should be heading for the door.

"We've been investigating Mr. Harlen for some time. We believe he's working with a South American drug cartel."

"That's hard to believe. He's rich. Got planes, yachts."

"He's wealthy, all right. But not from his waste management company. That's just a front. We think he got it from dealing."

"Oh." I had to let that sink in a minute. What did I know about Harlen? Actually, nothing.

"Where did Jorge fit in?"

"We don't know for sure. Apparently he was brought in by his sister..."

"He had a sister?"

"Carmelita Mendez. She and Harlen are...quite close."

"But why? Why was Jorge taking flying lessons?"

"We suspect it had something to do with flying in drugs."

"Using Mustangs? It doesn't make sense. They'd stick out like a sore thumb."

"Exactly. That's what we hoped to find out by watching Mendez."

I stood up and began pacing so I could think better. "That girl, Sharon, was training Jorge to fly a Mustang in air shows. But what could that have to do with smuggling dope?"

"We've been asking ourselves the same question."

I remembered something else Harlen had said and the memory was as though a fist had closed around my heart "Wait a minute. His instructor, Sharon Daadian. Harlen said she was part of his team. Do you suppose he meant the drug dealing?"

I held my breath, waiting for his answer, hoping against all odds that his answer would be no.

There was a long pause before he shook his head, and I was able to breath again. "She's buying that P-51 from Harlen. But we have no evidence that she's involved with his dealing. That's another thing we were hoping to find out. Now..." He ran his fingers through his hair. "Jorge's death puts us back to square one." He turned those chilling lenses on me. "Unless..."

There was an ominous tone in that word that brought my pacing to a quick halt, and again I wished I could see his eyes behind those dark glasses.

"Unless what?"

As soon as I asked I realized I'd made a tactical mistake. The proper move would have been to open the door and say goodbye and good luck. Too late.

"I understand Mr. Harlen suggested you take Jorge's place on his team."

Shock made me step toward him. "Where did you hear that?"

"The point is that he did ask."

Jack Blutcher! Damn his soul. There'd only been the three of us in the hanger, and I was damn sure Harlen wasn't going to tell the DEA. And neither would the girl if she were involved. It had to have been Jack. And with the realization, a lot of things fell into place. Bremm had said they were keeping an eye on Jorge. Who better to do that than Jack Blutcher. His flying service next to Sharon's put him in the heart of the situation.

"All right," I admitted. "He asked. But I'm sure as hell not going to get involved with selling dope. So what has it got to do with Mendez?"

He didn't answer right away, and I had the sinking sensation that I was about to be offered a proposition I should refuse. He slipped off his dark glasses and put them in his suit's handkerchief pocket. He stared at me a moment, and after I saw the speculation in his eyes, I wished he would put the dark glasses back on.

"I'm thinking about lives," he said. "Most people have no idea how many lives are ruined by addiction to drugs. Maybe they know one or two people who are addicted, or they hear about some celebrity who ends up in a detox center, but they rarely hear about the marriages, the homes that are broken up because someone put his addiction ahead of his family, his job, his children, even his life. No big deal. One guy. Or one woman. One teenager. Not mine. Not me. They want to ruin their lives, no skin off my nose. But multiply that by hundreds, thousands of kids, mothers, fathers, working people. If nothing else, think of the millions of job hours lost, the kids who'll end up on the street before they even get a job, or an education. The gangs that are sustained by dealing. The kids in those gangs."

"What about alcohol?" I said. "Same thing and it's legal."

He turned on me with more passion that I thought possible in a government employee. "It's not the same. Thousands, millions of people drink alcohol for years and it never adversely affects their lives. Most—I could say virtually all--don't drink to get high. Not like dopers. They always want to get high. And dope is insidious. They may not start out to get high. It sneaks up on them. Unlike alcohol. Some people can drink for years without progression. Not with dope. You can't use drugs for years without progression like you can alcohol. It always takes a little more to get that high. A few people can handle the progression. It doesn't noticeably affect their jobs or relationships. They're the exceptions. The number of people whose lives eventually are ruined by alcohol is nothing compared to those ruined by dope. That's why I stay in this job." He took a step toward me. "Would you help those people, those children, if you could?"

I wanted to say, 'No. I've got my own life to live,' because I knew that any hint of an affirmative reply would open a door that I didn't want to open even a crack. Instead, I waffled. "Well, I...of course, if I could, but-—"

He stuck his foot in the door before I could nail it shut. "Good. I knew we could count on your help."

"Hey, wait a minute," I yelped, fighting a horrible suspicion that he was about to put my neck in a noose. "What is it your suggesting? I don't..."

He held up his hand to stop me. "Nothing," he said, and I

began to relax a little. Then he continued and the suspicions came flooding back. "That is, nothing you haven't already said you'd like to do."

"And what would that be?" If my voice had been ice it would have given him frostbite.

He ignored the frostbite. Instead he put his dark glasses back on and smiled as though he were delivering a gift to a five-year-old. "Fly a P-51."

So Jack had told him about that, too. My resentment faded a little when I thought about what he'd said. Did he mean that he was offering me a chance to fly a Mustang? "I don't get the connection," I said, hoping there really was no connection, but knowing there would be and that it would be a connection I would not like.

"You could be a big help to us if you accepted Mr. Harlen's offer."

I was right. I didn't like it. My brief euphoria vanished in a dreadful realization. "You mean...take Jorge's place... with Harlen?"

"In effect, yes."

I went behind my desk and sat down. I needed time to think. If I made a bad decision now I could be involved with a drug dealer, which I did not want. Also—I sat up straighter as a sickening thought struck me--it could get me killed, which I definitely did not want.

"What you're saying..." I attempted to keep my voice really cool, as though I weren't seriously apprehensive. "You want me to go undercover. Be a spy for the DEA."

Bremm was much cooler than I. He calmly took a seat in my office chair and crossed one leg over the other as though it was a done deal and all we had to do was work out the details. "You're in the security business with,"---his voice took on a knife-like edge I could practically feel across my throat---"several government contracts. You could consider this another government operation."

He did not exactly state the obvious, but the tone of his voice implied that Roan Security's government contracts could be in serious jeopardy if I refused his offer. I weighed the impact on our business if we lost all, or most of, our government operations. If I accepted his proposal it could lead to additional government contracts, and at the same time, it would allow me to fulfill a very real desire to fly a Mustang——but a desire that could get me killed.

"I'm not sure it would work," I said. "Harlen knows about my company. He knows I do a lot of work for the government. If, as you say, he's involved with drugs, I'd be the last one he'd want to have on his payroll."

"So why did he make the offer?"

"Maybe he hadn't thought it through."

"That's not like Harlen. Look at it from his point of view: Jorge's death has got him worried. With a bunch of cops sniffing around, he's probably covering his ass. Having a boy scout with your credentials on his team would be proof he's not involved in dope."

"So, in a way, I'd be his insurance. Give his air show operation credibility."

"That's what we want him to think."

It sounded plausible, if it worked. And I would get to fly a P-51. I would even get paid for it, wouldn't I? "Let me get this straight," I said. "I'd be working under government contract."

"That's right."

"The contract will include reimbursement for the cost of my lessons..."

"Unless Harlen pays for them, as he did with Mendez."

"There'll be other expenses..."

"Let's just say 'cost plus.' You're actual costs."

I sat back, thinking. Cost plus meant that the government would reimburse Roan Security for all my expenses plus a substantial profit. Except for the danger involved in working undercover, it was a beautiful arrangement: I would get to fulfill my fantasy of learning to fly a P-51 and get paid for it. Even the chance of Harlen finding out I was a spy was minimal. And if he did, I could always run. What could be better? Except I sort of wished Bremm hadn't put on his dark glasses before he made the offer.

CHAPTER SIX

Less than a week later I was signing papers in Sharon Daadian's hanger office to begin flight training. Morris Harlen had already cleared the way after I'd signed on to be part of his flying team. It was a very small team consisting of Sharon, me, a mechanic and couple of ground crewmen. At least, those were the visible members. If Harlen really was a big time drug dealer there were undoubtedly many other team members lurking in the shadows, probably even a few hit men.

But could someone as gorgeous as Sharon knowingly be involved with a bunch of cutthroat thugs? It was possible. Many beautiful women were involved with drug dealers. And somebody had murdered Jorge Mendez. It could have been a woman. But Sharon? That was hard to believe.

I sat in a hard wooden chair next to Sharon's desk and sneaked peeks at her as she put the papers I'd just signed into a file cabinet. It was a four-drawer cabinet and she stood with her back to me, but it was still a lovely view. Until that moment I had been fighting doubts about this entire set up. Events had been moving so fast that I'd had little time to think—which could have been deliberate both on the part of Bremm and the DEA and Morris Harlen. But now that all the paper work had been cleared, and I'd arranged with my staff to be relatively incommunicado for a while, the doubts were beginning to overbalance my sense of adventure, especially when I considered the kind of unsavory characters who tended to be involved in dealing drugs.

But watching Sharon Daadian standing in front of the filing cabinet quickly took my mind off the job's perils, unless the perils consisted of the way she filled out her white flight coveralls. She was tall, close to six feet, and what some would consider athletically slender, expect for nicely rounded buns and hips that were just a little too feminine to be considered athletic. It was also easy to stare at the way the white coveralls highlighted the mass of dark curls cascading down her back. It had to be difficult to stuff all that hair under a flying helmet, but I'd certainly like to watch her do it.

She closed the file drawer and sat at her desk in front of a desktop computer's big monitor, and I got to study her face as she concentrated on the monitor and began working the mouse. It was not exactly a beautiful face like that of a Versace model. The cheekbones were high like a model's and the lips as full and petulant, but her eyes, while dark and deep, were too piercing to be considered sexy. And there was no softness in that face. While it may be beautiful, it was the face of a fighter, a face that came from a line of conquerors: Darius, Cyrus, Xerxes. Could it possibly be the face of a killer? It didn't seem possible.

The remarkable eyes turned to me and the lovely mouth said, "You think you're a hot-shot pilot, but here's the plane that's probably going to kill you."

I pulled my chair around so I could see the computer's monitor, thinking that she was wrong: The plane wouldn't kill me, but she might if she knew what I'd been thinking.

I expected the monitor to feature a sleek Mustang. Instead it featured a two-place Vultee AT-6 WWII trainer.

"That's not a P-51," I said.

"Right. We start with the T-six."

"Why? We could save time by going straight to the Mustang."

"You've been flying a Stearman. Going straight to a Mustang would be too big a jump. But the main thing is the instruments."

She used the computer mouse to begin playing a documentary film on the monitor, augmenting the film's narration from time to time with poignant comments as the film illustrated the procedures for checking out and flying the WWII trainer. She was right about one thing: it soon became obvious that it would even be a big jump from flying the Stearman to flying the AT-6 let alone a P-51. Even so, a plane is a plane. it might take me a little time, but I thought I could handle the big trainer, maybe even a Mustang if the weather was good.

After the film, I assumed we'd open the hanger doors, wheel the AT-6 out, and go for a check ride where I would whip the plane through a few loops, rolls, stalls and landings to prove I didn't need the intermediate training. I was ready for the big bird.

But instead of heading for the hanger door, she led the way directly to the AT-6 where it was sitting next to her sleek Mustang like an envious sibling. Not that the AT-6 was ugly. It was a beautiful image of practicality, but next to the P-15 it was like a tug boat sitting next to an America Cup yacht.

She began what sounded like a standard introductory speech: "This is an AT-6 'Texan,' built by North American Aviation for World War-two pilot training. Four hundred horse power engine, etc."

I listened to her rote dissertation, but my mind was more on the lovely way her lips moved as she spoke than on the words. I think she caught something in my expression because her lips stopped moving in the middle of a fascinating statistic about dual fuel tanks, and they lost a little of their charm when they sort of hardened into a thin line that scarcely moved as she growled, "Get in. "

I scampered up a short ladder that had been positioned next to the cockpit and nimbly climbed into the cockpit. It was my first time in the cockpit of a fully instrumented plane, and staring at the array of dials and knobs delivered a severe blow to my confidence. The old Stearman had managed to fly perfectly well with nothing more important than a compass, a tachometer and a fuel gauge, but wow! The AT-6 had more gauges than a new Mercedes.

Sharon climbed the ladder, and as she leaned into the cockpit, a faint scent of perfume destroyed my ability to concentrate on anything but her face so close to mine. When she began to speak I wrenched my thoughts back to reality. She was identifying each of the instruments, and I concentrated on memorizing their use and placement. She hadn't identified even half before my eyes began to glaze. How could anyone concentrate on flying when they had to monitor altimeter, air speed indicator, compass, turn and bank indicator, artificial horizon, tachometer, oil pressure, fuel gauge, etc. I was in instrument-shock before she finished the front panel, and she hadn't even started on the radio and all the buttons, switches and levers.

Her voice finally broke through my mental fog when she said, "They're all listed in the Flight Control Manual. When you've got them memorized we'll do a preflight check. As soon as you've memorized the check, we can start flying."

She climbed down the ladder, and I dutifully followed her back to her desk. She opened a desk drawer and tossed an AT-6 Flight Manual on the desk in front of me. I landed with a heavy splat that seemed to give a period to my chances of ever understanding any of its contents.

"Memorize this," she said. "I'll be asking questions."

My hands felt numb as I picked up the thick manual. Memorize the whole thing? She might just as well have asked me to memorize the Encyclopedia Britannica. I sat staring at the manual in a state of technology shock until she stood up and pushed her tumble of hair back behind her ears. The unconscious, utterly feminine gesture started my blood circulating again, slewing away the fog of doubt. If a gorgeous woman could memorize the manual, I should be able to handle it. And don't forget, in the urgent days of WWII, kids hardly out of high school were flying planes a lot more complicated than an AT-6 trainer. If they could do it, so could I.

But I had one huge obstacle they never had to face: an instructor so sexy it was difficult to think of anything so mundane as getting killed.

CHAPTER SEVEN

The next week sped by in a blur of activity. After I'd studied the manual for the AT-6 and answered Sharon's quiz to her satisfaction, we spent a day going over a ground checkout of the plane. Finally we took to the air with her in the front seat and me in the back.

Flying the 'Texan' was a quantum leap from flying the old Stearman biplane. I couldn't help wondering how some of those World War I aces like Richenbacker and Luke would have felt about giving up their light, agile Spad and Neuport biplanes for the heavy, powerful World War II trainer. They might have thrilled to the AT-6's increased speed and its stability as a gun platform, but they probably would have been less than thrilled with its lack of agility. But, then, rugged trainers weren't designed for air-to-air combat, even though elderly AT-6s had done heavy work as ground attack aircraft during the Korean War and the war in Vietnam.

Although at first the change from flying the agile Stearman to the heavier AT-6 felt strange, the actual flying proved to be relatively easy. The AT-6 was a steady, friendly platform. What really demanded concentration was the huge increase in instrumentation. There was very little flying by the seat of your pants as I had learned to do in the Stearman. With the AT-6 there was an array of instruments, levers, buttons and lights for just about every activity, including operation of the retractable landing gear. I discovered early on that forgetting to put the wheels down when coming in for a landing tended to bring out Sharon's worst side.

I knew, however, that while myriad, the variety of instruments was a far cry from what I would encounter in a P-51 Mustang, so I gave them my full attention with the idea that if using them became second nature on the AT-6 I wouldn't have to relearn their use in the Mustang.

But the real difference between the Stearman and the AT-6 was in their landing characteristics. Landing the Stearman with its light weight, huge wing surface, and close-together landing gear, was like trying to set a leaf on a saucer during a wind storm. Even though the heavy trainer came in faster, it tended to plop down on the runway like a duck landing on a lake. And once on the ground, every gust of wind didn't try to scatter you over the terrain like it did with the Stearman.

There was another aspect of the training I found enjoyable: day after day being close to Sharon. She was a tough taskmaster, but even when I screwed up and she displayed her disgust at my stupidity, it was like being chastised by Catherine Zeta-Jones. Her lovely eyes would blaze and her voice would become a whiplash of exasperation, but her face would still be beautiful, her lips exquisite, and her figure breathtaking. I couldn't help myself; I usually just listened with a stupid grin, much to her disgust.

Morris Harlen came around a couple of times to see how I was doing. After talking to Sharon, he seemed satisfied because he didn't kick me off the team. I figured that event would probably come later after I wrecked his million dollar P-51.

From time to time I checked in with Bremm, and he seemed satisfied with my progress. When I tried to make excuses about not having learned anything about Harlen's supposed drug dealing, he told me not to push it. The first thing was to gain Harlen's trust. Once I was firmly on the inside, Harlen's dealings in dope could be ferreted out. He didn't have to add that being too inquisitive could also cost my life.

The day I soloed in the AT-6 was a red letter day in several ways: First I had taken off, flown and landed the airplane without forgetting to put the landing gear down or becoming a smoking hole in the runway, and, second, Sharon took me to dinner to celebrate. Well, actually, I took her to dinner, but she did consent to join me which I considered a major victory since all week long she had acted like I was a peon and she was *El Jeffe*.

I introduced her to a restaurant called the Nuevo Bistro in Newport Beach near the pier. It was one of my favorite places when I wanted to impress a client because it had a French name and dark oak paneling, soft lights, individual booths upholstered with real leather, and service designed for royalty.

When I picked up Sharon in my ancient Corvette, I had a

chance to see where she lived in Laguna Beach. I'd rather expected her to have an upscale apartment with tons of security, but was delighted to find that she had a modest home. At least it was modest by Laguna Beach standards even though its back door opened onto a secluded beach just around a bluff from Laguna Beach's famous stretch of sand and surf. I couldn't help thinking how nice a moonlight dinner could be on her wide back porch, breathing the tangy sea air and listening to the surf. Then after dinner walking barefoot in the spindrift of waves washing up on the wide beach, hand in hand, shoulders touching, neither of us saying a word.

Well, it could happen. Since she was willing to join me for dinner at the Bistro after soloing in the AT-6, she surely wouldn't object to dinner at her place after I soloed in a Mustang.

But first I had to make a good impression. I began by astonishing her with my choice of wine for a before-dinner appetizer. A dilettante would have chosen champagne or a light chardonnay but I went for a robust claret. My hubris was rewarded by an appreciative lift of her eye brows when I told the sommelier: "Chateau Margaux, seventy-eight, s'il vous plaît."

He sort of lifted his chin and said, "Eighteen or nineteen seventy-eight?"

1878? Holy Molly! That would have to be at least fifty dollars a sip.

He read my expression perfectly. His voice carried a ton of disdain when he said, "The nineteen seventy-eight. Very good, sir."

The humiliation didn't really matter. My plan to astound Sharon with my witty repartee while enjoying the heady tang of the wine sort of fell apart when just looking at her tended to make me tongue tied.

During the day her hair was usually concealed by a helmet, but now it swirled around her face and down her back in its full glory. And usually she wore no makeup, but tonight she had done something to her lashes and shadowed her eyes that made looking into them like drowning in perfume.

And usually her lips were without gloss and generally engaged in berating me for some misfortune, but in the glow of a single candle, they glistened seductively, and when they formed words or, worse, when they smiled, I was lost in awe.

And her voice. Some stupid thing I'd done could cause it to sting like a whip lash, or reek with the despair of a Cassandra. But tonight her tone were dulcet, mesmerizing as the call of a Lorelei.

And if all that was not enough to turn my mind to mush, she had exchanged her flight coveralls for a satin-like mini-dress with a décolletage that made me afraid to take my eyes away from staring at her face. If I gave so much as one teeny thought to the view of her legs under the table with her mini-dress's skirt...

"How did you get involved in flying," I blurted. So much for clever repartee.

"My dad. He was a pilot in the Air Force. I grew up around planes."

"You were a military brat?"

"Not really. My dad was in the Iranian air force. After they came here,--legally, by the way--he flew commercial jets. We pretty well stayed in one place."

"Here? Laguna Beach?"

"Los Angeles. Then we moved down here. I went to UCI."

I breathed a sign of relief. She had put me on familiar ground. "You went to Irvine? So did I. At least for awhile."

I didn't think it was necessary to tell her I had dropped out of the university after two years when I had run out of tuition money.

"Oh," she said. "What was your major?"

"Business administration. I'll bet yours was a lot more fun."

"I doubt it. Aeronautical engineer. A lot of math and physics."

"How come you didn't join the Air Force? Maybe be an astronaut."

"My dad. He said the military was too structured. And astronauts don't really fly. If I wanted to fly like a bird I'd do better on my own."

"You think he was right?

"I've flown military jets. They don't compare with Mustangs. How about you?"

"Me?"

"What made you take up flying?"

What she had said about flying like a bird gave me the courage to tell the truth. "Like you, I guess. I wanted to be a bird. I tried hang gliding and skydiving, but it wasn't until Jack took me for a ride in his Stearman that I found what I was looking for."

She nodded. "I know."

Was I mistaken or was she feeling a little empathy. I was about to capitalize on the opening, when she said, "Jack's a strange guy. I think he was some sort of mercenary"

"He was. Originally Army Special Forces. I think they let him go when he got shot up. Then he spent a couple of years with the French Foreign Legion. After that he was all over the place: the Middle East, South America, Asia. I met him in Africa."

"You were a mercenary?"

"No, no. My company is involved in security. I was shepherding a computer to Uganda. It didn't go too well and Jack...uh...gave me some help."

She was silent for a moment, her eyes far away, her mind reliving some distant memory, and I searched for words that would return the mood of romance.

Before I could think of anything that would be both clever and romantic like 'I'll bet with those lips you can really kiss,' she said, "Have you heard anything more about Jorge?"

I sat stunned. What a reversal. I had to yank my thoughts into the new direction before I could even remember who Jorge was. "Uh, no. I guess the police are still working on it."

"It doesn't make sense. Why would anyone want to...why would they want him dead? He was just a pilot."

Reluctantly I decided that since her thoughts were centered on the murder, it might be a good time to see what I could learn.

"Tell me about Harlen. How did he happen to pick you for his team?"

She didn't answer immediately as though debating about how much she should tell me. She picked up her fork and toyed with it, looking at it to avoid looking at me. Did that mean she was forming lies? More likely the fork was more interesting than my face.

"He didn't exactly pick me. I picked him."

Well, that was a bad development. Did she mean she had been attracted to him? Were they lovers? He was handsome in a kind of superficial way, and he certainly was wealthy, but I hadn't sized her up as a person who would be drawn to looks or money. It was depressing to think I could be wrong, especially when I so much enjoyed watching the flickering candlelight play with her hair and the soft angles of her face.

"You picked him?" I repeated like a fool.

"When my father died, he left me the flying school, a Stearman, and the AT-6. His hospital bills ate up what cash we had. I had to sell the Stearman--to Jack. He gave me a good price, but the school wasn't doing that well, and when Harlen offered to sell me a Mustang, I jumped at it."

"A million dollars? That doesn't sound like you were doing so badly."

"A million, three hundred thousand. He owns me for twenty years."

"Oh."

She was buying the Mustang on time. That meant she was not totally in his debt. I felt better already. On the other hand, she could be holding back the real truth. Or maybe she actually was part of his drug cabal. I took a chance on overplaying the situation by asking, "Was being on his team part of the deal?"

I knew I was pushing it, but since we were on the subject, it might be my only chance to find out how far she was involved with Harlen.

She could have evaded the question, and I rather suspected she would. Instead, she answered without hesitation: "It was the only way I could swing it. You know how much it costs to fly and maintain a Mustang? And there's the AT-6. Without his help, I could never make it."

I sat back in my chair, happy as a clam. Her relations with Harlen were purely business.

Then the dark side of my personality kicked it. I'd once had a fortune cookie that said I think too much. It was right. Right now I couldn't stop thinking about her relationship with Harlen. Was it only business, business with ties to his dope dealing? Was she in love with Harlen? He was wealthy, handsome, big feet. Everything a girl could want. How many strings were attached to his deal? I would have to tailor my conversation carefully so she wouldn't suspect my real reasons for asking.

"This advertising scheme is going to cost him a fortune."

"I guess he knows what he's doing. He's been going to a lot of air shows."

"I've only heard about the big ones: Oshkosh, L.A., Reno..."

"I looked it up. There are about fifty in the U.S. Four or five in Canada. A couple in Mexico."

"Mexico? They have an air show?

"Mexico City, I think"

"I doubt they'd be interested in waste management in Mexico."

"I guess it'll be our job to make it happen."

Our job? Was it just a job to her?

I sipped my wine, my train of romantic fantasy derailed by an avalanche of reality. If Bremm was right and Harlen was dealing drugs, where did Harlen's sudden interest in air shows fit in? Or did it fit in at all? Maybe his advertising was legitimate and had no connection with his dealing---assuming he actually was dealing. And if Jorge was an important part of his team, why had he been murdered?

I studied Sharon, wishing there was some way I could read her mind. How could anyone so beautiful, so intelligent be involved with drug dealing?

The chilling thought made me shiver. I really didn't want to know. My job was to find out about Harlen and his involvement with drugs. His relationship with Sharon—unless it involved his dealing—had nothing to do with my task. Her personal life was none of my business and, in fact, I had better make sure it remained none of my business. Any romantic thoughts about Sharon Daadian could only end in heartbreak. Mine.

The remainder of the evening was nice, but a little short of being exhilarating. Sharon was just as beautiful, my conversation just as witty, her smile as breathtaking. But for me, suspicions about the depth of her involvement with Harlen had robbed the evening of its aura of impending romance, and try as I might, I couldn't get it back.

I needed more facts. And I didn't have the patience to sit back and wait for the information to drop in my lap as Bremm had suggested. I decided to go looking for it.

CHAPTER EIGHT

I got Carmelita Mendez's address from David Bremm. He asked why I wanted to see her, which I thought was a stupid question. I told him it was to ask if she had any idea why her brother would want to kill me, and he told me they'd already talked to her and had come up dry. I still wanted to see her, and he gave me her address while telling me I'd be wasting my time.

He was probably right. However, maybe she just didn't like talking to cops. Some people are like that.

The address was for a small clapboard house in the hills just north of Sunset Boulevard in L.A. near Dodger Stadium. All the homes in the area were probably built in the 1920s or 30s, and there wasn't a blonde within five miles in any direction. Most of the shops and stores in the area were identified with signs in Spanish. A mile or so south the signs were in Korean, and a couple of miles north a Little Armenia area was beginning to rival Big Armenia in Glendale.

I found a place to park about a block away from Carmelita's house on a steep side street, turning my old Corvette's wheels into the curb and setting the hand brake hard. I'd tried to call ahead, but there had been no answer at the number Bremm had given me. So I left a message I was coming to see her, and took a chance she'd be home around 5:00.

Climbing rickety wooden steps that led both to her house and a couple of others perched on the side of the hill, I listened to the sounds of the neighborhood. The area was full of life. I heard kids playing, voices raised in anger or laughter, dogs barking, cars whizzing by on nearby Sunset Boulevard, and others joyously challenging the steep side streets. There couldn't be much privacy in this neighborhood.

A small porch that struggled to keep its grip on the old frame house, creaked ominously as I crossed it. There was an ancient bell button next to a door with an outside screen. To my surprise when I pressed the button I heard it ring inside. In a moment I heard steps approaching. On the house's wooden floor, the steps sounded crisp, efficient, created by shoes with heels. The sound made me quickly change the mental picture I'd formed of Carmelita. They certainly were not the steps of an obese woman. I would even bet that the owner of such purposeful steps could not be ugly—homely maybe, but not ugly.

I waited with great anticipation when the steps stopped and the door was opened.

"Yes?" Her voice had the same crisp and efficient sound as her footsteps.

Her image was not much more than a shadow behind the old screen door, but she appeared to be tall, slender, wearing tight jeans and a loose white blouse with long sleeves. I'd been right about the shoes: she was wearing cowboy boots. She had straight, thick, dark hair that hung down her back almost to her waist like a silken waterfall. Her face was in shadow, but from what I could see it seemed to be all there and in the right places: nose, eyes, mouth.

Hoping that she was having as much trouble seeing my face as I was seeing hers, I grinned and said, "HI. Are you Jorge's sister?"

"What if I am?"

Her voice was so cold and guarded, she probably thought I'd heard about her brother's death and was here to sell her something. "Nothing, really," I said quickly. "I kind of met him at the flying school, and..."

I stopped talking when I realized I sounded like an idiot. I tried to start over before it was too late. "What I mean is...I'd kind of like to talk to you about him."

"You a cop?" Her voice hadn't thawed a degree, but her question took me by surprise. Did I look like a cop? I'm reasonably tall, wiry, with good shoulders and dark brown hair worn a little long and shaggy for a cop. And it couldn't be my clothes. I had on an almost new pair of chino pants and a short-sleeved polo shirt with the tail out. Maybe that was it. She probably thought I had a gun and badge on my belt under the shirt. "No, no," I said. "I'm a pilot. You know: airplanes."

"Oh."

Did I detect a little warmth there? "I'm kind of taking his place on Mr. Harlen's team. Morris Harlen. You know him?"

"What's your name?"

"Roan. Benjamin Roan."

For answer she unhooked the screen door and pushed it open. She did not ask me to come in, but when she walked away I assumed it was an invitation to enter, so I did.

There wasn't a lot of light coming through the room's small windows. which I thought was fairly typical for homes built in the 20s. Carmelita walked straight across the small room saying, "You want coffee or beer?"

"Uh, coffee."

She went through an open doorway into what I assumed was the kitchen, and I heard cabinet doors opening and closing and dishes rattling.

There wasn't much furniture in the room. Near the kitchen doorway was a dining table covered with a beautiful crocheted table cloth and with a potted rose bush precisely in the center. A couch flanked by a couple of overstuffed chairs faced a 24-inch TV. A couple of throw rugs added color to the polished wood floor that age had given a few undulations. Framed prints that appeared to be Mexican hung on the walls.

I pulled one of the wooden chairs away from the table and sat down. On the other side of the table was a window that looked out on a small back yard with a lawn and a few bushes needing water and an unpainted five foot high wooden fence that appeared to have been built about the same time as the house. On the other side of the fence the hill went up a few feet and supported another house. More small houses were stacked like that as far up the hill as I could see.

I was admiring the beautifully crotched table cloth when Carmelita came back in carrying a cup and saucer and two squares of paper toweling. She put one of the paper towels on the table cloth in front of me and set the coffee cup and its saucer on it. She put the other paper towel on the far side of the table. Straightening, she gave her head a little toss that swept her hair back away from her face and went back into the kitchen. I figured that with her long hair she must have to make that little gesture a lot.

In a moment she came back with another cup and saucer and a ceramic pot. She poured steaming black coffee from the pot into each cup then, with another of those little hair tosses, she sat down and stared at me. She didn't ask if I wanted sugar or cream.

The window behind her kept her face somewhat in shadow, but I could see I had been right: she wasn't ugly. Except for a nose that was a trifle thin and a mouth that was a shade too wide, she was so gorgeous I felt a little intimidated.

I had to look down at my coffee to keep from staring at her, but I managed to say, "I'm really sorry about your brother."

She did not answer.

I wished I had a spoon so I could stir the coffee as an excuse for not looking at her.

"Uh, I guess the police told you how it happened."

She did not answer.

I searched for something to say, but the thought that pounded through my mind was 'why the hell am I here?'

"Did the police tell you he tried to kill me?"

I heard her chair squeak as though she had leaned forward. "Why would he do that?"

With the conversation slightly thawed, I took a swig of coffee, staring at her over the cup. Jesus! I almost dropped the cup to clutch my scalded lips. My hand was shaking and my tongue laving my burning lips as, somehow, I set the cup in the saucer without slopping coffee all over the table. If I had, I was sure it would have set it on fire. I silently berated myself for not noticing the steam wafting from the cup.

"Sorry," she said. "I should have warned you. I like my coffee hot."

"Coffee?" I said. "I think it's molten lava."

She laughed and the spell was broken.

"I'll get you some ice.?

She got up and went into the kitchen. I heard a refrigerator door open and she came back with an ice cube held in a paper towel. I took it and gingerly held it to my lips, feeling like a fool.

She sat down watching me and sipping her coffee as though it were cool. Her lips had to be tough as leather.

"I don't believe you," she said.

"About your brother? It's true. I was flying a Stearman. He came after me in a Mustang. I got away from him and crash landed in a field. Then he came back and looked a couple of shots at me."

"Why would he do that?"

"I was kind of hoping you could tell me."

She shook her head and her shiny skein of hair undulated like a wave. "I don't know. Are you sure it was him? Jorge?"

"I'm sure. I got a good look at him when he shot at me."

She sipped a little of the scalding coffee. Maybe that was the secret: small sips. "When did this happen?"

"Just before he...uh...before he was killed."

"Did you do it?"

"Me? Gosh no. Why would I do that? I didn't even know him."

"If you didn't know him, why would he try to kill you?"

"Like I told the police, it might have been because I saw those two guys he was with."

"You saw them?" She carefully put her coffee cup in its saucer and leaned across the table. "What did they look like?"

"Latino, I guess. Dark hair, dark eyes. Black, short beards. They were well dressed. Suits and neckties. They got in a fight with Jorge."

"What language?"

Her question surprised me. No one else had questioned their language. But Jorge probably spoke Spanish, and if the two men were foreigners, probably Latino, why hadn't they been speaking Spanish?

"I couldn't tell. But it wasn't Spanish."

Instead of answering, she turned in her chair to look out the window as though she didn't want me to see her expression. Maybe this talk about Jorge had brought back painful memories, and she was crying.

But questions about their use of a foreign language nagged at me. I needed some answers. I assumed Jorge spoke Spanish or she wouldn't have asked her question. But his English, and hers, were without accents, so maybe Jorge didn't speak Spanish very well.

"Jorge was born here, wasn't he?"

She answered without turning. "We both were." Then she added as though to forestall an unpleasant query. "We're citizens."

"But your parents were from Mexico."

"No. Columbia." She turned back to face me. "They were naturalized citizens before we were born. They didn't even want us to speak Spanish." There was no signs on her face that she had been crying, but her voice reflected a faint bitterness as though she was tired of people thinking that all Latinos were illegals.

"So English was really your native language."

"Yes. Right off Alverado Boulevard"

Alverado was a nearby main street that ran through the heart of the West LA Latin district. The Spanish language was not as pervasive as it was in the huge Latin district in East LA, but until a few years ago one could have grown up on the western edge of downtown LA without hearing much English. Now, however, there were probably as many Koreans in the area as Latinos.

But even if Jorge's Spanish had been far from perfect, it seemed strange that their conversation had been in some other language, especially while arguing. When emotions are high, people tend to revert to the language that is easiest for them.

My analysis was interrupted by Carmelita asking, "You're

65

taking Jorge's place on the team?"

"Well, yes."

"Jorge hated flying."

Her words hit me with a jolt. "He did? So why did he do it?"

"That girl, Sharon. He was in love with her."

Another jolt. Now it was my turn to stare. "He was? Are you sure?"

"She's why he started flying, why he hung out with Harlen."

"Was she...uh...was she in love with him?"

I held my breath waiting for her answer. When I realized what I was doing I felt my face burn, wondering why her answer should matter.

"I don't think so. If they'd hooked up, I think Jorge would have stopped flying."

I got up and went over to study one of the pictures on the wall, not really seeing it, but not wanting Carmelita to see my face. "But he figured he had a chance...of hooking up?"

From the corner of my eye I saw her shrug. "It wouldn't have lasted. Apples and oranges. Flying is her life; he hated it."

I needed to think. My mind was struggling to sort through the information she'd given me. Besides, it was obvious she either knew nothing about Jorge's connection with the two men I'd seen, or if she did know, was not willing to talk about it.

"Well, thanks for talking to me." I moved to the door.

She got up and crossed the room, walking with the purposeful strides I'd heard before, her back straight, her head up, her eyes hooded, locked on me.

"If you hear anything...about Jorge...I want you to tell me."

"Oh, I will. Of course."

She stopped in front of me. "Promise?"

It was as much a threat as a query, and I realized she was not a person one wanted to have as an enemy.

It was not difficult to be totally sincere when I answered, "I will. Promise."

She pushed open the screen door. I had stepped onto the porch when she said, "Wait. I'll give you my cell phone number."

Without waiting for an answer she went back into the room. I waited on the porch, listening to the traffic on the unseen Sunset Boulevard. Mention Sunset Boulevard to most people and they would visualize Beverly Hills and the mansions of Bel Air, the purity of the Pacific Palisades, or the place where Sunset ended at the ocean near Malibu. They didn't realize there was an opposite end of Sunset, that heading east, after cleaving Hollywood, it cut through at least four ethnic areas, ending next to LA's China town.

The screen door squeaked open and Carmelita said, "Here's the number. Call me any time."

I took the piece of paper and put it in my shirt pocket. "Okay. Thanks for the coffee."

"How's your lip?"

For the first time she looked at me without her eyes burning and her lips drawn into hard lines. It was as though she became another person, Latina beautiful, her soft lips sensuous.

I tested my lip with the tip of my tongue. "Better. A little sore."

"Good." She touched my sore lip with the tip of her finger. "It'll help you remember me."

Talk about an understatement. I would be remembering her when I was in my grave, which, thinking about it as I walked down the steps to my car, might not be too long.

CHAPTER NINE

I had been soloing in the AT-6 for a week when Sharon handed me the pilot's manual for the P-51 Mustang. We had gone back to her office in the hanger after she watched me practice landings, and she slapped me in the chest with the thick manual.

"Read every word. A lot of it's boring, but as sure as you're born the day'll come when you'll wish you hadn't skipped something."

"Okay. I'll try to stay awake." Which for me, should be easy. Just the thought of flying the sleek plane was terrifying, kicking my heart rate into overdrive. Even more terrifying was the knowledge that it was a single place cockpit so my very first flight would be solo. If I made a mistake, there would be no one to help. Every flight would be a final exam. Pass, and you could do it again tomorrow. Fail, and there would be no tomorrow.

I clutched the manual as though it were a life raft. I would not only read it, I would memorize ever word, every figure, every diagram.

"Pay attention to landing instruction," Sharon said, moving toward a big white-board she used for drawing diagrams. "Anybody can fly a Mustang. The trick is taking off and landing."

She didn't have to tell me Landing was always the most difficult part of flying any plane. It just got more dangerous as the landing speed increased, and the P-51 came in at more than a hundred miles per hour. At that speed a little misjudgment could scatter plane and pilot over a considerable area.

Still, the Mustang had a wide landing gear and in case of trouble the 1,600 horses in the big Rolls-Royce Merlin engine could haul you back into the safety of the air in a hurry.

"If you get in trouble don't ram the throttle. You do and at slow speed the torque will flip you over."

Well, that was good to know. 1,600 horses might get you out of trouble, but they could also kill you.

"Full power wouldn't help much anyway. At slow speed the Mustang doesn't accelerate in a hurry. Lots of torque but not much thrust. So, if you have to go around, give it power slow and smooth. Get your gear and flaps up. The secret is don't let your speed get too low to begin with."

Listening to her I was reminded of the old saw that had been around as long as airplanes: 'Fly low and slow, the mother said to her darling air cadet. So he flew low and slow as his mother said, and they haven't found him yet.'

For the next few days she pounded away at me with tidbits of information not found in the manual, which, in itself, was a hodgepodge of instruction.

I, and many others, consider the Mustang one of the most beautiful airplanes ever built. But walking toward Sharon's P-51 the day of my first flight, the closer I got the more the beautiful plane began to look like a coffin. Was I ready? Would I soar like an eagle or would my first flight end in a million dollar pile of rubble?

If Sharon had any trepidations, she didn't show it. I was a bundle or nerves, but she kept right on talking as though we were going for a walk in the park. "Go to six thousand feet. Practice some air landings, the whole caboodle: gear down, full flaps, trim, throttle. Watch the air speed. Control tends to get heavy at slow speed. Don't get below a hundred knots. If it stalls, it wants to go over on its back, so watch it. Don't try to pour on power too fast or it'll snap roll. Remember: if you have to go around, easy on the throttle, but even at full throttle acceleration is slow, so stay on top of it. Keep your speed up. Better to land too fast than not at all."

By the time I finally buckled up in the Mustang's cramped cockpit my head was crammed with instructions. Fortunately, Sharon, standing on the wing so she could look over my shoulder, helped me with the preflight checklist, even though the last few days we'd already gone over it dozens of times. Again she talked me through starting the engine: battery on, radiators open, starter on, magnetos, fuel boost pumps, prime for four seconds, fire it up, mixture to normal, then sit and listen with awe to the purring mighty Merlin.

"Don't forget: easy on the throttle. Take your time with the before-takeoff check and the landing check. Okay?"

I think I answered with a nod and an "Okay." I was in such a combined state of terror and ecstasy at what I was about to do that my brain didn't know which way to spin.

She whacked me on the back and climbed down off the wing, and I was alone—totally alone in a million dollar airplane with more than 1,600 snorting horses, each of which was waiting for the chance to kill me.

Well, I could either fly the stupid plane or cut the engine and climb out. Since I was too big a coward to climb out, I released the brakes and eased the throttle forward gingerly as though it were a butterfly I didn't want to hurt. I was rewarded by a deepening roar from the huge Merlin engine, and to my horror the plane began rolling. Fortunately, my training kicked in and I was able to bring it out on the runway without ground looping, and I rumbled along toward the end, making jerky S-turns to I could see around the P-51's long nose and not ignominiously run off the runway.

At the head of the runway, I swung into position, and by referring to the takeoff check list from time to time, made sure my harness was securely locked, tail wheel locked, altimeter correctly set, rudder trim at 6-degrees to offset the takeoff torque, elevator and rudder trim set, canopy securely latched, carburetor set to ram air, radiator to automatic.

Done.

I had to take a deep breath before I was able to call the tower and squeak out a takeoff request. I was almost sorry when they gave it to me. Lordy, it was hot under the canopy. Even my hands were sweating.

Since I now had no recourse short of leaping out and running, I looked a deep breath, released the brakes and eased on power. The big plane responded, starting to roll. I was committed. I steadily increased power, listening to the powerful engine, half afraid I would hear a frightening burp or burble. As the speed increase, despite the 6-degrees of trim, I had to keep increasing pressure on the right rudder peddle to counter the big prop's gyroscopic torque that attempt to pull to the left.

With one eye on the airspeed, another eye watching the side of the runway, and another on the horizon, I eased the stick forward to lift the tail wheel and bring the nose level. Ahhh. Better. Now I could see straight ahead at the end of the runway that was rushing at me at about a gazillion miles an hour.

I was too traumatized at the sight to even think of looking at the air speed indicator. But I had to be going fast enough to fly a brick so I eased back on the stick and we were up and away.

Once in the air and climbing, I pulled the wheels up and the big bird surged skyward.

I'd done it! I was actually flying a Mustang! The wonder of it drained away my apprehension. Actually, once at altitude and with good airspeed, the plane was remarkably easy to fly.

At 6,000 feet I practices slow speed flight. Despite Sharon's warning, I was taken by surprise when at one time I stalled out and the big bird quickly rolled inverted. But I had plenty of altitude and time to build up speed before I regained control and tamed the beast.

"Ah ha," I told her. "You may be a big doll, but you're sneaky."

After twenty minutes of sheer delight pretending I was an eagle with an eleven-foot propeller, I called the tower and told them I was coming in.

Now I would have to prove I was a real pilot. I knew everyone on the ground would be watching, so all the time I was flying the approach I kept reminding myself what Sharon had said: "Keep your speed up." I also had to remember: gas to fullest tank, boost pump on, mixture normal, prop at 2,700 rpm, radiator auto, partial flaps. When speed was below 170 knots, I shoved the gear handle, and when the wheels came down the speed dropped so abruptly that for a moment I felt a surge of panic. Resisting an impulse to jam the throttle forward, I gingerly added a little power to hold at 150 knots with full flaps during the final.

Coasting in over the beginning of the runway at a little over 125 knots, holding my breath while trying to ignore the quiver in my legs, I chopped the power. My practice landings at altitude had given me a good feel for the Mustang's gliding capabilities, but I was still a little startled at how quickly she settled with very little ground effect, I smacked down harder than I wanted to but almost in the center of the runway, which I thought made up for the embarrassing bounce.

Still, I don't think I took a breath until I turned off onto the peripheral road where I paused for a moment to convince myself that I actually was on the ground. I had about the same feeling Sir Edmund Hillery must have felt standing on top of Mt. Everest as I S-turned my way back to the flight line in front of the hanger. Working more automatically than with purpose, I held the brakes and gave the Mustang a little throttle to get coolant in the tanks and to get the oil moving. Then it was fuel mixture to idle cut off, magnetos off, fuel shutoff to off, fairing door released, battery off, carburetor to unrammed air, unbuckle my harness, wipe sweat off face and listen to the incredible silence.

Climbing out of the cockpit I fought an impulse to run around turning handsprings. Instead I played the part of the cool World War II ace, preparing clever answers for Sharon's congratulations and her amazement at what a wonderful pilot I was. But it wasn't Sharon who walked out to meet me. It was Morris Harlen, and walking beside him, Carmelita Mendoza.

CHAPTER TEN

I loosened my parachute harness, feeling a little disappointed that Sharon hadn't even bothered to watch my almost perfect landing. It must mean that she had so much confidence in me she did not feel the need to watch.

Harlen, wearing a big grin, was striding along carrying a champagne bottle. Carmelita wore a mini-dress that displayed her magnificent legs. Despite three inch heels on her sandals, she matched Harlen stride for stride, her raven hair flowing in the breeze.

"Nice going," Harlen said. He held out the champagne bottle that was wet with condensed moisture. "Congratulations."

I would have preferred a Coke or, better yet, a hot fudge sundae, but bowing to tradition I took the icy bottle and swigged down a swallow. Carmelita had been carrying an empty champagne glass and she held it out for me to fill.

She raised the glass toward me. "Congratulations. It looks like you've made the team."

Harlen took the bottle from me and raised it high. "Here's to teamwork."

He took a swig and offered the bottle to me. I shook my head. "Thanks. Maybe later."

He refilled Carmelita's glass. Seeing the two of them together made me feel like a dunce. Carmelita and Harlen were obviously friends—or more. And I had talked to her as though she'd never heard of him. Had she told him about my visit? Harlen might wonder why I had taken it upon myself to talk to her. Could the visit have put a rent in my cover.

If it had, Harlen gave no sign, but I was relieved when he said, "This is Carmelita, Jorge's sister. Carmelita, Ben Roan, best damned pilot in the E.T.O."

So, she hadn't told him. I wondered why.

"E.T.O.?" she said.

"European Theatre of Operation. An old World War Two expression."

"Is he better than Jorge?"

"So far. Jorge bounced twice on his first landing."

She sipped the champagne, her smoldering eyes measuring me over the top of the glass. The intensity of her stare made me uneasy. I couldn't tell if it was filled with hate, amusement, or speculation. Hate about taking the place of her brother I could understand. Amusement, certainly. I often had that effect on beautiful women. But speculation? Speculation of what?

"I'm sorry about your brother," I said as though I'd just met her.

She lowered the glass with a slight nod. "Thank you."

"Come on," Harlen said. "I want to talk to you about a proposition. Something you'll like."

Walking with them toward Sharon's hanger, I thought about Harlen's words. We were already involved in a proposition, one that he had to assume I liked or I wouldn't have accepted. In one way I hoped this new proposition would be about his involvement with drugs. Bremm would be happy if I could bring him something that would confirm the DEA's suspicions. On the other hand, I hoped that Bremm was wrong and Harlen would turn out to be clean. Then I could work for him with a clear conscious because I wouldn't be spying.

Inside the hanger Sharon was sitting at her cluttered desk putting her signature on checks. When she saw us she got up and came around the desk with her hand out. "I see you're in one piece," she said. "How is my plane?"

"Buried," I said. "I landed six feel low. I had to dig my way out."

"I figured you would. I couldn't bear to watch."

74

Holding her hand I was again struck by the strength of her grip. You didn't get that kind of hand strength by flying. It pretty well confirmed my suspicion that she worked out on a regular basis.

Harlen chuckled. "He was great. Only one bounce."

"Well, that's a relief. I'll have the landing gear checked."

"It wasn't that bad," I said.

"He's going to be okay." Harlen pulled a chair around for Carmelita who sat down and crossed her legs. Harlen pulled up another chair which he indicated to me. "Sit down."

I sat, glad that I wasn't facing Carmelita and her crossed legs. Sharon went back behind her desk and for some reason glared at me as though I had damaged her airplane.

Harlen perched on the corner of the desk. Judging by the disapproving look on Sharon's face, it wouldn't surprise me if Harlen's pants didn't burst into flame.

"Well, how did you like it, flying the Mustang?" Harlen asked.

I gave him a quick thumbs up. "Great. Terrific plane."

"How would you like to own one?"

I stared at him, stunned. I knew enough about the antique warbirds to know you didn't just pluck them off trees.

"Well, sure," I said. "Who wouldn't?"

"They're available, for the right price."

I was well aware of their price. So I laughed, but without humor. "The right price for you maybe. But I'm just a poor working stiff. Way out of my league."

"Not necessarily. I'll give you the same deal I gave Sharon."

I stared at him, unable to believe my good fortune. Most pilots had to wait years to acquire one of the rare warbirds, provided they could even afford one. Still, I hesitated. There had to be a catch somewhere. Either Harlen was prepared to pay me a fantastic salary, or the kind of air show he expected would cancel my life insurance policy.

I probably looked as stupefied as I felt. I was like a starving kid being offered a whole carrot cake. I wanted to reach out and snatch it, but as a kid brought up on the mean streets of L.A. I knew that cake was either an illusion or the minute I reached for it, it would be snatched away.

On the other hand, Harlen had made a deal with Sharon regarding her plane. The deal he offered me would probably have the same string attached, one that would tie me to his drug dealing.

I shifted my stare to Sharon with the idea that if Harlen was trying to work some kind of scheme she would give me a warning. But she sat motionless, her expression blank.

Reasoning that I had nothing to lose by listening to Harlen's proposition, I said, "What kind of deal is that?"

"While you're making payments, you fly on my team. I take care of maintenance, hanger fees, fuel, insurance, everything."

"Sounds good, but we're still talking about a million dollar or more. That's a hefty payment every month. My business can't handle that."

"I'll pay you to fly the air shows, of course, and I think I can arrange some extra income." He looked at me as though my answer could spell the difference between life and death.

My pulse rate went up a few points. If Bremm was right Harlen might be offering me some kind of drug deal. Then I remembered he'd said I could have the same deal as Sharon and my blood chilled. She had to be dealing.

My voice was guarded when I asked, "Extra income? How? I don't have time---"

"Air shows."

"You mean air races?"

It gave me a thrill just thinking about zooming around a bunch of pylons at 500 miles an hour a few feet off the ground.

He shook his head. "Reno is the only place that has air races any more. I mean air shows. Big business all over the world. And they all want the warbirds. They bring in business. You fly in, let the people come by for a look. You shake a few hands, do a few flybys, fly back home."

"That's it?"

He held up both hands. "That's it."

"What do you get out of it?"

"Advertising. Your plane will be painted with my logo. Like those NASCARs. When people ask about it, we give them a brochure."

It kind of made sense. Companies as big as Harlen's spent big bucks on advertising. I did have one question, however.

"You own the planes. Why don't you just hire pilots to fly them to the shows."

"I tried that." He shook his head. "Didn't have the right mystic. The pilots are as important as their planes. I need pilots who want to own their own warbird, pilots who want to build a personal image."

"How do we do that?"

He shrugged. "A few shows. Your name---and my name---will get out there. That's what we want."

I glanced at Carmelita who uncrossed her legs and gave me a smile that on a billboard would have solved all of Harlen's advertising problems. I said, "Did you make the same offer to Jorge?"

Harlen hesitated. The question had taken him by surprise, but he recovered quickly. "Pretty much. Does it matter?"

"I guess not," I said, although I was curious about Jorge's qualifications to be a company spokesperson. He hadn't looked as though he smiled a lot.

Harlen pulled a business envelope out of his jacket pocket and offered it to me. "Here. Look over the contract. Give it some thought. Think of the fun you'll have at those air shows. People all love warbird aces."

I reached for the envelope. He was right about the fun. I could already see myself zooming around in front of those big air show crowds. And it couldn't hurt Roan Security's business either. I'd have to figure a way to include a pitch for my company that wouldn't get Harlen's nose out of joint. I'd also have to talk over the deal with Bremm. I didn't think he would turn it down. It seemed to me it would fit right in with our plan to infiltrate Harlen's operations.

"I'll have my attorney take a look at it," I told him.

He pushed off the desk and held out his hand. As I shook it, he said, "Don't take too long. Those Mustangs don't stay on the market long."

"Okay." I was sure he was right. Although more than 16,000 P-51s had been manufactured during WWII, it is estimated that only a little more than 100 are still flying, and as usual with vintage machines, each day that passed make it more difficult to obtain spare parts. In a few years almost all the old planes would either be in museums or hauled to the air shows on flatbed trucks. I only hoped it wouldn't be in my lifetime.

Harlen was moving away when Carmelita uncoiled her legs and got up. "Have they heard anything more about my brother?" she asked.

"Not a thing," I told her. "Not that I know of."

"Let me know if you find out anything."

"Okay."

She hurried to catch up with Harlen, her heels clicking like castanets and her short skirt swinging like it belonged to a haughty flamenco dancer.

My eyes were still watching her when Sharon said, "More?"

Reluctantly my eyes turned away from Carmelita. "What?"

"She said let her know if you hear anything 'more' about her brother. What did she mean by that?"

Darn. I would have preferred that Sharon didn't know I'd talked to Carmelita. Jorge's murder was supposed to be none of my business. "I thought she was asking both of us," I lied. "I just assumed you hadn't heard anything more. Have you?"

My diversion was weak, and the look in her probing eyes gave me the feeling that it hadn't really fooled her, but to my relief she chose not to pursue the subject. "No," she said. She got up and held out her hand. "The contract. Mind if I take a look?"

"Nope."

I handed her Harlen's envelope. It wasn't sealed and she took out the contract. She sat in her chair and snapped on a desk lamp. Holding the contract in the light, she began reading. I moved around to look over her shoulder, my head close to hers. The contract appeared to be a high quality printout from a computerized document. The rate she flipped through the three pages led me to believe it was familiar, except for the numbers probably a copy of her own contract with Harlen.

When she did peruse a particular paragraph, she read slowly, sometimes using her finger to follow a complex passage. I wouldn't have minded if she had taken the remainder of the afternoon. With her hair brushing my cheek, I was acutely conscious of her subtle perfume.

I sort of hung there, in suspended animation, breathing in that mesmerizing scent until she finished reading and slipped the contract back in the envelope. Turning her head to hand the envelope to me brought her lips within striking distance, and if I hadn't already been paralyzed I would have made a total fool of myself.

I guess she didn't realizing her peril because she did not immediately recoil. Or maybe the perfume was affecting her, too, because her eyes kind of locked on mine and her lips parted a little. After what seemed like a couple of eternities but was probably no more than a millisecond, I forced myself to blink and jerked my head away .

Straightening, fumbling the envelope, I cleared my throat. "Did..." My lips felt stiff, dry as a California arroyo. "Did it look all right?"

Was I mistaken or did she look disappointed? Could it be because I hadn't taken advantage of my chance to kiss her, or because she didn't want me to become involved with Harlen? "Depends on what you mean by 'all right,'" she said. "It'll put you in Harlen's back pocket for a few years."

I wished I could tell her it was exactly what I wanted—or rather what David Bremm wanted. But I just managed a wry grin.

"The story of my life. It's always somebody."

Her face sort of hardened as though I had said something she didn't want to hear. "Tomorrow," she said. "You can shoot a few landings. Nine o'clock."

I stepped back, resisting an impulse to salute. "Right. Nine o'clock. A.M."

I walked toward the side door leading to the pilot's locker room. I wanted to look back to see if she was watching me walk away, except I didn't want to find out the truth, which probably was that she couldn't care less.

CHAPTER ELEVEN

When I called David Bremm he told me to meet him in the giant parking lot of the Orange County mall in front of Denny's restaurant. He didn't want to take the chance of someone seeing me going into the DEA offices. Actually, I preferred meeting him at the mall; it saved me a long drive to Santa Ana in heavy traffic, and while ordinarily I don't mind traffic, by three o'clock in the afternoon the traffic was a mad house. Besides, the DEA could afford burning up gasoline sitting stalled in traffic better than I.

I thought Bremm would be driving a big government limousine with the DEA logo on the side and maybe a couple of pennants on the front fenders to warn away slow drivers. Instead, he pulled up in a two year old Toyota Camry sedan. I walked over and got in the passenger seat.

He had on a dark suit and darker glasses. He carried an automatic pistol under his jacket in a shoulder holster. It looked like a .40 Beretta Cougar.

"What's this about a contract?" he said.

I handed him the envelope. "Harlen made an offer to sell me a Mustang."

"Like the one he's selling Daadian?"

"That's right. From what I gather, pretty much the same deal."

He gave the contract a desultory perusal. At one point he reached up and took` his dark glasses off so he could get a better look. I knew he had come to the price.

"Holy shit!" he said. "A million three?"

"A bargain. The real cost is in maintenance and aviation gas."

"Damn. He give any indication on how this ties into his

dealing?"

"Not really. He said he wants us to participate in air shows, but I don't know how that could connect to dealing drugs."

He folded the contract and inserted it back in the envelope. "Okay. It'll have to go down this way: sign the contract, buy the plane, make the payments, the whole enchilada. I'll arrange reimbursement."

"Might not be necessary. I'll get paid for performing at the air shows. And he said he can arrange for me to make some extra money."

"Extra, huh? If he's setting up something, he'll give you plenty of slack."

"Like he gave Jorge?"

Bremm had the good manners to look uncomfortable. "We have no evidence that Harlen had anything to do with that."

"Do you have any evidence that he didn't?"

He spread his fingers. "Not at this time."

I wondered if he would tell me when they did have some concrete information. I doubted it. But there was something he could tell me. "What do you know about Jorge's sister?"

"Carmelita? Not much. She works for Harlen."

"Works for him? I thought she was his girl friend."

"She is. But she's on his payroll. We think she's also involved in his dealing."

"Maybe she didn't approve of her brother's involvement with Harlen's operation."

"She got him his job. Why wouldn't she approve?"

"Maybe she thought it was just flying. Maybe he thought so, too."

"So?"

"So maybe when he found out about the drug dealing, he wanted out."

Bremm's face pulled into a skeptical scowl. "So Harlen killed him? More likely he wouldn't like his sister involved with Harlen."

"That would be a motive for Jorge to kill Harlen, not the other way around."

"I don't know. If Harlen made a play for my sister, I'd want to kill him. If I had a sister.

"What you're saying is you don't have any ideas why he was killed."

Bremm started the car's engine, which I took as a sign the meeting was terminated. I opened the car door and got out.

"Keep me up to date," he said.

"Yeah, sure."

Watching him drive away the thought that gave me a headache was that I was not only going to be on the hook for more than a million dollars, I was also being sucked deeper into a pit of quicksand that could end up with me breathing mud.

CHAPTER TWELVE

A week later on a gorgeous California morning I finished shooting landings in Sharon's Mustang and was on the flight line talking to Jack Blutcher. Standing next to Sharon's sleek plane in my flight coveralls and chute harness and with my helmet under my arm, I felt like a WWII fighter pilot after a tough mission. I sort of wished the P-51 sported a few bullet holes and had half a wing missing.

I gave Jack a crooked, fighter-pilot grin. "Gas her up," I said. "I'm going up again."

"No, you're not. You're time's up. She's got another student."

"Oh." So much for saving the world.

"You almost screwed up a couple of those go-arounds. You've got to get a better feel for the throttle."

"I can handle it."

He spit on the tarmac in disgust. "A couple of months ago a better pilot than you aborted a landing. He manhandled the throttle. The torque rolled him on his back. He went in upside down."

I'd read about the deadly crash. The mental picture of what had happened—and how quickly it could happen--sobered me, that plus the fact that I had wrestled the Mustang out of a similar tendency to roll during one of the practice landings. "Okay," I said. "Next time up I'll work on the throttle from five or six thousand feet."

"Better make it eight or ten. Jam the throttle. See how fast it snaps over. Then if you over-control, how fast it'll snap back the other way. You'll probably end up in a split S or a spin so you'll need the altitude."

I was well aware of the plane's idiosyncrasy. I'd never told Jack that it had already happened to me. I turned to look at the P-51. It should have been called a Tiger instead of a Mustang. It appeared so benign. Sitting placidly on the tarmac, it was hard to believe it was a born killer, designed to bring down prey. And like a natural killer, if taken for granted, it could just as quickly kill its master.

But that was true of most powerful machines. The trick was to master the machine so well you could use it with joy while never forgetting that it was capable of turning on you.

"Good idea," I told Jack. "I'll do that."

I was considerably more subdued when I headed for the pilot's locker room. Before I reached the door, Sharon came out of her hanger and motioned to me. I changed course and went to meet her. Waiting for me in her white coveralls with one hand on her hip, her hair swirling in an infinitesimal breeze, and her eyes glowing, she kind of reminded me of the Mustang: a great joy if mastered, but one that could kill if not properly handled.

"Harlen wants us to join him for lunch," she said.

I shook my head. "Can't do it today. I've got some things at my office—"

"Harlen wants us to join him for lunch." Her voice did not raise in volume, but it made me realize the statement was a command, not a request.

"Right," I said. "Lunch. Come as you are or should I drop off my chute harness?"

"Suit yourself," she said. "I'll be in my car in fifteen minutes."

She went back in the hanger and, for once, I didn't take the time to watch her walk away.

Fifteen minutes later, wearing blue jeans, short-sleeved golf shirt and pilot's jodhpurs, I slipped into the passenger seat of her vintage 450 SEC Mercedes and she headed for the highway where she turned right toward Newport.

`Although she gave no sign of wanting conversation, it was seldom lately I had the chance to talk to her so I decided to take advantage of the opportunity to play detective.

"How long have you known Harlen?" I began.

"Not long."

"I thought maybe he was an old boy friend?"

"Not my type."

"What is your type?"

"Nobody I know."

I was beginning to think my detective skills were a little rusty. Not only had I learned nothing, but I'd gotten completely off track.

"Tell me about Harlen," I said.

Even though her glance was quick I detected a gleam of disgust. "You should have done your due diligence before you signed the contract."

"I'm not worried about the contract. I know all about his offices in Newport Center and his holdings. I just don't know much about him as a person."

"What makes you think I do?"

"Well, you've obviously known him longer than I have."

She concentrated on a car that cut in front of us, expertly avoiding a collision. "From what I've learned, he was a dock worker in New Jersey. Got to be head of their union branch. Then—I think with union help--he bought out a waste management company. Put his own name on it. Now he operates in several states."

"You think the union is still involved?"

"No. I don't think so."

I'd have to ask Bremm about that. He would surely know. But I still didn't know how close her relationship was—or had been—with Harlen. I couldn't ask directly, so I said, "What's he like to work for? Any, uh, problems?"

She caught the nuance in my voice and hesitated. "He's never tried to hit on me. Always been all business. No pressure. But I get the feeling it wouldn't be a good idea to cross him."

"You think Jorge might have tried?"

"Jorge? As far as I know he had no reason to."

"This whole deal with airplanes. It's got to be costing him a fortune. Hard to believe it's just for the advertising."

"Oh," she said. "Why do you think he's doing it?"

"I asked you first."

She lifted one hand from the steering wheel. "Who knows? A lot of wealthy guys are into warbirds. What about you? Why are you into them?"

Obviously, she didn't want to talk about Harlen. Was it because she was involved in his dealing? Whatever her reasons I doubted that I would get more information from her. Right now I wasn't much more than a total stranger. She probably wouldn't let me in on any of her secrets until I gained her trust, which might mean convincing her I was up to my eyeballs in Harlen's drug dealing.

"Well, it's kind of an accident," I said. "Jack bought the Stearmans and that got me interested in learning to fly. I thought they were about as good as I could afford. But when Harlen made his offer... well, who wouldn't fly a Mustang if he got the chance?"

"The strings didn't bother you?"

"Strings?"

"Being on Harlen's team. Doing what he tells you."

My interrogation had taken a nasty turn. Now she was the one asking the questions. But right now I wasn't any more ready to open up to her than she was to me.

"He hasn't told me anything. What about you? Has he put pressure on you to do anything you didn't want to?"

She shook her head. "No."

"You think he might?"

"If he makes a pass I'll shove his Mustang up..."

She cut off the thought, but I thought that if I were Harlen I wouldn't want to pull the wrong string. Still, she had avoided answering questions about Harlen's drug dealing.

We were both silent during the remainder of the fifteen minute drive. She was a good driver, instinctively choosing the lane of traffic that was moving the fastest. I had to admire her concentration. I've ridden with drivers who kept my toes curled. Her mind had to be churning with questions about Harlen and his motives, but she was still able to drive with such precision I was able to relax and concentrate on my own thoughts. I wished I knew what was going through her mind. I would also like to know how much she knew about Harlen's hidden occupation, or if she knew anything at all. Maybe during the coming meeting she or Harlen would let something slip that would give me a clue.

We met Harlen at a Mexican restaurant in Newport Center that was surrounded by what in California passed for skyscrapers. Harlen had brought Carmelita with him, and the presence of two gorgeous brunettes gave the lunch a definite exotic aura.

We chewed our way through some terrific Mexican dishes. Some were a little too picante for my tastes, but both Carmelita and Sharon seemed to enjoy the dishes that set my mouth on fire.

I said to Sharon, "If it's too spicy, they probably make dishes more suited for Anglos."

She shook her head. "I love it. A lot of Middle East food is hotter than this."

Carmelita said, "That's right. You should try *khoresht.*"

Sharon gave her an odd look. "You've had *khoresht?*"

Carmelita hesitated, then said. "I enjoy different cuisine."

"If you want hot," Harley said with his mouth full, "you should try real Indian curry."

I listened to them discussing spicy cuisines of the world. I knew that many Hispanics enjoyed food that would burn a hole through a steel plate, but I didn't realize that some Middle Eastern and Asian cultures also enjoy very spicy cuisine. It seemed that every nation in the world went in for heavily spiced food except those of European descent. Maybe that's what made their girl's dark eyes like black smoke from hot internal fires.

I noticed that Harlen, despite his knowledge regarding spicy Indian and Chinese food, steered clear of the hottest dishes. It made me curious about his background. What was Harlen's culture? Sharon said he had been a dock worker. Maybe he was Irish. Or Italian. Or

Polish. I'd have to ask Bremm? They should have a file on him a couple of inches thick.

On the other hand, did I really want to know? It would be like making friends with a fellow soldier. If he were to be wounded or killed, you didn't want him to be a close friend. If I had to be responsible for bringing Harlen down, I certainly didn't want to become a friend.

Looking at Sharon I felt a stab of dismay, because the same thing applied to my growing attraction to her. If I brought Harlen down, it would also bring down his associates, all those involved with his drug dealing cartel. And that would probably include Carmelita and Sharon.

The thought almost spoiled my appetite. It did put a damper on my usual witty repartee. I allowed Harlen to dominate the conversation, expecting him to talk about why he had called the meeting, but he rambled on, mostly about airplanes and famous aces and dogfights, with never a hint about why we were here. It wasn't until a bus boy was clearing away the detritus that Harlen dispelled any doubts that this was definitely a business meeting.

Pouring himself the last of his bottle of Corona beer, he said, "I love this Mexican beer: Corona, Dos Equis, Pacifica. It's all good."

"It's the water," Sharon said with a wry smile. "Something in the water."

"Right," Harlen said. "Don't drink the water, only the beer." The tone of his voice changed, losing all sense of humor, when he said to Sharon, "You ever been to Mexico?"

Sharon caught the sudden hardening of his tone, and her own voice was flat and noncommittal as she replied, "A couple of times."

"Acapulco?"

She shook her head. "No."

His voice lightened again. "You'll love it, won't she, Carmelita."

"One of my favorite places," she said.

Harlen's ability to change character with a chameleon-like

rapidity amazed me. I supposed it was one reason why he was such a success in business: competitors would have a difficult time keeping up with his changes, always keeping them off balance. I cautioned myself never to be caught up in his moods because they could change in an instant. And I couldn't be sure which held the most menace, his jovial humor or his flat, deadly tone.

Sharon continued to stare at Harlen as though she, too, was puzzled by his abrupt mood swings. "Why should I?" she asked.

He made a tight little smile, "You're going to fly your Mustang to Acapulco." "

Her eyes didn't so much as blink, but her voice did. "Oh? Why?"

Instead of answering her directly, he looked at me. "You and Jack Blucher fly down commercial."

"To Acapulco? Mexico?"

"Right."

Maybe Sharon hadn't been shaken by the command, but I certainly was. The look of incredulity on my face prompted Harlen to add, "You pick up your Mustang there."

I was too dumbfounded to speak. I hadn't given much thought to how or where I would take delivery of the Mustang. In some childlike corner of my mind I sort of expected that it would miraculously appear on the flight line some morning, maybe with a red ribbon around it. But Mexico? That was way out of the dream.

Even Sharon sounded a little incredulous when she said, "Why do you want me to go?"

"Why?" He gave her the same dark look that guy in the movies got when he was asked, 'You talkin' tuh me?'

Sharon ignored Harlen's displeasure at being questioned. "He picks up the plane; he flies it back. There's nothing I can do.

Harlen hesitated before answering as though saying anything would undermine his absolute authority. Then he smiled. "Acapulco's Alextrimo Air Show. It's one of the biggest in Mexico. I want both of you to participate."

"Participate?" I said. "You mean fly? In the air show?"

He turned his eyes on me. They were as hard as his voice when he said, "Is that going to be a problem?"

I turned up my palms. "Not for me."

Sharon asked, "Is this part of your advertising plan?"

"Right," Harlen said with a broad smile. "The inauguration."

Sharon continued to probe: "Why Mexico? Isn't that a little out of your territory?"

Could she be talking about Harlen's waste management business--or his drug dealing?

Harlen answered my unspoken question. "I want to expand my operations in Mexico. We could use the advertising and the good will."

That made sense. "Show the flag, so to speak," I said.

"Exactly. My associates down there will handle the details. Blutcher will certify the plane is airworthy as promised. After the show, you'll both fly your planes back here."

'Your planes.' That had a lovely ring.

"That's about fifteen hundred miles," Sharon said. "They don't have the range."

"Drop tanks. You can do it."

I made some mental calculations. During World War II, P-51s with drop tanks had flown six hour missions escorting bombers deep into Germany as far a Berlin. That was almost 1,500 miles around trip, and they still had enough fuel in their internal tanks to engage in dog fights after they jettisoned the drop tanks. But Acapulco was a long jump, more than 1,500 hundred miles as the crow flies, provided the crow didn't run into bad weather. I'd have to ask Jack if he thought it could be done, although it's hard to believe Harlen hadn't already done the arithmetic.

Since I was committed to Harlen's orders wherever they took me, I gave him a big smile. "Right," I said. "I've always wanted to see Acapulco."

"When is this air show?" Sharon asked.

"Next week?"

Next week! Whoa. That was going to be a problem.

I quickly made some mental calculations. I would have to reschedule some Roan Security business meetings, but if we didn't have to spend too much time in Mexico it could be done without too much damage.

"Only one little problem," I said. Harlen frowned as though it were up to him to decide whether there was a problem or not. "I can't speak Spanish."

"Me neither," Sharon said. There was a trace of relief in her voice. It seemed she wasn't hilariously excited about partying in Acapulco."

"No problem," Harlen said. "Most of my contacts speak English. And Carmelita'll be there if there are any problems."

I glanced at Carmelita. It appeared that she was more than just a girl friend to Harlen. She sat impassively, but with Harlen's words, her face that had seemed so beautiful had taken on a decidedly deadly cast.

Sharon also sat quietly sipping her Carona, and I wondered what was going through her mind. Had she known about Carmelita's business ties with Harlen? And what were the dimensions of her own association with Harlen? Could she refuse the trip to Mexico? She'd made it clear she had no romantic interest in Harlen. But was it true? Did she considered Carmelita a rival for Harlen's affections? If so, the news that Carmelita was a business as well as a romantic rival must have come as a shock.

"I assume you both have passports?"

Sharon nodded, and I said, "Yes."

I made a mental note to make sure my passport was still valid. I rarely used it, but now that a passport was required for virtually any trip outside the U.S., it would be a good idea to have it renewed. If its validity had indeed lapsed, I'd have to get Bremm to pull strings to expedite the procedure.

92

Harlen extracted several folded papers from his jacket pocket and pushed aside glasses and dishes to spread them on the white table cloth. "These are clearance forms for flying into Mexico and back. Sign them and I'll turn a copy in to the Mexican consulate."

After a desultory glance at the papers, I signed my copies and pushed them back to Harlen. Sharon sat staring at her copies, and I thought for a moment she was going to refuse to sign. Then, abruptly, with the set of her mouth showing more resignation than satisfaction, she signed the papers. She did not give them back to Harlen; he had to reach across the table and gather them up.

"Carmelita'll fill you in on the air show. I suggest the two of you work out the routines you'll fly."

He leaned back in his chair and picked up his half empty glass of Mexican beer. "So. Here's to Acapulco."

We all joined in the toast, but watching Sharon's face, I had the impression she was about as enchanted as Sleeping Beauty would have been to wake up and find that the prince who had just kissed her was Quasimodo.

CHAPTER THIRTEEN

When Sharon saw the paint job Harlen had ordered for her beautiful silver Mustang, her moment of shock gave way to clinched jaws of anger. Then, realizing that the decision was out of her hands, the anger was replaced by sagging shoulders and an expression of dismay and resignation.

Actually, it didn't look too bad. The Mustang's prop-spinner and the forward nose had been painted bright red. A long slash, sort of like the Nike swoosh, ran from the nose to the tail. If it wasn't for Harlen's logo--a big green trash truck lifting a big Dumpster and rainbowed by the words 'M. H. Waste Management'—that took up most of the plane's aft fuselage, it would have looked rather jaunty. I assumed that the Mustang I was to pick up in Acapulco would have the same motif. The paint job certainly did advertise Harlen's company. Seeing the two planes roaring side by side over Acapulco Bay, I'd be tempted to run out and sign up for Harlen's waste management myself.

Sharon was still muttering to herself when she had begun her long flight to Acapulco. Her plane had been fitted with a 150-gallon fuel tank under each wing. But even with the drop tanks and full wing and behind-the-seat internal tanks, I wasn't sure she could make it non-stop.

"Will she have any trouble?" I said to Jack sitting beside me on a United Airlines' flight from LAX to Mexico City. ""That's a long flight."

"Shouldn't have if she doesn't push it. She keeps her altitude around twelve angels and cruise around three hundred knots it won't be a problem."

I eased the seat back and relaxed, visualizing Sharon in the cramped cockpit of the Mustang. P-51s were built for fighting not for pilot comfort. Sharon was close to six feet and weighted around 130 pounds, which was a little thinner than most WWII pilots. Even so, being strapped in so tight you could hardly move while sitting on an unyielding parachute pack was bad enough for two or three hours, but by the end of six or seven hours it could be numbing.

Harlen had been too frugal to buy Jack and me first class tickets; even so, on the commercial jet we could move around, and were supplied with food, drink and entertainment while Sharon would have nothing to eat or drink, unless she took along a goodie bag and a bottle of water. And her only entertainment would be in the form of sheer panic if her engine misfired over Mexico's Sierra Madre Occidental range. The advent of the Global Positioning System had taken the anxiety out of navigation, but the thrill of flying could be considerably dulled by worry over every little fluctuation in any one of the instruments.

If Harlen came through on his promise to deliver my Mustang in Acapulco, I would soon be facing the same uneasy flight while heading back north. I couldn't help but think about the problems faced by pilots flying during WWII. If I had to make a forced landing, I wouldn't have to worry about death by irate citizens or long years in a German Stalag.

"I wonder why Mexico," I mused aloud.

Jack looked up from the inflight magazine he'd been reading. "Why Mexico what?"

"Why I'm to pick up the plane in Mexico."

"Makes sense. After the war, the Army scrapped most of their piston-engine aircraft, including all but a couple of hundred P-51s. A few were used in the Korean war. Some were sold to foreign countries. Guatemala had a bunch of them. Those turn up once in a while. They're usually a piece of shit if they fly at all. I'll bet yours is one of them."

That was Jack: always the optimist. "He wants me to fly it in the Acapulco air show. I couldn't do that if it wasn't flyable."

"It's you life, not his."

"Well, if it's that bad, I'm not going to fly it."

Jack made one of his smiles that was supposed to be

humorous but which made him look more like Vlad the Impaler smiling at the advancing Turkish army. "Your own plane. You'd fly if it was a bucket of bolts."

I would have laughed if he hadn't been right. I'd fallen in love with the famous Mustang the minute I'd seen one. Flying Sharon's had only deepened my affection. I loved every minute I was in the air. In fact, I would have changed places with Sharon and flown her plane to Acapulco myself if she had trusted me not to end up as scorpion bait in the middle of the Sonora desert.

Still, later in the day I was prepared for the worst when Jack and I got out of the taxi that had brought us to an ancient but neatly maintained airport about ten miles east of Acapulco. A number of private planes were parked on the freshly surfaced tarmac of the flight line bordering the single runway. Most had probably been flown in for their owners to attend the air show. Some had just arrived, their engines still running. Airport personnel were busy servicing the planes, while golf carts shuttled pilots and passengers between the planes and a small passenger terminal next to a two-storied airport traffic tower.

Jack and I watched a Cessna business jet land followed closely by an old C-47 transport as we walked toward one of the hangers that had a rusty sheet-metal roof. The front of the hanger supported what was left of a sign with peeling paint that had once read "Gomez Aero Servicio." Several smaller buildings fronting the flight line appeared to be machine shops and shops selling aircraft parts.

Looking at the signs in Spanish made me remember that we were emissaries of a drug dealer. If Harlen had enemies in the drug cartels of Mexico, this entire episode of selling him a P-51 might be nothing but a scam to get him and anyone connected to his organization into Mexico. When Jack and I walked into the old hanger it was possible we'd be greeted either by gun fire or the Federale Policia.

My apprehension was not helped when I pulled open the small personnel door in the front of the hanger, and it announced our arrival with a shrill squeal. I was prepared to duck and run as Jack and I stepped onto the hanger's concrete floor. I guess Jack had been harboring the same thought because he quickly moved away from the open door. What little light there was in the hanger oozed in through

96

rows of grimy windows high up on the sides? Coming from brilliant sunshine into the relative darkness of the hanger, I could see little. But to my relief, nothing happened.

My eyes adjusted quickly to the darkness, and I saw that the hanger was empty except for a canvas-covered plane near the far wall.

I tensed when I heard the click of approaching footsteps, but they were the steps of one person. It didn't seem likely that there would be an ambush with only one man. Man? They sounded more like the footsteps of a woman. She came out of the shadows, striding with the bouncy gait of a runway model, wearing a colorful mini-dress over blue tights. Carmelita. And the crisp footsteps had sounded from the heels of her cowboy boots.

"Buenos tardes," she said. "I was beginning to worry about you."

"Sorry," I said. "It was hard to find a taxi."

She held out her hand to Jack. "You must be Jack Blucher."

"Correctimente," Jack said, taking her hand. "And you've got to be Carmelita."

"Verdad. I've heard a lot about you, Mr. Blutcher."

"Call me Jack."

Jack's smile showed teeth I didn't even know he had, and my opinion of him went up a few notches. I had never known him to show much appreciation for any form of beauty—either human or mechanical--that couldn't kill. But then, one glance at Carmelita's calculating eyes made me realize Jack hadn't changed. He recognized Carmelita as someone who could probably kill in as many ways as he could--and one more.

"I'm sorry about your brother," Jack said.

For a moment Carmelita's eyes misted. "Gracias," she said. "I miss him."

"Where is Mister Harlen?" I asked.

"No reason for him to come. I run the operation here."

I wondered which operation she was referring to: participation in the air show or his drug dealing. Most likely it was both.

Jack pointed to the canvas covered airplane. "That the Mustang?"

"Yes." Carmelita walked toward it and we followed. "I had it covered. There are those who might try to take it if they knew it was here."

"Tiene razon," Jack agreed.

Working together Jack and I peeled off the tarp. Before it was half off I could see why the plane cost so much. It appeared to be in perfect condition. It had obviously been either restored or carefully cared for. It had been painted identical to Sharon's with the M. H. Waste Management's logo and the red racing stripe from nose to tail. The remainder had been left polished silver aluminum. Even in the dim light it gleamed like an angel.

When the tarp was completely removed, Jack walked around the plane, not touching but giving it a careful examination. Checking the tires he said, "Looks like it came right out of the factory. Even got new tires."

"It never went to war," Carmelita said. "It was one of several surplus airplanes sold to Sweden, then to Guatemala. It was in storage for several years when Harlen heard about it. He had some restoration work done to make it flyable."

Jack ran his fingers along the leading edge of the three-bladed propeller. "New. I'd like to hear that engine."

"Whenever you're ready," she said. "The air show starts tomorrow, Sabado, but you don't fly until Sunday."

"Good," Jack said. "Give us time to wring out the kinks."

"Too late today," she answered. "Have you checked into your hotel?"

"Not really," I told her. "We dropped off our bags and came straight out here."

"Bueno. If you'll put the cover back, I'll check with my security."

"Security?" Jack said. "Maybe I should stay."

"Not necessary. We've got people who can handle it."

I said nothing, but if Harlen really was involved with Mexican drugs, I imagine Carmelita would have her pick of some very tough guards. If he wasn't connected...well, American dollars could buy a lot of security.

Taxis and buses were continually coming and going between the auxiliary airport and Acapulco's major hotels so we had no problem finding transportation back to the city.

Harlen's company had made arrangements for us to stay at Las Brisis. Known as the pink palace, Las Brisis is one of Acapulco's most famous hotels. From my spacious suite on the fourth floor I had a perfect view of Acapulco Bay, one of the largest and most beautiful ocean bays in the world.

My pink telephone rang, and when I answered, it was Sharon. She had landed at Acapulco's General Juan N. Alvarez International airport a couple of hours before and was now getting settled in Las Brisis, also on the fourth floor. I told her Carmelita had made arrangements for us to have dinner at some big restaurant in Acapulco's notorious Gold District. Jack and I would pick her up in an hour and we could ride in together.

A P-51 was not manufactured with a baggage compartment. Only a small bag could be jammed in behind the pilot's seat. So I didn't expect Sharon to bring any clothing not designed for work, but somehow she had either brought with her or had obtained a low-cut, thigh-length dress, sandals with high heels, a white, sequined jacket that she wore loose over her shoulders, and long, dangly earrings. Her hair tumbled in ebony waves across her shoulders and down her back. No person, alive or dead, who didn't know her would have guessed she could pilot a gut-wrenching warbird.

Jack, wearing a navy blue jacket and dress shirt with no tie, was obviously in awe because he was unusually quiet during the taxi ride to the restaurant.

Actually, I thought I looked pretty good myself. By flying commercial, I had no restriction on luggage, and I had cleverly thought ahead about Acapulco's night life. I was dressed in black pants and shoes with a white tuxedo shirt, a black cummerbund and a white tux jacket. But instead of a bow tie I wore a white silk necktie tied in a double Windsor knot. A handkerchief in the jacket's handkerchief pocket would have been tacky. Instead I left the pocket empty so I had a place to stow my pilot's amber glasses with the end sticking out just enough to show that I had them. Another nice touch: I hadn't shaved, so my two day growth of beard gave me a decided macho look.

I knew I looked great because Sharon's eyes widened in appreciation when she first saw me. Even Jack muttered, "Jesus."

The restaurant was an impressive example of Mexican motif. A large central dining area was surrounded by a balcony whose railing was draped with colorful blankets and serapes. Huge murals on the wall, painted by very good artists, depicted impressive vistas and scenes of Mexican life during the time of the great haciendas with their horse-mounted Dons and caballeros and senoritas with sexy eyes and swirling skirts with their dark hair caught up in tall combs draped with mantillas.

On a small stage a band of musicians wearing black mariachi uniforms and incredibly wide-brimmed conical-crowned hats was spewing out spirited mariachi music. From time to time they left the stage and played while wandered among the diners to make sure they were appreciated.

Sharon created quite a stir when we followed the maitre d' to a table. Within seconds all the musicians had clustered around our table, making the air vibrate with a happy rendition of Cuando Caliente El Sol.

"How was the trip?" I asked Sharon when the musicians had moved away. "Any problems?"

"Not really. Some bad cumulus over the desert, but I was able to get around them."

"What about fuel?" Jack said. "Those drop tanks work okay?"

"No problem. I even had a couple of gallons left when I got here."

"No problem landing with the tanks?"

"Not really. Might have been hairy if they'd been full."

"I was thinking about that runway at the auxiliary field," I said. "It looked short."

100

"It's short, all right," Jack said. "You'll never get off with full drop tanks."

"Maybe we can leave from the international airport."

Jack nodded. "Have to."

"Maybe not," Sharon said. "They asked me about my drop tanks before they gave me clearance to land. If they'd been full, I don't think they would have let me."

"What could you have done?" I asked.

"Jettison them over the ocean, I guess."

The thought of throwing away two expensive tanks, even empty ones, gave me heartburn.

"Which means they might not let us take off with full tanks," I said.

"I'll check with Harlen," Sharon answered. "If I know him, he'll have something worked out."

The mariachi music trailed off in a ragged death knell, and I looked up to see why. It was Carmelita. She followed the maitre d' toward our table with the fingers of one hand resting lightly on the arm of a tall, slender man with silver hair and mustache who wore an expensive dark gray suit. But the eyes of everyone in the room were on Carmelita's gorgeous legs that were displayed like works of art below a tight mini-skirt. Above a bare midriff decorated with a small rose tattoo, her breasts struggled to escape from an equally mini-blouse. Her straight black hair had been pulled back and hung down her back in a long braid. This allowed large circular earrings to swing free. With her hair pulled severely back, her lovely lips and feral eyes were on full display like a painting by an inspired Goya.

At our table Jack and I leaped to our feet while the maitre d' held a chair for her. Before she sat down, she introduced her escort to us. He was Señor Alfredo Nuñez, an associate director of the Alextrimo Air Show.

He knew all about our planed performance and as we sampled excellent Margaritas, he unfolded a map of the Acapulco area that he spread on the table.

"You will take off from the auxiliary airport at thirteen-thirty-five and rendezvous at five thousand feet at this location ten kilometers south-east of the airport. There will be a beacon marking the location...."

He continued giving details of the mission while Sharon and I made notes. He concluded by saying, "...Tomorrow morning at oh-nine-hundred there will be a briefing of all performers. Films will be shown of last year's program." He folded the map and passed it across the table toward me. "I must caution you that at some points in your demonstration you will be flying over or very near high rise structures located on the perimeter of the bay. Safety is always the first consideration."

Sharon and I muttered our 'of courses' and Nuñez sat back in his chair. "I am a pilot myself," he said. "Some day I hope to fly a Mustang. To me, that would be el ultimo."

"Come to California," Sharon said with a smile. "We can arrange lessons."

"I will do that," Nuñez said. "As soon as possible. Allow me to give you my card."

He took a card case from his jacket pocket and extracted a business card. He handed it to Sharon saying, "When next you come to Acapulco it would be my pleasure to be your escort."

Sharon looked at the card. "Sounds like a plan."

Looking at the card Sharon couldn't see Carmelita's face, but I could. Her lips had pulled into a thin line of exasperation, but her eyes radiated pure jealousy, and I wondered whether her relationship with Nuñez was all business.

Her stormy attitude was not helped when the musicians segued into a saucy salsa number and Nuñez asked Sharon to dance. Sharon proved to be as expert as Nuñez, and watching the two of them gyrate on the crowded floor, I felt a few twinges of jealousy myself. I'm not sure whether it was because Nuñez was not only a better dancer than I or because he was able to bring a smile to Sharon's face, a feat that thus far had eluded me. Still, I did pretty well with the dancing when Carmelita grabbed my hand and practically dragged me out on the dance floor even though it turned out that all I had to do was wiggle my hips and hold Carmelita's hand once in a while as she salsaed around me like a berserk TV contestant. I got so fascinated watching her feet cha-cha-chaing and her hips undulating I even forgot that I was not the object of the crowd we attracted. But when you're aiding and abetting sheer perfection, who cares that you're strictly a supernumerary. For the moment you too are a star.

The glow didn't last long. When the music stopped and we made our way back to our seats, my brain slowly returned to normal, and I thought this might be a good opportunity to learn more about Carmelita and her place in Morris Harlen's organization.

It was not to be. She didn't even have time to sit down before Señor Nuñez grabbed her hand and hustled her back out on the dance floor. Watching them I had to admit that Señor Nuñez put on a better show than I did. He at least moved his feet once in a while and pretty much in sync with the beat of the music. But I thought I had him beat with the hip gyrations and the arm waving. He probably would have done better with a tango where getting your legs tangled up like a Gordian knot was the whole show.

When I gave up watching and turned back to Sharon, I caught her studying me, and she quickly looked away, her face faintly flushed with embarrassment. I would dearly love to know what she had been thinking. I was not so egotistical as to believe her mind had been filled with admiration. More likely, she was wondering how I had managed to survive in a world that was not particularly kind to doofases.

I thought I might be able to take advantage of her momentary confusion with a few questions that she probably wouldn't answer if she thought about it.

"Your situation with Morris Harlen," I said. "How long have you been involved with him?"

Her momentary confusion vanished so fast I thought someone had yelled, "Fire!" "Involved?" she snapped. "What do you mean by involved?"

Her riposte had been so quick it looked me a second to respond. "I mean have you known him long? Like maybe high school or college?"

There was still a lingering resentment in her voice when she answered, "I didn't know him at all until I heard he was looking for an instructor for Jorge. I got the job."

"But you didn't own a Mustang at the time?"

"That's right."

"So it was Harlen's idea."

"He wanted Jorge to fly a Mustang. I gave him some names." She gave a slight deprecatory shrug. "He wanted me."

"To give him lessons."

Her eyes narrowed. "What else?"

I quickly shied away from what I was thinking. "And to do that, of course, you had to have a Mustang."

"That's right."

"He hasn't suggested taking it back, has he? Since Jorge is..uh...kind of hors de combat."

"He can't. Not as long as I make the payments."

Which brought me around to the question of why she was at Harlen's beck and call when he had nothing to hold over her head.

As though she'd read my mind, she said, "It costs a fortune to fly and maintain. As long as he pays the freight, I'll go along with this air show scheme of his."

"Yeah. Me too."

She stared at me a second with a look that dared me to make anything more of her relationship with Harlen, but I was happy to close that book, if indeed it was closed. If there was anything between Harlen and her that wasn't strictly business, I didn't want to know about it.

She dropped the entire subject by saying, "I think the best thing for tomorrow is for you to hold formation off my left wing. Just do everything I tell you."

I smiled to allay any fears she might have that I was one of those macho types who wouldn't take kindly to having a woman leader. "Sounds like a plan," I said. "Just don't get too wild."

"Don't worry. We'll make a couple of low level passes. Maybe a slow roll on the climb out. Try to stay with me. If we get separated, be sure to watch your air speed. If you wipe out, hit the water. We don't want to hurt anybody."

"Hit the water. Right."

She apparently thought she had shaken my confidence because she added, "Not that you will, of course. You'll be fine."

"Sure, I will. Look." I held my hands out above the table and made them tremble. "Hardly shaking."

She smiled. She actually smiled. "Just what I need: a comedian." Our conversation had brought us forward in our chairs. Now she leaned back and lifted her Margarita. I couldn't help but admire the grace of her every movement and the way her beautiful hands held the glass. I decided to show off my knowledge of the Middle East. "So you're Persian," I said, hoping she would pick up on the fact that I'd called Iran by its original name.

"That's right," she answered, not sounding impressed.

I hit her with my knockout punch. "Shite or Sunni?"

"Most Iranians are Shiia. Except I'm Christian."

"I didn't know there were Christian Iranians."

"A lot here in the U.S. Not many in Iran. Not any more."

"With the present government. I imagine their lives are a little hazardous."

"It always has been. That's why my folks left."

"You were born there?"

"Nope. Los Angels. San Fernando Valley."

"You're a Valley girl?"

She smiled. "Van Nuys High School."

"You don't sound like a Valley girl."

"You're thinking of the movie version. We don't totally talk like that, fer sure."

I laughed and it was as though some wall between us suddenly collapsed. I could feel it in the way she relaxed and in the way the timbre of her voice became decidedly warmer.

"I thought your father had that flying school," I said.

"He did. After he retired flying commercial. He started giving lessons at Whiteman Airport in the Valley. It got too crowded so we moved. He opened the place I have now."

"So now you live in Laguna."

"Yes. How about you?"

"Newport Beach."

"I mean where are you from?"

"Oh." Discussing my background—or lack of it—always made me uneasy, so my reply was somewhat abrupt. "Grew up in Orange County. Santa Ana High. Cal State Irvine."

"Another California native. Not too many of us."

"Well, kind of."

She didn't pick up on my evasive answer. Or maybe she did because she sort of cocked her head and waited, her eyes probing.

"I was an orphan," I explained. "Don't know exactly where I was born."

"Oh." Her eyes got that look of sympathy I hated. "You never knew your parents?"

"No." My voice was more than a little curt. But she chose to ignore it.

"It must be awful," she said, "not to have a culture."

"A culture?" I thought she was going to say it must be awful not to have a family, although 'awful' was not really the word I would have chosen. In truth, I had never been sure what word would have been correct because the feeling of not having a family had always been impossible for me to describe. It was like trying to explain to an Eskimo what it was like to be African.

"The feeling of belonging," she said. "Like being Irish, or

Mexican or French. The holidays. The people. Your people."

"I have that. I'm American."

"So am I. That isn't want I meant."

"I manage."

She must have caught the tone in my voice that told her I did not enjoy talking about family because she ended the interrogation by saying with a smile, "In that case, I'll make you an honorary Persian."

"Sounds good to me." I tried to think of a way to suggest an intimate initiation ceremony that wouldn't get me thrown out before I was even in, but the best thing I could come up with was: "Do we seal it with a kiss?"

She was too quick for me. She said, "We mingle our blood. Give me your hand." She picked up a fork. "This may hurt."

She clutched the fork like a dagger, and I wasn't really sure she was joking. "Thanks," I said. "I think I'll just wait for the dancing and the feast. I love baklava."

"Won't be the same," she said, but she lowered the fork. "Maybe we'd better wait. Wouldn't want you wounded for tomorrow."

It wasn't until I was lying in the hotel bed that night that I realized I'd missed my chance to question Carmelita about her brother and the two killers. I would also like to know why Harlen was paying for Jorge's pilot lessons. I couldn't make myself believe it was simply so he could advertise Harlen's waste management company in air shows. How many people in Mexico would be interested in waste management? Carmelita probably knew why. But I had been so intrigued by the side of Sharon I had not seen before that I had forgotten Carmelita and my mission. I was still puzzling about it when I fell into a restless sleep.

CHAPTER FOURTEEN

Sunday, the final day of the air show, the weather was perfect. A light onshore breeze had swept the air crystal clear. By 10:00 a.m., the beaches all around the bay were packed with colorful crowds waiting for the flight demonstrations.

They weren't disappointed. The show started with sky divers performing heart stopping maneuvers as they plunged toward the bay, at the last second swooping in to land on the beach. Then came precision flying by the Mexican Air Force, followed by the U.S. Navy's Eagles, then the Canadian Snow Birds. These were followed by aerial acrobatics. Planes such as the Pitts 111B biplane and the Russian built Sukhoi SU26M, the world's premier aerobatic aircraft, put on a spectacular show, with smoke generators marking their trails as they danced across the azure sky. I would liked to have seen them myself, but Sharon and I went to the airport early to preflight our Mustangs. Jack Blutcher had slept in the hanger with the two planes, both to make sure they were safe and so he could get an early start checking out the engines.

Jack and I had checked out my plane on Saturday as much as possible without actually flying it and it had performed perfectly, but I still had to fight a heavy apprehension. All planes, like anything mechanical, had their own idiosyncrasies. I only hoped this one's aberration did not crop up when I was flying at about 300 mph about 50 feet in the air.

"Let me know about the center-of-gravity," Jack said. "As far as I could tell it's close to stock. But you never know for sure until you get in the air."

We planned to take off an hour before we were scheduled to perform to give me time to get acquainted with the plane. Sharon and I had worked out a routine that didn't demand any really difficult or dangerous maneuvers so I didn't expect any problems. Our flight cues required constant radio contact so we made sure our radios were in perfect order. During my preflight check with Jack, Sharon came by.

She also harbored some apprehensions about the new plane because she said, "Why don't you let me fly this one. You're more familiar with mine."

That was, of course, the logical thing to do. She was an experienced P-51 pilot while I was an almost total novice. But the old hot-pilot machismo wouldn't let me do anything so logical.

"Thanks," I heard myself saying. "I can handle it."

Jack said, "She's right, Ben. It would be better if—

"Hey," I interrupted, even more miffed. "I said I can handle it."

Jack made a face like he'd taken a bite out of old broccoli and lifted his hands. "Okay, hot shot. But if something goes wrong, don't come crying to me."

"Don't worry. Nothing's going to go wrong."

Even as I spoke I had the sinking feeling I was challenging the devil, and I fought the urge to turn around three times and spit on the ground.

Sharon obviously had a lot of experience with male egos because she didn't argue. "Just concentrate on our routine," she said. "Keep your eye on me. You'll be okay." She glanced at her watch. "We'd better get going." She started to walk away, then turned back. "This runway is really too short for Mustangs. I'll go first. When you take off you'll want to give it power too quick. But remember what you learned about torque. Watch yourself."

At the mental picture her words gave me of my plane cart wheeling across the runway, my apprehension came flooding back so strong my "Roger" wasn't much more than a croak. She gave me a sharp look before she continued toward her plane.

Jack didn't help much. "There's no wind, so you don't have to worry about that. Keep the brake on and build up to about thirty inches MP. Don't forget: six degrees right rudder trim. When you take the brake off, watch it. It'll come out fast, pulling hard left. Get those rpm up fast, but don't let her get away from you. You want to be at forty-five MP by the time you reach the middle of the runway. That should give you plenty of airspeed by the time you hit the end of the runway."

"Should?"

"You do it right, you'll be Okay."

His warning echoed in my ears all during engine start and check. Jack had the engine nicely warmed up so it went smoothly. Even the radio check with Sharon came through loud and clear.

During taxi out to the runway, I settled into the cockpit. Although it was the mirror image of Sharon's Mustang, the cockpit felt different. It reminded me that a lot of little things were doing to feel different, and I'd better be ready for them. The hour of flight we had before the show would give me plenty of time to work out the bugs.

Sitting at the end of the runway, my plane's nose turned a little so I could watch Sharon, I followed her lead in running up our engines to 2,300 rpm to clear the spark plugs.

After Sharon got takeoff permission from the tower, I sat watching her with my engine idling. Listening to the smooth purr of the Package-built V-12 Rolls Royce Merlin made me shiver with pleasure. It never ceased to amaze me that a piece of machinery with twenty-four spark plugs firing hundreds of times per second, valves slamming open and closed, each of the twelve piston reversing direction hundreds of times per second, spinning the crankshaft thousands of rpm, expelling exhaust gas at high velocity, pumping gallons of oil and coolant through the engine and radiators, could do all this so smoothly that the only sound was a soul-satisfying purr.

Sharon lifted off yards from the end of the runway, so I assumed the take off would not be as close to disaster as I imagined. I had my mind changed in a hurry when it was my turn. Holding the brakes, I revved the engine to 2,000 rpm. Even sitting still I could feel the torque, with the big propeller trying to twist the nose off the plane. When I released the brakes the Mustang shot forward like it had been fired out of a gun with the powerful torque yanking the plane to the left, and the right wing coming up like it wanted to roll over. Jack and Sharon's warning saved me because, although surprised at the quickness and power of the maneuver, I was ready with my right foot trying to push the rudder peddle through the floor and the stick a fast right.

It was a combination of instinct and terror that allowed me to get the plane straightened before it ran off the runway. It was shaving the left side of the runway, the engine screaming in frustration as I charged ahead, too afraid to attempt a change of direction to get back in the middle of the tarmac. When I was able to get my brain back in focus, I was startled to find that the tail wheel had come up, and the end of the runway was rushing toward me like the monster from under the bed. I fed in throttle as fast as I dared, too fascinated by the sight of the onrushing fence at the end of the runway to check my airspeed, praying I would be going at least a hundred twenty before I ran out of tarmac.

When I decided it was now or never I eased back on the stick and the beautiful Mustang surged toward the sun. I cleared the fence at the end of the runway by at least forty feet, giving all the credit to adrenaline.

Sharon's voice in my earphones brought my elation back to normal. "Good job. You might consider raising your flaps and gear."

"Uh, roger," I answered. I'd throttled back at a couple of thousand feet and was climbing nicely but I'd forgotten to bring in my wheels. How embarrassing. I milked the flaps up and hit the gear level and, as the wheels came up, the air speed increased.

I picked up Sharon's plane and discovered I was closing in fast. I checked my airspeed. 250 knots already. Wow. I eased back and slid into position off her left wing. She looked over at me and waved. I waved back and we were as one.

We headed out over the ocean where the sky was all ours and for the next forty-five minutes we practiced: formation flying, rolls, diving, climbing, low level flight. Sharon warned me again on the radio not to allow my airspeed to drop below 120 knots. We would be flying too low to get out of trouble in a stall. Just stay with her and I'd be all right.

When we got the word on our radio that we were up, we were at 3,000 feet and within sight of Acapulco Bay with its shoreline of high-rise hotels and office building and its distinctive huge rock jutting out of the bay's vivid blue waters. I was already sweating and the idea of flying a few feet off the water at more than 300 knots so close to all the people on the beach didn't help my nerves.

The tower told us we were clear and Sharon said, "Here we go. Stay with me."

"Roger," I answered, my voice displaying all the confidence of a duck heading south in the hunting season.

Sharon edged the speed up and began a shallow dive toward the bay with me glued to her left wing. By keeping my eyes and my mind on maintaining formation I didn't have to look at the suicide-prone people clustered on the beach.

We came in low and fast, so low I thought our props were going to chop the tops off the whitecaps and so fast we left a turbulent wake on the water. Talk about a thrill! My heart had to be pounding at about a million beats a minute. For a moment I had a mental picture of WWII and the two of us flying low to strafe a German airfield. All we needed to ratchet up the thrill was the zing of bullets and 20mm shells punching holes in our wings.

After the show that had been put on by the aerobatic planes I wasn't sure how much of a thrill it was for the spectators to see two planes streaking across the water, but if they were like me, just the incredible sound of those big V-12 Merlin engines would send shivers up their spines. I hoped they got a good look at Harlen's waste management logo.

Then, with the cliffs rushing toward us so fast I began to think our show was going to have a fiery finish, Sharon pulled up into a near-vertical climb, and on her command, she began her planned slow roll to the right. I did the same to the left, although my roll was pretty sloppy because at our speed the controls where a little stiffer than I expected.

But I got through the maneuver okay, and formed back up with Sharon. We didn't want to get out of sight of the spectators, so we made a fast climbing turn. At its peak we executed a split-S half roll and dived back for the bay. Too close to the water to suit me, we half-rolled upright and streaked back over the water in the opposite direction.

By the time we made two more passes I was beginning to get the hang of it, and I couldn't help pulling a slow roll as we streaked across the bay with the tips of my wings so close to the water I thought I might fricassee a few dolphins.

I was still grinning with self-satisfaction when I pulled back in formation with Sharon. She looked over at me, and she was not smiling. She did wave. Well, it wasn't exactly a wave; it was more like a gesture. But as I always say: It's the thought that counts.

CHAPTER FIFTEEN

The next day did not start out well. To be truthful, the previous night had not gone all that well either. Sharon had been a little testy about my—as she called it—stupid slow roll.

She was right, of course. It had been stupid. It is an aerodynamic characteristic that in a roll a plane's nose wants to dip. I had practiced enough rolls in the Stearman, the AT-6 and Sharon's P-51 to be aware of the tendency and knew to correct for it. But every plane has its own eccentricities, and I really hadn't been sufficiently acquainted with the new Mustang to know how it would handle. So it had been stupid, an impulsive display of machismo that could have gotten us both killed. So I guess it was only natural that she was miffed.

But it sure had been fun.

And spectacular. Even Jack—who had been watching with binoculars—said it had given him a thrill, except that 'thrill' wasn't the word he used.

At the alternate airport——where we had landed successfully, much to the disappointment, I was sure, of observers who had collected to watch---most of the flying crowd had packed up their planes and gone home so the flight line was almost deserted. Our two Mustangs were in the hanger where Jack and a couple of Harlen's mechanics were checking them out. I was gratified to see they were making a thorough check. It would be a long flight back to California, and the mountains and deserts of northern Mexico were not friendly to machines that dropped in.

Then, a real problem. The mechanics had been fitting both planes with 150 gallon drop tanks. Gasoline, like water, weights about 6 pounds per gallon. With 150 gallons under each wing, plus the weight of the tanks themselves, we'd be carrying around 2,000 extra pounds. A Mexican FAA official took one look at the short runway and denied permission to take off with the gasoline-loaded tanks. We suggested flying over to International Airport with empty tanks and filling up there. Taking off from their two-mile-long runway, even with the extra weight, would not be a problem. But he had refused on the grounds that taking off from the International Airport in the gasoline-loaded P-51's posed too much danger to the surrounding community. We pointed out that since the airport was located at an angle on a peninsular we'd be taking off over water in either direction and, therefore, would pose no danger to anyone. No matter. We were still refused.

We were sitting inside the hanger admiring our certificates of appreciation from the city of Acapulco for our air show and trying to resolve the short-runway situation when Sharon said, "Harlen knew the situation when he sent us down here. I thought he had everything covered."

"That inspector is full of shit," Jack said. "Even with 165-gallon drop tanks it'd be a piece of cake."

"On this runway?" I said.

"Sure. It could be done."

I thought back to my takeoff for the air show and knew he was exaggerating a bit. With 150-gallon tanks it would really be dicey. Still, if Jack said it could be done... So the refusal had to be some other reason. "Maybe he was looking for a little"—I rubbed my thumb over my fingers—-"you know, propina."

"Naaa. I tried that." Jack shook his head. "It don't make sense. He acted like he was scared to take it?"

Carmelita had been listening to our complaints, calmly using an emery board on her carmine toenails displayed by her high-heeled sandals, which had her leaning over in a way that made it difficult for me to concentrate on the takeoff problem. Without straightening she said, "The solution is simple."

"Simple?" Sharon said.

Carmelita straightened and began using the emery board on her fingernails. "You take off with empty drop tanks. You fly to another airport--up north. Then fill up the drop tanks and fly home."

She was right: it was simple.

Then Jack shot it down. "The only places you can find 100 L.L. fuel are all FAA controlled."

"Not all of them."

"If you're talking about some dirt field, they don't carry high octane fuel."

Carmelita was unperturbed. "There is such a place."

"Where?" Jack said.

"North of Guadalajara."

"How far north?" Sharon said. "It'd have to be in range of our internal tanks."

"It is," Carmelita assured us. "And they have the proper fuel."

Jack said nothing, staring at Carmelita. Like me, he realized she had come up with the only possible solution, but was wondering how much of it had been planned in advance.

I was the one who said, "Wait a minute. If this place is far enough north, we won't even need the drop tanks. If they can refuel the main tanks, they should be able to get us home."

Carmelita quickly shook her head. "No. The weather is bad up around the border. You'll probably need the drop tanks."

"Why take a chance?" Jack said. "You don't use it Harlen'll have a couple of hundred gallons of cheap gas."

"Okay," Sharon said. "If you can guarantee they'll have the fuel."

Carmelita's smile was the smile of someone who wouldn't be overly concerned if Sharon ran out of fuel in the middle of nowhere. "Don't worry," she said. "They'll have it."

Her Cheshire smile and the way she said it, with total confidence, made me certain that Harlen had planned the entire operation long before the air show. But why? Just to advertise his company? It didn't make sense.

I waited until I could find a place behind the hanger where

116

nobody could hear me and called Agent Bremm on my cell phone and told him my suspicions.

I ended by saying, "I think Harlen's got some plan to use our planes to move dope across the border."

"Sure sounds like it. You'll probably pick it up at that field where Carmelita wants you to refuel."

"What happens to us if they hide a couple of kilos of dope in our planes?"

"I hope they do. It'll prove Harlen is dirty."

"But what happens to us: Sharon and me?"

"Don't worry. We'll handle it."

When a government agent says 'don't worry,' that's when I start.

"What about the Mexican Federalies? Can you handle them?"

"I'm sure Harlen's got that worked out. You just go along with whatever Carmelita suggests."

I didn't have to give that much thought. I wasn't sure what kind of trouble I would run into if Bremm didn't keep his word, but I was darn sure what kind of trouble I would find if Harlen thought I was screwing him. Of the two evils, the U.S. government sounded positively angelic.

CHAPTER SIXTEEN

The next morning I was sitting in the cockpit of my Mustang with its engine warming up while I gave a last look at the map Carmelita had given me (with a copy to Sharon). Our planes had been fitted with the 150-gallon drop tanks and the Mexican official had made sure they were empty.

Jack stood on the wing watching the instruments. "I wish the hell," he said, "this had come with one of those RCAT systems. I could do a hell of a lot better job of system checks."

"You mean electronic checkout, like those on new cars?"

"Better. On cars you've got to plug 'em in. RCATS use telemetry. I could keep track of all your systems when you're in the air, including g-forces."

"Wouldn't do much good. We'll be out of range in a couple of minutes."

"Yeah. I don't like this whole damned setup."

"If Harlen's got some dope deal up his sleeve, he won't want anything to happen to us."

"It ain't just Harlen. If he's involved in runnin' dope, he'd better be playin' ball with the Mexican gangs. If he ain't... Well, you and Sharon watch your asses at that field."

I grinned at him. "I'll watch hers if she'll watch mine."

"Smart ass," he said. "You just watch yourself. Planes like this are getting scarce."

He scrambled down from the wing. I folded the map and stowed it in the leg pocket of my coveralls where it would be handy. Sharon and I got clearance from the tower to taxi. While we headed for the end of the runway I tried to put Jack's warning out of my mind so I could concentrate on the instruments and the sound of the engine. I noticed that the deep purr of the big Merlins had attracted quite a crowd. There must have been a fifty or sixty people standing by the flight line when Sharon and I pulled into position at the end of the runway.

The runway was too narrow for a side-by-side takeoff, and she had permission to go first. We made our final checks, then she stood on her brakes and built up power. A Mustang is not noted for fast acceleration, but when she released the brakes and blasted down the runway she was moving like a jet with its afterburner fired up. She was off and climbing long before she reached the end of the short runway.

I'm sure it was for my benefit, but she had only climbed about a hundred feet when she executed a lovely slow roll. I could almost hear Jack Blucher's scatological comment.

Not to be outdone, when I blasted off I had to do the same thing only I did mine with four points. The fact that the roll was rather sloppy I attributed to the unfamiliar drag of the drop tanks. Even so, since I didn't end up as a hole in the ground, I was sure Jack Blucher was proud of me.

It took me about five minutes to pull into position off Sharon's left wing. She looked over at me and put her hand over her eyes so I knew she had been watching. I had probably made her very happy. After all, she was my instructor.

When we reached 11,000 feet——not quite the ideal altitude for fuel conservation, but low enough that we wouldn't have to go on oxygen——we throttled back to 325 knots cruising speed. I tried to set the throttle, propeller pitch and trim tabs so the plane would practically fly itself. I soon found, however, that the Mustang was either too sensitive or had too many variables to fly hands off. I had to stay on top of it, continually tweaking the tabs and throttle to keep in trim and in formation with Sharon. I didn't pay much attention to navigation. If we got lost, it would be her fault.

I settled back in the seat and tried to relax. It was going to take more than three hours to reach Carmelita's designated field, which gave me plenty of time to wonder about what I'd gotten myself involved in. This business of not being allowed to take off with fuel in the drop tanks so we'd have to stop for refueling sounded contrived.

There had to be some subterfuge behind the required stop. If Bremm was right and Harlen was a major dealer, it probably had something to do with drugs. And if it did, and my suspicions proved correct, we would be loaded with dope when we crossed the U.S./Mexican border. It certainly would explain Harlen's sudden interest in foreign air shows. But since Bremm had okayed it, I would be off the hook for whatever it was.

One of those 'on the other hand' thoughts wiped out my complacency: suppose Bremm denied giving me instructions to follow Harlen's orders? Suppose he denied even knowing me? What evidence did I have that I was working for DEA? I had our contract, of course. But the contract was somewhat vague (deliberately, I was sure), so it might not be much proof. If push ever came to shove, Jack could testify on my behalf. But suppose they didn't believe him either. I should get some definitive form of evidence about my association with the DEA, something that would stand up in court if I ever needed it. That would be the first thing on my agenda when I got home.

With that settled I began to enjoy the flight. Despite the P-51 requiring constant attention, it was still a joy to fly, riding the air with the grace of an eagle. And like an eagle, I had the feeling that if I wished I could turn the elegant beauty into a deadly predator in an instant. This had to be how a WWII pilot felt, easing along close to the sun, watching for game. And when it was sighted, pouncing for the kill.

I looked toward the ground, half expecting to see the green forests and fields of Germany with a gaggle of FW 190s or ME 109s trying to sneak up on a squadron of B-17 bombers. Instead I saw the brown hills of central Mexico dotted with small villages and scattered green fields.

The terrain of rolling hills, green with brush and fields green with produce, did not appear suitable for an emergency landing, and, although the Merlin engine was purring like a big cat, I was reminded of a quote made by an old pilot: 'Always keep a place to land in your pocket.'

As time and miles slipped away, the topography gradually changed from green to a sandy brown, rumpled with the treacherous hills and deep arroyos of Mexico's Sierra Madre range. Fortunately, the good weather continued to hold. The few clouds we encountered were mostly fluffy white cumulous. Occasionally, strong thermals rising from the heated earth, built into a towering cumulonimbus, some topped with an ominous anvil-shape while the black shadow of rain spewed from the dark base. It's a really bad idea to fly into a cumulonimbus cloud. The torrential winds inside the towering cloud could tear the wings off a plane, even one as strong as a Mustang. And flashes of lightning inside the dense mass warned any intruder that if the hurricane force winds didn't destroy you, the lighting could. However, after three hours of monotonous flight I wouldn't have minded the excitement of a little brush with disaster.

It was not to be. Sharon deftly eased us around every potentially deadly monster. She also had a good instinct for avoiding invisible thermals that had not yet formed into visible clouds, and except for being bounced around a little once in a while, the flight was generally pretty monotonous.

From time to time I pulled the map out of my pocket and tried a little pilotage navigation, but it didn't do much good. Except for a lake now and then, there were no really outstanding landmarks I could use for a positive visual fix.

We'd figured it would be about a three hour flight, and right on schedule she called me: "Mustang Alpha twelve to Mustang Bravo twenty-one."

"Bravo twenty-one. Roger."

"I'm changing frequency to pick up their beacon."

"Roger that."

I also changed frequencies to the one we'd been given for the field's control tower, and in a couple of minutes I heard Sharon asking for landing instructions. The voice that answered spoke English with an accent, but his approach and landing instructions were easy to understand.

In about a minute I spotted the field. In was a single strip of narrow black asphalt surrounded by desert with a long dirt strip at either end and flanked by three wooden hangers and a few dilapidated houses. The runway had been constructed for light aircraft and looked awfully short for anything that had to land at more than fifty miles per hour.

Still, I figured that if we ran off the end of the runway, the dirt would help bring us to a stop.

Sharon went in first, dropping her gear early and easing in as slow as possible. She touched down expertly at the very beginning of the asphalt and by putting a strain on her brakes, was able to stop before reaching the end.

I wasn't quite so lucky. I touched down about where she did, but I guess I was going a little faster and even though I almost set fire to my brakes, I ran off the end of the runway in a cloud of dust. When I finally turned to head for the parking area, I kicked up enough dust to blot out the sun, much of which found some way to get into the cockpit. I manually closed the radiator doors to keep the dust out, taking a chance I wouldn't overheat before reaching the place where some guy wearing a baseball cap was signaling me to park.

It worked out okay. But before I cut the engine, the cloud of dust I kicked up went sweeping over the field like a Sahara dust storm. The signal guy's cap flew off and tumbled away on its way to Guadalajara. The way he clutched at his shirt I thought it might take off after the cap.

When the dust cleared he glared at me like it was my fault. Actually, with the temperature about 110 degrees, he should have been grateful for the breeze.

The way Sharon stood next to her plane, gagging and choking, she probably felt the same as he did.

I walked over to her and said, "Welcome to Mexico."

"Is there any of it left?" Her tone was a little snide, which I thought was uncalled for since I had managed to land without running into anything.

"'olla," someone with a deep raspy voice said. "Muy bueno. Right on time." It was the same voice we'd heard on the radio, and it belonged to a short but husky man with a face that hadn't been shaved for a few hours and squinty eyes that smiled but didn't look like they meant it. His hair, which had been glossy black until it collected all the dust that hadn't blown away, was straight and neatly trimmed. He wore baggy blue jeans with scruffy cowboy boots and a once-white

122

Guayanna shirt with short sleeves. I sensed that the shirt concealed a pistol stuck in his belt. He held out a hand that was attached to a hairy wrist that looked like it was designed for lifting weights. The way he squeezed my hand proved I was right.

"You are *Señor* Roan, no?"

"*Correctomente*," I said.

He turned to Sharon. "And you are *Señorita* Sharon Daadian. Señor Harlen told me much about you."

"Are you Juan Castillo?" she asked.

"At your service."

He was more gentle shaking Sharon's hand then he'd been with mine, at the same time giving a little bow which I was sure was so he could get a good look at her chest. I guess he liked what he saw because when he straightened he was showing a lot of brown teeth in a smile.

"How was the trip?" he asked. "Any *problemas?*"

"No," Sharon said. She glanced at her watch. "How long will it take to refuel?"

"Not long. An hour. Maybe two."

"Two hours? What are you going to use? A tin cup?"

"The drop tanks," he said. "They take a little *tiempo*."

"We'll use the main tanks," Sharon answered. "We won't need the drop tanks filled."

Juan's lips twisted in chagrin, and he made a small shrug. "*Señor* Harlen asked us to fill the tanks."

"Why?" I said. "The main tanks will get us home."

Again he made the shrug, this time accompanied by moving his hands apart. "Maybe because gasoline is cheaper here."

"Oh, yeah," I chimed in. He had to be right about that. Mexico was a major oil producer and sold gasoline for a fraction of the U.S. price, although the way Harlen spent money I didn't think he'd be trying to save a few dollars on the price of gas.

"Come to the cantina," he said. "You are just in time for *almuerizo* and, perhaps, *un vaso de cerveza.*"

Sharon looked at me, and I shrugged. I didn't want the beer, but I thought getting out of the boiling sun might be a good idea.

"Okay," she said. She indicated the Mustangs where an old, brown fuel truck was just pulling up. "Could you rig a cover over the cockpits. That sun's going to turn them into ovens."

Castillo said, "Oh, *si.*" He moved a couple of steps toward the men working on the planes and yelled a string of Spanish. They stared at him blankly, and he yelled louder, punctuating the command with a few words I recognized, such as '*estupido.*' Judging from their expressions when they nodded and turned away, they thought the extra work in the hot sun was *estupido.*

Castillo yelled a few more choice words at them before he led us to one of the buildings that looked newer than the others. There was a steel water tower behind the building, and I wondered what was growing inside the tank in the desert heat. The water probably harbored a greater variety of bacteria than all the Petri dishes at Amgen.

] Approaching the door I smelled food cooking, and my salivary glands reminded me that I hadn't eaten since early morning. This would probably be my chance to taste some authentic Mexican cuisine.

Before we entered the cantina, I glanced back at our planes. I stopped. "Hey," I said. "What are they doing?"

At our planes the brown-painted gasoline tanker had pulled up and several men where covering the two planes with tarps that had been painted to resemble the desert ground.

Castillo showed the palms of his hands. "You wanted the cockpits covered."

Sharon said. "Covered, yes. But why the camouflage?"

Castillo showed his brown teeth again. "It is—*como se dice*—better safe than sorry."

"Safe from what?" Sharon asked.

He shrugged as though we were the *estupido* ones.

"Competition. There are certain people who do not like free enterprise."

"Competition for what?" Sharon said. "We're not selling anything."

Castillo laughed. "*Por supuesto. Señor* Harlen takes care of everything."

Before I could give his answer much thought, he put his big hands behind our backs and practically pushed us into the cantina.

Dusty windows and overhead fluorescent tubes illuminated several wooden tables and chairs and a worn wooden floor. A big fan in the ceiling languidly stirred the stale air as though the heat had sapped it of desire. A small bar had been built in one corner. Shelves behind the bar displayed bottles whose labels indicated that most held tequila or rum. The wooden floor was partially covered by linoleum that was curling along the edges. An opening in the back with no door led to the kitchen. I resisted a strong desire to make a sanitary inspection before I ordered lunch.

I hadn't seen any power lines, and I wondered where they got their electricity until I became aware of the faint sound of a gas motor that I assumed ran a generator.

Castillo flopped into a chair at one of the tables, and one of his shaggy eyebrows lifted when I held Sharon's chair for her. If I'd been able to see Sharon's face my guess was that both her exquisite eyebrows were also up around her hairline.

"You'd better tell them not to fill those drop tanks to the top," Sharon said. "We're going to need all that runway as it is."

"Already considered," Castillo assured her. "You will have no trouble."

"Who considered?" I asked. "*Señor* Harlen?"

"*Sí.*" He laughed. "*El Jefe.* He has made all arrangements."

A plump girl wearing a white blouse and long, full, red skirt came out of the kitchen. She had a face that would have been beautiful if she dropped a few pounds. Castillo gave her instructions in Spanish. Before returning to the kitchen she went behind the bar and lifted three bottles of Dos Equis beer from a freezer, opened them and

125

brought them to the table along with three glasses.

Sharon hesitated, looking at the bottle. She had the same thought I did: The flight home would take more than three hours, and P-51's had not been built with restrooms. Smart pilots did not partake of liquids before such long flights.

But it had been more than three hours since we'd had anything to drink, and she had to be as thirsty as I was because she filled her glass. But she only took a swallow.

She stood up and said, "*Donde esta el baño?*"

Castillo pointed to a door near the bar. "*Alli.* Need any help?"

"I'll let you know," she said. "Wait here."

Castillo must have thought she was serious because the smile that creased his face as he stared at her walking away was filled with hope. Apparently he had spent so much time in warm climates he could not recognize an iceberg when he saw one. Like the Titanic, if he so much as touched this one it would send him to a deep, cold grave.

But he had to be hedging his bets because he jerked his head toward the door of the baño. "Where she live? California?"

"Right A place called Tehachapi. You've heard of it?"

"Everybody know that place. They got big prison there."

"Right. She works there. A guard. Mean. Killed two men."

His eyes widened satisfactorily. "Two men?" Then he grinned. "How she killed them." He made his hands into fists and jerked his hips suggestively.

I gave up trying to dissuade him. He was so wonderfully animalistic that nothing short of a cattle prod would take his mind off sex as long as there was a woman around. Well, maybe there was one thing: *dinero.*

"How do you happen to know *Señor* Harlen?"

"Happen? Oh, *si.* Friends. We do business with him."

"Smuggling gasoline?"

He showed me the evil grin that was becoming familiar.

"Gasoline, *sí*. We do business with mucho 'gasoline.'"

"With the increased border patrol, it must be getting tougher to get the stuff over the border."

"*Verdad*. Those stupid illegals. They got the border shut down. Trucks, planes, tunnels. Hard to get through. Last week we lose five tons." He tapped his temple with a blunt forefinger. "But *Señor* Harlen is *muy intellihente*. He come up with this idea. Nobody stop your planes."

"Yeah, but those tanks only hold a hundred fifty gallons. That's hardly worth the trip."

He stared at me a moment, his expression calculating as though he was trying to decide if I were joking or just being stupid. His eyes bore so much malevolence, I almost wished he would give me that evil grin. "That not my problem," he said. Then his eyes did something I wouldn't have thought possible: they became even more malevolent when he added, "Or yours."

"Right," I hastened to reply. I charmed him with one of my own famous grins and lifted my hands in the air. "Not my *problema*. I just fly the stupid airplane and collect my *dinero*."

It was the word '*dinero*' that did the trick. It was a word that explained everything. To my relief, his evil grin reappeared. "*Verdad*," he said. "Show me the money."

Use of the famous movie line broke him up, and he reached across the table and slapped me on the shoulder.

But just as I was basking in his camaraderie, his mood changed so quickly I was left with my smile pasted on. "Watch out," he growled. "There are those who might try to stop you."

"Those? You mean border patrol?"

His lips pulled into a frown that was even more evil than his grin. "No! Some people don't like the business *Señor* Harlen make."

"Competitors?"

"Competitors, *sí*. *Ladróns*. Robbers."

"Yeah, well don't worry about it. Once we're in the air, nobody's going to catch us."

"Bueno. You got good planes. One thousand miles an hour."

"Well, not quite—"

The *baño* door opened and Sharon came back. She'd put on makeup and combed her hair, and Castillo forgot all about competitor or, for that matter, me. He leaped to his feet and pulled out her chair.

"*Aye, chihuahua,*" he said. "*Muy guapa.*"

Sharon must have understood his Spanish because she gave him a look that was considerably warmer than her usual icy stare. Instead of sitting down, however, she glanced at her watch. "If your men have finished," she said, "we should get moving."

Castillo spread his hands. "No *prisa.* You will stay for the *fiesta esta noche,* no?"

"Fiesta?" I said. 'Fiesta' meant 'party' and my experience with Hispanic parties had always been better than pleasant, so I continued, "*Como no?* There's always *mañana.*"

Sharon must also have had some experience with Hispanic parties, especially the kind that Castillo probably had in mind, because her eyes frosted over and she said, "Thanks. But we have to get back." She looked at me out of the side of her eyes as though she did not trust turning away from Castillo. "Isn't that right, Mister Roan?"

I quickly weighed one night in heaven against a lifetime in hell and said, "Right. We've got to get back. *Señor* Harlen said hurry back."

But Castillo did not give up so easily, "You would enjoy the fiesta," he said to Sharon. He gave her a look at his beguiling grin, "We could do business together."

"I'll take it up with Harlen," she said. "I understand he has many very important *amigos* in Mexico."

I expected to witness an interesting courting ritual with Castillo enumerating his many highly placed friends, but Castillo threw in the towel before the conquest was hardly started as though he recognized that this female would never be captivated by one-upmanship. "Ah, yes," he said. "When you see *Señor* Harlen, tell him how quickly we prepared the delivery."

I took my turn in what passed as the restroom while Sharon

walked to the flight line with Castillo.

By the time I joined them, the tarps had been removed from the planes, Sharon was completing her preflight check, and Castillo was admiring her P-51, the first he had ever seen.

"How fast it fly?" he asked, running his hand over the smooth aluminum skin of the fuselage.

"It cruises at around three-twenty-five. Top speed is over four-hundred."

Castillo's eyes glistened as though he were calculating the number of trips he could make to the U.S. at 400 knots. He thumped one of the drop tanks. "They make these *mas grande*? More big?"

"Bigger and smaller," Sharon explained. "These are 150 gallons. They make 85 gallon and 180 gallon tanks."

There was something about the sound when Castillo had thumped the drop tank that when Castillo and Sharon moved away made me linger to take a look at it. The expression 'drop tank' is a misnomer, at least when applied to commercial or private aircraft. Only military aircraft would ever actually jettison their tanks. For one thing, the metal tanks were expensive, costing several hundred dollars. If filled with fuel the cost could be more than a thousand dollars each. And in an emergency, you couldn't drop just one; you had to jettison both to keep the plane in trim. And a jettisoned tank, even if recovered later, could not be reused. Then there was the damage a loaded tank could cause if it hit a populated area, especially if it caught fire.

During WWII the tanks used on fighters were made of paper lined with rubber because they were almost always jettisoned. But modern fuel tanks are reusable so they're made of steel, and when you thump a metal tank filled with liquid, it makes a solid sound like a full metal pot sounds different from an empty one. When Castillo had rapped on the tank it had made a sound that could not have come from a tank filled with liquid. A close look at the top of the tank confirmed my suspicions. Next to the filler cap a large door had been cut into the tank. It had been cleverly done with such a perfect fit that it could only be detected by a close inspection. But the door certainly wouldn't contain high octane fuel sloshing around.

So if the tanks didn't contain fuel, what did they contain?

The answer was easy. Harlen was in the drug business. Most drugs in the U.S. came in from Mexico. But the DEA was not stupid. They were constantly discovering and closing the dealers' methods of smuggling in dope. So dealers were always trying to find new ways. Obviously Harlen had found a new one. Planes that participated in air shows were typically given carte blanche clearances to cross borders. But the small aerobatic planes could not carry heavy external tanks. Military planes were too closely supervised to be used. Only the rugged, powerful WWII Warbirds could carry heavy payloads for long distances, and most were already designed with attach points for external tanks. Each 150 gallon tank could probably be crammed with more than 1000 pounds of packaged dope. Two Mustangs, four tanks, two tons of dope. In its pure form, that much dope would represent millions of dollars.

No wonder Harlen had made sure we would be carrying empty tanks when we left Acapulco. It insured that we would have to make a stop to refuel. The refueling would allow Camarillo's men time to switch the real drop tanks with the fake ones. And we could easily make it back to Newport on the fuel in our internal tanks.

But the thought that created a heavy feeling in my chest was that the two Mustang pilots, unless they were really, really stupid, would have to be in on the deal. The plane's fuel gauges would clearly indicate there was no fuel in the drop tanks. There was no way the pilot could not tell that something was rotten in Denmark.

Sharon had to know, which meant she was drug dealing with Harlen.

It was the only explanation. Harlen thought he had me under his thumb so I was no problem. But he also had to be sure of Sharon. If not, he could have just put the fake tanks on my plane and left the real ones on hers. She would never have known.

But the tanks on her plane were supposedly filled with aviation fuel. If she didn't know already, she would certainly know they were fake the minute she made her preflight fuel check.

I would have to watch her, wait for her reaction. I could only pray that when she realized the deception she would leap out of the cockpit screaming like a double-crossed banshee.

130

A short time later, with the hot sun making an oven of the planes' cockpits, we ran through our preflight checks. My attention was divided between running my checks and watching Sharon in her cockpit as she worked her way through her checks. Everything seemed to be going smoothly except that she often turned her head to look over at me.

When I ran my own fuel check, the drop tank gauges indicated empty as expected. Sharon should be making her fuel check any moment, and I glancing over at her to catch her reaction. She had paused in her checkout to stare at me, her eyes wide, intense as though she expected something terrible to happen.

I had a sudden terrifying impulse to leap out of the cockpit. A bomb? Had Harlen discovered my connection with the DEA? Was my plane meant to explode in a ball flame?

Sharon must have seen my expression of abject terror because she tapped her earphones. I switched on my radio and went to our frequency.

"Yeah?" I said. Or I tried to say it. It took me two tries with my voice breaking like an adolescent passing through puberty.

"You okay?" she asked. Her voice sounded fine, calm, sexy as ever, which meant that either she hadn't made her fuel check, or had made it an found exactly as she expected.

"Great," I said. Then, because I had to know, I added, "How's your fuel."

"Okay." A fraction of a pause. "How yours?"

The flood of emotion that washed over me was part relief that she hadn't expected me to blow up and a dark disappointment that she had completed her fuel check and was not alarmed by the results.

"Okay," I said while watching her carefully. "No problem."

She turned her face away. I couldn't read her expression, but when she answered, "Uh-roger. Let's do it," her voice sounded dry, dead, as though my answer had slammed some secret door in her mind.

I knew exactly how she felt. She must have harbored some small hope that I was not part of Harlen's drug cartel, that my only connection with Harlen was as an innocent dupe, which was exactly what I had hoped about her. She was as dejected about learning the truth about me as I was about her. The one difference was that she was dead wrong.

Flickering through my dark funk was one tiny spark of joy: she appeared to be acutely disappointed by her seeming discovery that I approved of Harlen's plan. If I meant nothing to her, why would she care? But my euphoria was tempered by the proof that she was, indeed, part of Harlen's 'team.' My one remaining hope was that no one as beautiful, as vivacious as Sharon could willingly be involved with dealing dope. If she were dealing, it had to be because Harlen had some hold over her more powerful than just payments on a Mustang. All I had to do was find out what it was, and rescue her. Putting Harlen in prison would set us both free.

I clung so fiercely to this thought I almost lost everything during takeoff. I'd never flown a plane carrying a payload weighing close to 2,000 pounds, and was not prepared for the unfamiliar feel of the controls and the extra speed it required to lift off. But I made it into the air without destroying any of the prickly Joshua trees near the end of the runway and charged after Sharon. Due to the extra weight and aerodynamic drag of the drop tanks, the controls had a slightly sluggish feel. I had been flying a sports car, now I was flying a sedan. It only took a few minutes however, before I was able to adjust, and I soon had the Mustang trimmed up and skimming the air side by side with Sharon.

Making adjustments to my mood, however, was not so easy. I flew in a semi-stupor, performing automatically, fighting doubts about Sharon and her relationship with Harlen. But every way I twisted the facts, they always came up with the same conclusion: how could she not know? Was she willingly working for Harlen? And if so, how many other times had she performed smuggling missions of one kind or another?

Sharon made no attempt to contact me. I wondered if she was fighting through the same thoughts about me as I was about her. Probably not. Why would she possibly care about me one way or the other? She might be a little disappointed to find that one of her students, someone she might considered a friend---even though an extremely minor friend---was willingly working for a dope dealer. For

132

me, it was going to be a long flight.

We leveled off at 11,500 feet. I paid little attention to our flight path, trusting the navigation to Sharon. It was not difficult, however, to now observe our progress through pilotage. From our almost 12,000 foot perch I could see a vast stretch of Mexico's heartland stretching away to our right, its desert-brown vistas dotted with oasis-like green patches surrounding small towns and villages. To our left the rugged mountains and deep, rocky canyons of the Sierra Madre Occidental range separated the heartland from a far smudge of blue that was the Pacific Ocean where it began to form the Gulf of California. I thought of the people frolicking in the tony spas and casinos at the southern tip of the 800 mile long Baja Peninsula. At one time I would have envied them. Not now. Now I was an eagle and they were ground-pounders. They could have their yachts and power boats. They could only cavort over the blue surface of the wide Pacific; never would they own the blue of a vaulted sky. Never would they feel the thrill of so much power, so much freedom, so much pure joy. If I had been alone I would have done cartwheels across the infinite meadow of the sky.

By keeping the gulf to our left we could hardly get lost. When the gulf ended we would be close to the U.S. border. From -there it was a straight north-west shot across southern Arizona and California to Newport. Barring having to circle around a really bad band of towering cumulous clouds building up over the Santa Anas, we should make it with fuel to spare.

As the flight wore on I began to feel better. It was difficult to remain depressed while fulfilling a dream. In front of me the propeller was a hypnotic blur; the drone of the Merlin engine a siren song. Above me the blue sky beckoned. All I had to do was pull back on the stick and my magic chariot would carry me to the heavens. Instead, I churned along next to Sharon, adjusting my trim tabs from time to time as the Mustang consumed fuel altered its center of gravity, dreaming of being a fighter pilot patrolling the dark skies above Germany, protecting my flocks of B-17 and B-24 bombers.

My dream almost came to a sickening conclusion when a stream of tiny objects zipped past, just missing my right wing. Hornets? Killer Bees? Up this high?

Possibilities ripped through my mind before the truth hit: bullets. German's! Focke Wulf-190 or ME-109 fighters. Every fifth bullet was a tracer. They're what I'd seen.

I kicked the rudder and skidded to the left at the same time pressing the mike button and screaming, "Break right! Break right!"

God. What a woman. She did not ask why? With the instincts of a fighter pilot she whipped over in a ninety-degree bank so quickly she almost left me hanging.

I had my Mustang almost on its back following her down when from the corner of my eyes I saw a dark object flash past, moving so fast I had only a glimpse of wings and a fire-streaming tailpipe. A jet? That sure as hell was no WWII fighter. If Sharon had hesitated an instant she would have been dead meat.

Sharon's voice in my ears. "What? What?"

"Jet. Shooting at us. Keep your eyes open. One o'clock."

She pulled out of the dive, and I pulled into position beside her, twisting my head, searching for the jet, hoping desperately he was alone.

"You sure? I don't—"

Her call broke off abruptly as she saw the sun glint from the jet curving around ahead of us. Its wings formed a perfect silhouette as it came around for another pass.

"Jesus," she said. "An F-sixteen."

If she were going to say more, the thought abruptly cut off. The F-16 came straight at us, head on, the closure rate at close to 800 mph. Winks of light came from its wings and a stream of bullets passed overhead, searching for our unarmed Mustangs.

Sharon broke left and I went right. The jet shot past, moving almost as fast as the bullets.

I didn't know about Sharon, but I headed for the ground. We'd lost several hundred feet on our first break, but we were still high enough to give the nimble fighter plenty of room to maneuver. Up here he could pick us off one at a time.

He was already banking around for another pass.

"Get on the deck," I yelled.

"Go," she said. "I'll pull him off."

She was going to sacrifice herself for me? The thrill that shot through me was almost as excruciating as being hit by a bullet. On the other hand, maybe she felt she was good enough to out-maneuver him.

A Mustang against a modern jet? And us with no guns? We might be able to escape for a few seconds, turning inside him, but eventually our destruction was inevitable, especially with our maneuverability restricted by the drop tanks.

We had to jettison the tanks. Harlen might kill us if we dropped his dope, but if we didn't, the jet would surely kill us. Shit! He would anyway.

I was about to yell at Sharon to jetton the tanks and the hell with Harlen when I realized: the drop tanks! They were our only weapons.

"Sharon," I yelled. "Don't drop your tanks. Follow me."

"Got to," she said, calm as Sunday morning. "He's on my tail."

I saw her then. She was above me, diving and rolling, the jet closing on her. I couldn't see them, but I knew that .50 caliber bullets had to be jabbing at the sky all around her. But she still had her tanks.

I jammed the throttle to the wall, full emergency, and sixteen hundred horses made a sound like a wounded dragon. Mustangs are not known for quick acceleration, but sudden g-forces pinned me back against the seat and momentarily blurred my vision. Fighting torque, I pulled up in a climbing turn to intercept the jet.

When my vision cleared, I had climbed slightly above and ahead of Sharon and the following F-16. They charged toward me, Sharon rolling frantically only a few hundred yards ahead of the jet.

"Break left," I shouted. "Left."

She broke, a turn so steep I was afraid the g-forces would black her out. Then, as I'd hoped, the jet broke with her, making a wide turn that brought him off my right wing. I turned into him in a diving turn, trying to time my maneuver to intercept.

He was so concentrated on Sharon he didn't see me coming, and he held his turn like he was on a rail, giving me the chance to judge my timing. He straightened, boring in on Sharon. Oh God. Faster. I had to go faster. I was already in emergency power, but I tried to shove the throttle through the instrument panel. Three more seconds, Lord. Just give me three seconds! I steepened my diving turn, moving at close to 500 knots when I sliced over his cockpit so close I though my prop might shatter his canopy.

He was so startled he must have yanked the stick back because when I backed off of the throttle and pulled out of my diving turn, he was fighting to pull out of a spin. Even as I watched he controlled the spin and leveled off.

I spotted Sharon way below me and I went after her.

"Hit the deck," I said. "Cut off his maneuver room."

"Roger," she said. "I see a good canyon."

"Right with you."

I caught her just as she slipped between the rocky walls of a deep canyon with a thin, brush-fringed stream at the bottom. Fortunately, the twists and turns in the canyon were gentle and we were able to hold a speed at close to 250 knots. Sharon, in the lead, skimmed just above the stream, dodging the precipitous canyon walls so close I couldn't look, except, following her, I had to do the same. I thought I had been scared in my life, but they were usually short, sharp spikes of terror. But seeing my wing tips flashing past the canyon walls so close they practically scratched rocks was a sustained terror that had my heart pounding and sweat burning my eyes and soaking my clothes. The terror was not helped by the realization that if we pulled up out of the canyon the jet would scatter us across the rugged landscape. In effect, we were quintessential examples of being caught between the rocks and the hard place.

I wanted to look for the jet, but was afraid to shift my gaze even an inch. But I knew he was there, sitting up in the safe, blue sky, waiting to pounce. He didn't have to follow us through the canyon. All he had to do was wait for us to come up, or for the canyon to straighten so he could come in behind us for an easy shot.

I desperately hoped he would lose patience and when he had a chance, come in for the kill. It was our only chance, and a slim one at that.

And there it was. The killing zone. The narrow canyon ran straight and true for a couple of miles, time enough for him to come down on us like a hawk after rabbits.

Now, in the wider part of the canyon, I could chance a look over my shoulder. He was there. Behind me. Skimming the bottom of the canyon. Closing fast. We had five second to live, maybe less.

"Sharon," I called. "On my mark. Pull up. Jettison tanks. Ready! Now!"

She heard me! I saw her pull up and her tanks tumble away, directly in front of me! I yanked the stick back as hard as I dared and jettisoned my tanks. The instant they fell away, the Mustang leaped like a bronco, and I shot past Sharon's two tumbling tanks, and up over the rim of the canyon.

Still climbing, I looked back. A ball of smoke and flame exploded out of the canyon like the eruption of a volcano.

Closing at high speed the jet had tried to avoid the tumbling tanks just as I had. Only he had four to dodge and at his speed, no time to maneuver. He had either hit one of the tanks or the canyon wall. Either way, sayonara.

Sharon had seen it too and she said in a voice unbelievably calm, "Harlen is going to be mad as hell."

She didn't fool me. Her breath had to be coming in gasps just like mine. I also knew her clothes would be plastered to her clammy body and sweat would be stinging her eyes.

I eased into formation, and as we began the long, slow climb back to cruising altitude I didn't look over at her. Mister cool. Just another day at the office. Thank heavens she couldn't see the way my hands were shaking.

CHAPTER SEVENTEEN

She had been right about Harlen being mad as hell. When he had seen us land without his precious drop tanks he might have been apoplectic, but the time it took us to pull up on the parking ramp and run through the shut down procedures gave him time to get a grip on his desire to kill us, and a few minutes later, sitting in Sharon's hanger office, he was grimly calm while he listened to our explanation.

"An F-sixteen?" he said. "Are you sure?"

"Yes," Sharon answered. "I'm sure."

"Any markings?"

"No. None I could see."

Harlen's hard gaze swiveled toward me. I shook my head. "No markings. But it carried at least four fifty caliber guns. Had to be government"

"Why would the Mexican government want to shoot you down? You're flight plans were filed. They knew where you'd been, where you were going. What the hell had you been up to?"

"Nothing. We hadn't done a thing." I turned my head to give Sharon an accusative stare. "At least I hadn't."

She chose to ignore my jibe, saying, "Maybe it belonged to one of those drug cartels."

Inwardly I winced. Why had she brought up the subject of drugs. I didn't want Harlen to get any ideas we—or I—knew what we were carrying.

I quickly tried to change the conversation's direction by asking, "Drug dealers don't fly F-sixteen fighters."

"Why not?" she answered. "They've got the money. They could probably buy one of those F-one-seventeen stealth fighters if they wanted to."

Harlen's expression didn't change, but his voice had a different edge when he said, "That doesn't answer the question: why would they want to shoot you down?"

"Beats me," she said. "The only thing we carried was aviation fuel."

Harlen thought for a moment. I could guess what was going through his mind: He knew we were in denial about the content of the tanks. So he could either admit what was really in them or keep up the pretense that it had all been some kind of mistake. He would surely suspect, however, that the F-16 belonged to one of his rival drug cartels who either wanted the drugs we were carrying, or they didn't like Harlen meddling in their business. Either way he had to come up with another explanation for the attack. And it wouldn't be because we were supposedly carrying aviation gas. Mexico had enough gas to fuel the entire army. I leaned forward in my chair. What would Harlen come up with? This should be good.

"They might have been after your planes," he said. "Those cartels are always looking for fast planes."

I sat back, as much astonished as chagrinned. Damn. He'd done it. A plausible excuse.

But Sharon didn't buy it. "I doubt it," she said. "If he shot us down in that terrain there wouldn't be enough left of our planes to build a tinker toy."

"Maybe he wasn't trying to shoot you down. Maybe he just wanted you to land so they could grab the planes."

"I don't think so," she said. "He was trying to kill us."

"Well, we'll never know," Harlen said. "You're damned lucky to be alive."

Not a word about the lose of his dope. I was beginning to wonder if I'd been mistaken about what was in those tanks when he said, "I've got contacts in the Mexican government. I'm going to get to the bottom of this. Can you pinpoint exactly where that F-sixteen went down?"

Sharon said, "Pretty close."

Inside, I smiled. Harlen might want to know the exact coordinates of the F-16's crash site for political purposes, but I doubted it. More likely he wanted to attempt a recovery of the drop tanks and what they had carried, which sure couldn't have been gasoline.

On the other hand, if it really had been an F-16 of the Mexican Air Force or some government agency, they were probably searching for it. If they succeeded in locating the crash site, they might also find the drop tanks and what they had contained. If so, Harlen would not want to have any connection with the incident.

He would have to rely on his Mexican 'connections' to find out who owned the F-16. If it were government, he would want to find out why it was interfering with his dope delivery. If it belonged to a rival cartel, he would have to collect the spilled dope before they did.

Sharon unbuttoned the flap on a leg pocket of her coveralls and brought out a map of Mexico. It was still soggy with sweat and she unfolded it carefully. If it had been in my pocket the odor of stale sweat would have driven us from the room, but hers only exuded a faint aroma that reminded me of roses. Or was it orange blossoms?

The map was marked with a plot-line of our course. She studied it a moment, then took a pen from a coffee mug containing a variety of pens and pencils and made a small X on the map.

"I can't be sure of the exact point. We were wheeling and dealing over a lot of terrain. But it's in a canyon with a straight gorge about two miles long."

"Okay," Harlen said. He carefully folded the map. "I'll see what I can find out."

"Sorry about losing your 'gas,'" she said.

If Harlen detected the touch of sarcasm in her voice, he gave no indication. He waved the thought aside as though losing what I assumed would amount to millions of dollars was not important. "Plenty more where that came from. The important thing is: you didn't have any trouble getting over the border coming back."

I had been fidgeting in my chair, hoping to cut the meeting short not only so I could change out of my sweaty clothes, but so I could call Bremm and tell him what happened. But Harlen's words brought my attention back to him full strength.

Sharon must have also been puzzled by his statement because she straightened in her chair. "Almost all the planes in the air show were from out of the country. Crossing the border is taken care of when you file a flight plan. You know how that works."

Of course he did. That's why he had sent us to Mexico. He wanted to find out if we would have to stop at the border either going or coming back.

"The point is: you proved it can be done. And,"—he almost smiled—"you're alive." He got up and came around the desk. "The Sarnia Air Show is coming up. Start making your plans."

Sharon stood up. "Sarnia? Canada? Why should we go there?"

On his way to the hanger exit, Harlen stopped and turned back. There was a bite in his voice when he said, "Because I want you to."

I got up. "That's a long trip. What's the point?"

Harlen lifted his hand. "Name recognition—for M. H. Waste Management."

"Nane recognition?" Sharon said. "In Canada? That's why we went to Acapulco."

Harlen smiled and shook his head as though we were children too immature to understand. "I've got big plans. Besides, you'll love Sarnia. Right across the river from Detroit." He turned and strode away.

Sharon looked at me with a puzzled frown. "Waste Management--in Canada?" Even frowning, her lips looked inviting.

I knew why Harlen wanted to cross borders, but I didn't want to share it with Sharon. I still wasn't sure where she fit in the picture. Looking at her now, her hair tumbling around her face as she searched for something in the drawers of her desk, I tried to divorce my thoughts from the sure, graceful way she moved and from the way she made even the shapeless, perspiration stained coveralls seen like the latest creation of a haute couture designer. Even in the insignificant task of opening desk drawers, she was all business, the planes of her perfect features composed, her dark eyes clear of abstraction, concentrating on her search with an intensity of purpose that almost transcended her beauty. Almost. It didn't seem possible that such perfection could be stained by the filth of Harlen's drug dealing. But I could not keep from thinking that her story about her connection to Harlen was suspect. All evidence thus far indicated she was a willing part of his cartel.

I wanted to walk away from her, walk away from the doubts that seared my mind. If she were in league with Harlen, I didn't want to know, didn't want to deal with it, now or ever.

And, yet, the events of the last few days had developed a semi-symbiotic relationship between us. She no longer looked at me as though I were some sort of bad luck that had to be endured until it went away. I should exploit her change of attitude, show her I was a heroic person and former boy scout who she could not only trust, but who would be a valuable friend. But how was I ever going to convince her of that?

With the decision to strike while the iron was at least a little warm, I said, "Can I help you with that?"

She looked up without straightening, her tangle of dark hair partially covering her face. She brushed it aside with an unconscious gesture. "It's my purse. I was sure I left it in my desk."

"You didn't lock it up? Maybe in your locker?"

"No. There's nothing in it. I keep anything of value in my wallet."

"Well, it'll turn up. If you're short of money, I'll take you to dinner."

I'd kept my voice firm, friendly but business-like, devoid of any hint of seduction, and she straightened giving the idea a little thought as though she wasn't too charmed by the offer. She glanced at her watch. "I didn't realize it was so late. Okay. We need to talk." Her voice had the same flat, noncommittal tone she would have used addressing a board of directors.

So much for seduction. "Great. Where do you want me to pick you up?"

I hoped she would say at her home so we would end up there

later. Instead, she said, "Here. How long will it take you to be ready?"

How long would it take me? I couldn't recall the last time I hadn't had to wait for a woman to be ready. Not that I was really surprised by her answer. I was certain she would have been ready if I'd said five minutes. But now I had to make a decision. If I chose a four star restaurant with soft music and dim lights, I would have to go home to change to appropriate clothes. On the other hand, the clothes I had in my locker would only be suitable for something between a McDonald's and Barney's Beanery. I decided I didn't want to give her enough time to up the anti on short notice. "Forty-five minutes?" I said, expecting her to add a few minutes.

She didn't hesitate. "Okay. Right here. Forty-five minutes."

Damn. I should have suggested a half hour, maybe even fifteen minutes. "Right," I said. "Leave the light on."

I almost ran to the pilot's locker room. Forty-five minutes would be cutting it close even for me, especially since I would have to be in a cold shower for at least twenty minutes or I wouldn't be in shape to take her anywhere except my house.

CHAPTER EIGHTEEN

In the locker room, after checking to be sure I was alone, I used up ten minutes talking to David Bremm. I gave him the details about the pit stop in Northern Mexico and my suspicions about the drop tanks being filled with dope instead of gasoline.

"So that's what he's been up to," Bremm said. "Very clever. I'll have to check it out, but I don't believe planes used in air shows are ever stopped or searched when they cross borders."

"He wants us to go to some show in Canada."

"Canada? That's not like him. He usually deals through Mexico."

"Should I go?"

"Hell yes. We've got to know what's going on."

"Okay. At least we won't have to deal with the Mexican Air Force."

Bremm's voice sharpened. "What about the Mexican Air Force."

"One of their planes tried to shoot us down."

There was a brief pause. "How do you know it was Air Force?"

"Who else would have an armed F-sixteen?"

Bremm's laugh was humorless. "Every dealer south of Tijuana." He paused. "Tried to shoot you down? How come you're here?"

"Hey," I said, a little miffed. "I can take care of myself."

"Against an armed jet? What'd he do, run out of gas?"

"We brought him down."

"We? You had help?"

"Sharon and me. We were coming back together."

"I'm surprised he didn't kill you both. How'd you do it?"

"Dropped Harlen's dope on him."

"Both of you?"

"Yeah."

He laughed again, this time with real pleasure. "I'll bet Harlen liked that."

"He didn't seem too upset. I guess he's got plenty more."

"True. He's probably using you and Daadian to check out bringing it in by air. Canada, you said."

"That's right. There's an air show some place called Sarnia."

"I'll look it up."

"Then we should do it."

"Right. Just let me know where you make the drop. We'll pick it up. You won't be involved."

There it was again: I won't be involved. I wished I could have made him give me Scout's honor.

After our conversation I didn't need a cold shower to keep my mind off Sharon. Worry drove away all thoughts of romance. It was too late to back out. Besides, I loved the flying. And I certainly wanted to hold onto the P-51. Still, I had no desire to be dead. If Harlen were involved in some kind of turf war with other cartels, I could be caught in the middle. And if something went wrong, would Bremm and the U.S. DEA come to my rescue, especially if it happened in Canada? I wouldn't bet on it.

On the other hand, I couldn't simply walk away without making a lot of enemies in high places? Was Bremm the vindictive type? Did he have enough influence to have my company's security clearance cancelled? Probably yes on both counts. Like a leaf ripped from a nice secure tree and driven by hurricane-force winds, I had no control over where the mission took me.

Except that this leaf wasn't dead. Not yet. Maybe there was something I could do to regain control of at least a semblance of my destiny: I could find out who had murdered Jorge Mendez and why. Maybe that would give me enough leverage to pry myself loose from Bremm before I became road kill like a valiant wolverine flattened on a Canadian highway.

But where to start? My only links to Jorge Mendez were Harlen, Carmelita and——I hated to admit it---Sharon.

I could rule out Harlen as a source of information. And Sharon? How deep was she involved? Was she as much a victim as I? How much of what she had told me was true? If she were lying, did I want to know the truth?

That left Carmelita. Beautiful, sexy Carmelita. She was obviously deeply involved with Harlen's drug operations. She seemed to be my only hope. One good thing: being alone with her for awhile couldn't be all bad.

CHAPTER NINETEEN

Sharon must have had a portable boutique in her office because when I meet her a little later I thought at first I was in the wrong hanger. How she was able to create such a transformation in such a short time was beyond my comprehension. It was almost dark inside the hanger and standing beside her desk, she was illuminated by the soft glow of a lamp reflected off the glass that topped her desk. She had uncoiled her hair and was standing with her head inclined to the side so she could run a brush through her hair's amazing fall of curls. Each pull of the brush brought a wave of light that burnished the lustrous strands. She had exchanged her coveralls for a no-sleeve, knee-length dress of some shimmering material that clung as thought it were in love with her lithe, sensuous body. And she had discarded her boots for sandals with stiletto heels that made me keenly aware she had legs. And such legs.

She saw me standing with my mouth hanging open and straightened. When she picked up her purse from the desk and placed the brush inside, I noticed she hid a little smile. She knew darn well that she had me just the way she wanted me, her own little pillar of mush.

I chose a restaurant on the ocean side of Newport Beach for two reasons: despite the darkness, it presented a mesmerizing view of white breakers rushing in to lave the wide beach, and, in case Sharon fell under my spell, it was close to my house on an island in the bay.

Well, actually there was another reason: I thought the place was kind of romantic. The sound of soft music and the faint boom of distant breakers were as subdued as the light from a single candle on the table. I'd learned that if I wanted to impress a girl it didn't pay to have too much light, especially when I was seated across the table from her with her face about two feet from mine. Sharon would look terrific even in the glare of a police lineup, but I was sure that after the long, exhausting flight, my face sagged like a deflated balloon. A near blackout would definitely work in my favor.

But with Sharon, the warm candlelight on her bronze skin failed to reveal a line or wrinkle. The flickering light only deepened the depths of her fathomless eyes. And her lips...each faint smile, each tiny frown, each touch of her tongue to her lips, mesmerized me, proving again how difficult it is to stare without seeming to do so. In a vain attempt to break the spell, I concentrated on her hands, again finding it astonishing that hands that could cradle a glass of Solutre Pouilly chardonnay with the delicate touch of a lover, could also control a 6,000 pound warbird pulling 6Gs.

During dinner I tiptoed up to the subject of Harlen and his sub-rosa occupation by first talking about her life, a subject I found infinitely more pleasant.

"Daadian. That doesn't sound Iranian."

"But it is. Daadian was one of the ancient Aryan kings. In those days it meant 'justice.'"

"Aryan? I thought Iranians were Arabic."

"Don't let them hear you say that. Persians were the original Ayrians. Out of Eastern Europe. Some even have red hair."

This was my chance to deliberately stare at her hair. "Personally," I said, "I prefer gorgeous black."

She smiled and kind of ducked her head demurely. "Thanks."

I allowed the compliment to sink in a little. Then I said, "Iranian. I don't believe I ever heard of a female Iranian pilot."

"There aren't any that I know of, expect me." Her voice turned bitter. "Certainly not in Iran."

"Have you spent much time there?"

"Not really. My parents wanted me to be a true blue American. I barely speak the language."

"Your folks must really love this country."

"More than most natives. They've seen the other side."

"I guess that's true of most immigrants. We do tend to take it for granted."

148

"Maybe it just seems that way. People like to boast about their home country, even those who want to be Americans. But I've noticed that real Americans don't brag much. It takes something like nine-eleven before they'll show their patriotism."

"It didn't take long for that to fade out."

"Oh, it's still there. Even in the immigrants. It may not seem like it sometimes, but they like to be considered Americans."

"When you go to Iran, do the people there consider you Iranian or American?"

She smiled, and I lost interest in her hands. "American. And not just there. You can speak English with an accent so thick you could cut it with a knife, but you go to a foreign country, you're an American."

"How about when your folks go back? Are they considered American?"

"Well, they speak Farsi like natives, of course. But they pretty much let everybody know they're Americans now.

"You have many relatives here?"

"Not really. There's a big Iranian community, but they're pretty clannish. My folks came from a small village so they don't have many close friends here." She looked down for a moment then drank a little wine as though to put an end to that line of conversation. I tried to think of a way to turn the conversation to Harlen and his 'team,' but she exploited my hesitation by saying, "What about your folks? Did you ever try to find out who they were?"

I wasn't too thrilled by the question. When women begin looking at a man as a possible father to their children, they want to know what kind of blood runs through his veins and whether there is insanity in his family, and especially, whether their kids are going to be cute or ugly. So I usually try to hold off discussing my background until I had them so hooked by my devastating personality they didn't really care much if I had relatives who where Caribbean pirates or descendents of Jack the Ripper.

But since I was sure I had as much chance of stealing this one's heart as I had of winning the lottery, it wouldn't make much difference what I said, so I might as well tell the truth. Besides, I'd learned long ago that if I said it just right, with a touch of hopeless bitterness in my voice, I could often make some real brownie points.

So I kind of sighed and stared down at the table. "Not really," I said softly. "They certainly made no attempt to contact me. I decided that it they didn't want me, I didn't want them. As far as I'm concerned I have no family. No brothers, no sisters, nobody." I looked up with my best martyr-like smile. "I try not to think about who my parents were."

Was I mistaken or did a hint of compassion appear in her eyes? My suspicion was confirmed when she reached across the table and touched the back of my hand. "I'm so sorry," she said. "It must be awful not to know."

As I'd hoped, the truth was working better than a lie. "It is pretty devastating," I murmured. "Not knowing. Not having anyone." I turned my hand over and pulled her hand into mine. "Not having anyone I can turn to when I need a friend."

She extracted her hand from mine, but gently. "You have Jack. I understand you've been friends for quite a while."

Jack? What the devil happened? So much for romance.

"Oh, sure. We linked up a couple of years ago when I was doing some work in Africa."

"He's a pretty good mechanic."

"He's pretty good at everything." I didn't elaborate. If Jack wanted her to know about his mercenary soldiering, he could tell her himself.

"In a way," she said, "he's kind of responsible for my buying my Mustang from Harlen."

I jerked to attention. "He was? Jack?"

"He found out Harlen had a Mustang he would consider selling. He told me about it. The rest is history."

There was no going back now. All the little intimacies of romance had been kicked out by the mention of Harlen. Well, this was my raison sociale for the dinner, wasn't it?

"Were you giving lessons to Jorge at that time?"

"No. Giving him lessons was part of the deal. I guess he wanted to make sure I had a paying customer to protect his investment."

"I wish he'd bring a couple of customers for me."

Her perfect eyebrows lifted. "I thought you owned a business. Something about security."

"I do, but..." I didn't want her to know that Harlen didn't have his hooks into me the way he did her. "Business hasn't been that good."

"So that's why you didn't say anything about what was in those drop tanks."

It was my turn to raise my eyebrows. "You knew about that?"

"It was pretty obvious."

I didn't know what point there was in asking, but I had to know. "But you were willing to bring it in?"

"I didn't like it. But I figured the little grass we could bring in was a drop in the bucket."

Marijuana? She'd thought it was grass. That did make her willingness to cooperate with a drug dealer a little less onerous. "Oh, yeah. That's what I figured, too."

"I wonder if that's why he wants us to go to that air show in Canada?"

"Probably."

"I understand Harlen's got a lot of organizations. You can probably get him to throw some business your way."

"Good idea. I'll ask him." I made an attempt to turn the conversation back to her involvement with Harlen. "Maybe he'll bring in more students for you, like Jorge."

"Maybe."

"Or even find a spot for you in his other operations."

She thought a moment, looking out the big picture window

toward the white foam of distant breakers. But she wasn't thinking about the view. "Well, once we get our planes paid off we can do what we want."

"Yeah, right."

Staring at her I felt a dark chill. Didn't she realize that with what she knew about Harlen's operations, he couldn't afford to let her quit. I had a way out. But she would likely end up firmly in Harlen's grip or dead. He probably already had some plan that would sink the hook in so deep she couldn't afford to quit. It might even have something to do with the air show in Canada.

I resumed eating, but the joy had gone out of the evening, and all the candlelight in the world couldn't bring it back. I didn't want to go to Canada. Nothing good could come of it for me and certainly not for Sharon. But I had no choice. Not only would Bremm insist on it, but I also wanted to know what Harlen was up to. There might even be some way I could stop him from dragging Sharon in so deep she couldn't get out. That alone might be worth the risk.

CHAPTER TWENTY

For the next two days I couldn't shake off a feeling of dread. My Mustang sat in the hanger space I rented from Jack while I tried to concentrate on work at my office. But I might just as well have stayed home. Instead of concentrating on office work, my mind, like a dog with a bone, wouldn't stop worrying about Harlen's plans for us in Canada. Would it be the same routine we'd used in Mexico? Or did he have something bigger in mind, something that would suck Sharon and me deeper into his cesspool?

I also gave a lot of thought about how I could get Carmelita to tell me what she knew about Harlen and his operations. She had a suspicious quality that would be difficult to penetrate. Actually, the idea of getting her to talk made me want to laugh. She couldn't be a major player in Harlen's operations if he wasn't certain she wouldn't betray him.

But she had to have an Achilles' heel somewhere. I'd just have to find out what it was. If Bremm could help me discover who murdered her brother, it would go a long way toward penetrating her tough shell. Hopefully, she had information about Harlen that would wind this thing up, and we wouldn't have to make the trip to Canada. All I had to do was get it.

I was getting ready for bed and out of habit I checked my phone for messages. I had a one from Jack. I considered waiting for morning to call him. It was nearing midnight and my body was beginning to feel the effect of tension and lack of exercise, but knowing Jack, he wouldn't have called if it wasn't important.

When he answered his phone he sounded as thought I woke him up. "Carmelita's been trying to get in touch with you."

"Oh? She back from Mexico?"

"Yeah. You got her number?"

"No, but...you mean now?"

"She said as soon as possible."

A glimmer of hope cut through my malaise. Maybe her call was social. Maybe I'd made a better impression on her than I thought. Maybe the old charm was going to pay off.

"Okay," I said. "She leave a number?"

I hadn't memorized her number, but the one he gave me didn't sound familiar. Jack added, "If you need me, give me a call."

"Why would I need you?"

"Depend on how she plans to kill you."

"Thanks a bunch," I said. "If it isn't with a gun, I'll need all the help I can get."

He laughed and hung up.

I called the number. Carmelita answered on the first ring. Her "Hello" sounded guarded like any woman would sound upon getting a call in the dead of night. When I told her it was me, relief flooded her voice, causing me to wonder whether her guarded 'hello' might have been because she was afraid I might be someone else calling, someone she knew and feared.

"I've got to see you?" she said.

"Okay. I'll come over in the morning..."

"No," she interrupted. "Now. It's important."

Now? I pictured the long drive into L.A. and hesitated. There wouldn't be much traffic at this time of the night, but it would still take an hour or more. "Can you tell me on the phone? I'm pretty beat—"

"No, no. It's something I've got to show you. Something from Jorge."

Her words sloughed away my tired feeling like a cold shower. "You're brother? What'd he say?"

"It's not a note. It's something he gave me."

I finally recognized what I was hearing in her voice. Fear.

"You'd better call the police. They'll want—"

"No police. No. You come. I'll give it to you."

I wanted to argue with her. I was tired. Whatever it was it could surely wait for morning. But the fear in her voice was not amenable to reason. "Okay," I said. "I'll be there in--"

"Wait," she said quickly. "I'm not home. I'm in a motel."

That brought me up short. Her fear had to be strong to drive her out of her home. She gave me the name and address of a motel on Hollywood Boulevard near Western Avenue, and I told her I'd be there in less than an hour.

It's almost fifty miles from Newport to Hollywood. Using the Interstate 5 and 101 freeways, I didn't push my elderly Corvette over 70, rationalizing that if I got stopped by the highway patrol I would lose more time than if I keep my speed down. Besides she was hidden away in a motel. What was the big rush?

Fortunately, the late hour had reduced the perpetual traffic on the freeway to the point I didn't have to spend every second concentrating on my driving because I drove automatically, thoughts spinning through my mind crowding out all but the basic driving instincts. Why me? If Carmelita had information about the death of her brother, why hadn't she called the detectives working on the case? That didn't take a rocket scientist to figure out. As involved as she was in Harlen's drug dealing, she wouldn't want the police messing around in her life. And if her brother had also been involved in Harlen's operations, Harlen wouldn't be too happy about calling in the police either. But why me? If she had some big secret, what did she expect me to do with it? As far as she knew, I was nothing more than a destitute pilot who was willing to sell his soul for a Mustang. Maybe Harlen had told her about my being owner of Roan Security. Even if he had, I couldn't believe she wanted to tell me about some big secret she couldn't tell the police...or Harlen.

Unless it was about Harlen.

But why tell me? She had no way of knowing I was working with the DEA? Did she? How could she possibly know?

My rampaging thoughts were interrupted by a sign indicating that Western Avenue was the next exit. It was a good thing I'd seen the sign. I'd been so caught up in the mystery I'd have driven past the exit.

I headed north toward the Hollywood sign I could just make out high in the hills.

Western is usually a maelstrom of cars and delivery trucks, but the approach of midnight had almost cleared the broad avenue. After passing Sunset I kept a close watch for Hollywood Boulevard where I turned east and began checking building numbers. The center of Hollywood, a little more than a mile west, had been undergoing a huge modernization program, but this was an old rundown section of Hollywood with no connection to the motion picture or music studios, peopled by tourists and want-a-be actors, singers and musician. The area had been slowly morphing into an Armenia district, and the signs on some of the shops and stores were in both English and Armenian as though the merchants didn't want to take the chance of missing any potential customers. Actually, they should have added Spanish and Korean since two of L.A.'s ubiquitous Latino and Korean districts were creeping up on them from the south and east.

In a couple of blocks, densely packed with small shops in fifty year old buildings, I spotted the motel's neon sign. The motel, sandwiched between a furniture store and a clothing store, consisted of a two-story, U-shaped building with a balcony on the second floor. The central parking area was about half filled with cars. The place looked peaceful, sleeping as wearily as its occupants.

Jack had once told me to be suspicious of anything and everything in an area that might turn out to be a battle scene, so I drove past and parked in a small, dark lot next to the closed furniture store. I walked back toward the motel past the front of the furniture store, trying to look like a normal pedestrian hurrying to get off the deserted sidewalk. I slowed my pace while passing the motel's entrance to the parking area, surreptitiously surveying the area without turning my head. The place looked just as one would expect a third-rate motel to look in the middle of the night: quiet, playing host to lovers, monetarily-challenged tourists and generations of termites. Light from low wattage floodlights on the roof scarcely illuminated the parking area as though the motel's owners knew that most of their clients didn't want to be seen. Near the front of the parking area, a small office was illuminated by a single lamp on a counter. The office looked deserted, and I assumed the manager had adjacent quarters and would appear in his pajamas if anyone entered.

I turner abruptly, entering the parking area, and walked between cars toward a flight of wooden stairs at the rear of the lot. The only sound was the soft crunch of my footsteps on the old, cracked macadam and the swoosh of passing cars in the street.

The rooms on the ground floor all had numbers beginning with the number one, which led me to believe that the room number Carmelita had given me, 204, had to be on the second floor, and I climbed the wooden stairs as silently as possible. At the top I paused to listen. I heard the faint sound of music and voices from two different rooms where light from television programs spilled from beneath blinds on the front windows.

Assuming the rooms were numbered from front to rear, room 204 would be near the front of the motel. I eased along the right wing of the balcony walkway, checking room numbers on doors. When I found 204, I stopped next to the door, my back against the wall, listening. Thin drapes drawn across the front window did not reveal any light from inside. I pressed my ear against the door. Nothing.

I pictured Carmelita sitting in the dark, staring at the door. If she were as terrified as her voice had suggested, she would be alert to the faintest sound, so I rapped on the door softly. There was no answer, no sound of movement from inside. I rapped again, slightly louder. Nothing. No sound. No movement.

A rising prickling sensation at the nape of my neck, told me to turn and leave. She was expecting me. She should have heard my knock. She should be opening the door and leaping into my arms, sobbing with relief.

But maybe she couldn't. Maybe whatever she had been afraid of had already happened. Maybe she was lying on the floor, wounded, unconscious, dying.

I gently tried the door knob, expecting it to be locked. But it turned easily. The hair on the nap of my neck lifted another fraction of an inch, and my gut instinct screamed at me to run. Against all rational thought, I eased the door open, trying to peer inside. There was just enough light from the parking lot lights filtering through the window's thin drapes for me to make out a double bed, a dresser with a mirror over it, and a couple of chairs. The room smelled faintly of stale cigarettes and Clorox antiseptic. There was no sign of a body, either dead or alive.

But at the other side of the room a thin streak of light came from beneath a door that I assumed was the door to the bathroom. That explained it. Carmelita had to be huddled in the bathroom with the door locked. She probably hadn't heard my soft raps on the door. Strange she hadn't locked the front door, unless she was too frightened to know what she was doing.

Easing inside, closing the door behind me, I quickly crossed to the bathroom door. I had my hand on the doorknob when from the corner of my eye I saw a dark form come off the floor on the far side of the bed. He was on me in instant, his hands up, slipping a noose around my neck.

If my body hadn't already been saturated with adrenalin, he might have been able to wrap the thin cord around my neck, but with fear-driven speed I ducked away, spinning, my hands twisting inside the cord, allowing his rush to drive me to the floor, dragging him with me, where I used his momentum to catapult him over my head. He hit the front of the dresser hard, and flopped to the floor.

I ripped the cord from his slack fingers and struck at his neck with the ridged edge of my palm. But he was already turning, pushing to his feet, and my blow hit him below the shoulder. I felt his collarbone snap, and he grunted with pain. Surging to his feet, he drove a shoulder into my stomach driving me back. My legs hit the edge of the bed and I flopped backward on the bed, rolling away from an expected blow.

The blow never landed. The man, holding one arm folded against his chest, leaped to the front door, wrenched it open. I had a brief glimpse of his face in the dim light of the parking lot lights before he bolted for the balcony stairs.

I started for the door, thinking of trying to catch him, but stopped abruptly when it occurred to me he might have a gun. He might not have wanted to use it when he thought he could kill me with the garrote, but if I chased him, he might change his mind.

Another thought also stopped me.

Where was Carmelita? The bathroom!

I yanked at the bathroom door, expecting it to be locked. It opened so easily it threw me off balance, and I stumbled, expecting an attack.

Nothing happened. Recovering my balance, I warily looked in the bathroom, steeling myself for the sight of Carmelita's body sprawled on the tile floor.

The room was empty, glaringly empty in the bright light. I ripped aside the shower curtains, prepared for the horror of seeing her bloody body in the stark white of the bathtub. Nothing.

I clicked the light off and returned to the other room. I turned on a bedside lamp and took a quick glance around the small room. Nothing. Where was Camelita? Only one other possibility: the closet.

Gritting my teeth, I opened the door to the small closet. Empty, except for a single bent wire clothes hanger.

There were no other places to look inside the room. Could she possibly have escaped and was outside?

Warily, I stepped outside onto the balcony, peering into the darkness, listening for the sound of stealthy footsteps. If the guy came back I didn't want to be surprised. There was no sign of him, no sound. The area was as quiet as before. Evidently, sounds of violence in the motel's rooms were not out of the ordinary.

I went back in the room, closed and locked the door. The cord was on the floor and I picked it up. It was thin, but strong, about two feet long with knots on the ends to give a good grip, designed for garroting.

Where was Carmelita? Was she dead, her body dumped somewhere? If so, she probably hadn't been killed in the room. There was no blood, so signs of violence except those caused by my fight with the man.

I stood just inside the door, holding the garrote, thinking.

This was the second time someone had tried to kill me. Maybe Carmelita wasn't the target. Maybe she had been forced to call me, lure me to the room. It seemed that the room had been set up to trap me. The man had been hiding behind the bed, knowing the light under the bathroom door would draw me toward it. If I hadn't been so charged up, he would have easily slipped the cord over my head, and with the noose cutting off the blood supply to my brain, it would have been almost impossible to break free before I lost conscious.

The question that nagged at me was about Carmelita. Had she called me willingly, or had she been forced to call? Maybe I should call the police. If she had been forced to call, she would need help.

Two things stopped me from calling: my suspicions that she was part of the set up, and my reluctance to get the police involved. Just dealing with David Bremm was bad enough. How could I explain to the police why someone wanted me dead? I didn't even know myself.

But if Carmelita was behind the attempt, why? Maybe she thought I was responsible for her brother's murder and she wanted revenge. Or—and the thought sent a chill up my spine—Harlen had found out about my ties to the DEA. If that were the case, they would probably try again.

I walked around the room, wiping my fingerprints off anything I'd touched, not forgetting the shower curtain. When I left I closed and locked the door.

Walking to my car, I kept out of sight of anyone who might be at the reservation desk.

I drove a couple of blocks and parked at the side of the boulevard. Using my cell phone I called Carmelita's home, trying to decide whether I would be happy if she answered or not. If she answered, it would prove she was alive, but would it also prove she was part of the set up?

I was almost disappointed when her sleepy voice said, "*Como?*"

There was a decided pause before I was able to say, "Carmelita. It's me, Ben Roan."

"Oh, Ben." She was alert now and I pictured her sitting up in bed, turning on a beside light. "Is something wrong?"

"No, no. I was just...when I talked to you, I thought you were in some kind of trouble."

"Talked to me? When?"

I almost dropped my phone. "A couple of hours ago. You told me—"

"I didn't talk to you."

I couldn't believe what I was hearing. It had been her. I would have bet on it. And yet?... Could I have been wrong?

"I got a message to call you. At another number. I thought it was you. You..uh..she---whoever it was---asked me to meet her."

"I've been home all evening. It wasn't me."

Was she lying? Now that I thought about it, I hadn't really questioned the call. I'd simply assumed that that it was authentic, because the person said she was Carmelita and had sounded like her.

"Okay," I said. "I guess I was mistaken."

"Are you all right?" The concern in her voice couldn't have been false and, despite my doubts, it gave me a thrill of pleasure to know she was worried about me.

"I'm fine," I said. "I'll...uh...see you tomorrow maybe."

"All right," she said. "Take care."

After I logged off, I sat holding the phone, trying to decide whether or not she was lying. It didn't seem likely that if she'd set me up for a killer, she would be home sleeping peacefully. Assuming, of course, that she had been sleeping. The one thing certain was that she had been home. Or had she? The number I had for her could be her cell phone, meaning she could be anywhere, maybe even somewhere at the motel waiting for the good news that I was room temperature.

On the other hand, she had sounded sleepy. But if she were the one who had called me, she had to be a darn good actress. So I couldn't be sure of anything, which seemed to be happening to me a lot lately.

But there was one thing of which I was certain. Someone wanted me dead.

I decided this was something Bremm should know so I called him.

When he answered his voice didn't sound a bit sleepy. Maybe

161

he never slept. With his responsibilities he probably sat holding the phone twenty-four hours a day.

"It's me," I said, assuming that by this time he'd know my voice.

"Yeah?" His voice was noncommittal so I couldn't be sure if he recognized me.

"Roan. Ben Roan."

"Ben?" His voice suddenly crackled with anticipation. "What's going on?"

"Somebody just tried to kill me."

There was an instant of silence. "What happened?"

I was more than a little chagrin that he didn't inquire about my health. He didn't even sound particularly surprised. Maybe he expected it to happen sooner or later. I told him what had happened.

"Damn," he said. "Sorry about that."

The concern in his voice sort of mollified my smoldering disgust.

"I called her," I said. "She said it wasn't her I talked to."

"Oh? You think it was?"

"I did. Now I'm not so sure."

"But it could have been."

"Well, yeah, but—"

"You think she, or Harlen, made you?"

"Made me?"

"Found out you're working with the us."

So. His concern wasn't for me. It was for the mission. Without me he had nothing. I tried to keep my disgust out of my voice when I said, "Either that or she thinks I'm responsible for her brother getting killed. And that was before I hooked up with you."

"Why would she think that?

"I don't know. Maybe because I kind of took his place."

162

There was a pause while Bremm weighed the possibilities. Then he said, "So she might not know."

"It's possible."

"But if she does know, Harlen probably knows, too."

"Probably. Why would she keep it to herself?"

"Good question." This time he was the one who paused before he said, "What do you want to do?"

He was asking if I wanted to quit. I hadn't seriously considered it until that moment, but now my various choices and their possible consequences flashed through my mind. If I quit the DEA would probably catch up with Harlen sooner or later, but he would damage a lot of lives before they did. On the other hand, if I didn't quit, I could end up dead. It wouldn't matter much whether it was because Carmelita was trying to avenge her brother, or because she—or Harlen—had found out I was working for Bremm.

But if I did quit, gave up flying and concentrated on my company, would Carmelita stop trying to kill me? How vindictive was she? Would Harlen believe that I had washed my hands of the entire sordid affair and leave me alone? I didn't think so.

In short, I was damned if I did and damned if I didn't. The only difference was that if I continued working for Bremm it would be over soon, one way or the other. If I walked away, I'd have to worry about a hit man—or woman—lurking around every dark corner for years. As Shakespeare put it: 'Better to bear the ills we have than those we know not of.'

There was one other consideration that kept pushing aside all the others: if I quit, I'd probably never see Sharon again. And if she wasn't part of Harlen's cartel, she also could be in danger. Did I want to abandon her? Was she worth my life?

Before I let the thought destroy my resolve, I told Bremm, "I'll finish what we started."

I hoped he believed I wanted to stay because I was the machismo type who felt no fear, only a burning desire for justice.

"Good," he answered. "Give me the address of that motel. We'll look into it."

I gave him the address and the room number. "I left the garrote rope there. Maybe you can get something from it."

"We'll see. But it's unlikely."

I agreed with him. Modern forensics can perform miracles, but the guy who had been waiting for me was probably no amateur. I seriously doubted they would find anything that would lead to his identity.

Then I remembered: "Oh, I think. I think I broke his collarbone."

"Good. We'll check the hospitals. But I should tell you, it probably won't do any good."

"I understand." I was growing a little tired of his negative attitude, although I knew he was right. Still, I couldn't help myself when I added peevishly, "The next time he tries I'll ask for his name."

To his credit Bremm didn't bite back. He didn't answer right away, when he did his voice was sympathetic. "Sorry, Ben. I really didn't think it'd get this hairy. I wouldn't blame you if you wanted out."

"No," I said. "I'd like to catch this guy, and whoever's behind him."

"Okay. I'll let you know if we get anything."

"Okay. Me too."

"Keep in touch." He hung up.

One thing was certain: the next time I saw Harlen or Carmelita, I would pay close attention to their demeanor. What was it Hamlet said? 'If they but blench, I'll know my course.' But then, Hamlet didn't have to worry about someone killing him.

By the time I arrived back at my house in Newport Bay, fatigue had virtually closed down all my bodily functions. Usually when I returned home after dark, I enjoyed standing near my boat dock for a few minutes admiring the way the various colored lights around the bay sent shimmering shafts of light across the dark, still waters. But tonight—what little night there was left—I had other things on my mind.

Entering the dark house I tried to be alert in case the guy

who'd tried to kill me had a friend. He would have had an easy score. I was moving like a medieval knight in rusty armor. Even so, when I fell into bed, I tossed and turned for a couple of seconds before I was able to ignore a nagging apprehension and fall into a restive sleep. The thought that wouldn't go away, and one that triggered nasty nightmares, was that from now on I'd have to keep a careful watch on my back.

CHAPTER TWENTY-ONE

I hadn't talked to Jack since returning from Mexico so I was glad when he asked me to meet him for lunch at one of our favorite restaurants: a little roadside place off MacArthur Boulevard that specialized in hot dogs.

As many times as I'd driven MacArthur, I'd never noticed the small restaurant that specialized in hot dogs until Jack introduced me to the place. It became one of my favorite restaurants because chili dogs hold a dear place in my heart. When I was fifteen or sixteen I had an after school job as janitor in a church. There had been a hamburger/hot dog stand down the block and I could just afford a big, fat chili dog and a cola for dinner. I considered it a major accomplishment when I became so skilled I could eat a chili dogs without spilling a drop of chili or losing a single bean. In most cases, I didn't even have to lick my fingers. When you're constantly hungry you don't waste even a drop of food.

The first time Jack and I had lunch there I was delighted to find out I hadn't lost my skill. But Jack was not impressed. He was a real slob with his own chili dog, dribbling chili down his chin and on his fingers. I guess it proved once again that you develop skills in activities that are either essential to survival or essential to attaining desired goals. Jack, for instance, possessed great skill in various forms of combat. I, on the other hand, had spent my formative years learning to survive on the mean streets and how to eat chili dogs without wasting a single bean.

Jack had taught me some of his more deadly combat skills, and I had, through practice, achieved a modicum of skill. But no matter how many hours I spent breaking boards with my bare hands or trying to kick holes in a heavy punching bag, I could never achieve his deadly perfection. Fortunately, the few times I'd had to use what little skill I had achieved in order to survive, the other guy had turned out to be even more combat challenged. It seemed that most would-be bad guys

166

spent more time building up their abs and biceps than they did on perfecting hand-to-hand combat skills. They would rather twist your head off than kick it off.

Another thing Jack could do better than I. He could listen without interrupting. Before I started telling him about my midnight adventure, I told him what had happened coming back from Mexico and my theory about the extent of Sharon's involvement with Harlen.

He listened patiently, chewing on his chili dog and licking his fingers before he said, "So it looks like Sharon really is on Harlen's payroll."

I thought I detected disappointment in his voice. Jack wasn't one to give away his emotions, but I knew he considered Sharon a friend, and my story had probably hurt him as much as if I'd stuck a knife in his back. I tried to make him feel better with the same rationalization I'd used to ease my own disappointment: "She didn't have much choice. She has to go along with Harlen or lose her plane and, probably, her entire business."

He grunted in answer, but I could tell he was disappointed. Even if it were true that she had been coerced into cooperating with Harlen, her image as a vestal angel was badly tarnished.

He wasn't nearly as surprised or upset when I told him the result of Carmelita's call, beginning with, "It was a set up."

He shook his head. "You sure? She sounded scared when she called me."

"She said it was about her brother. She asked me to meet her at a motel in Hollywood. When I got there some guy tried to kill me?"

Jack stiffened, and his eyes got their old snake-killer look like he was sorry he'd missed the fun. "I should have gone with you."

"There were a couple of seconds there when I was kind of wishing you had, too."

"Did you kill him?"

"No. He got away. I was glad to see him go."

His laugh was a short bark. "Maybe he'll try again"

He sounded happy, and I knew I wouldn't have to ask him to

stick close. He seemed to spend his time hoping somebody would try to kill him—or me.

"I called Carmelita. She denied the whole thing. Said I'd never talked to her."

He shrugged. "It was a setup. What dud you expect her to say?"

"Yeah, But if somebody was impersonating her, maybe she wasn't in on it."

"That's the kind of a 'maybe' that could get you killed."

I nodded, unhappily. "If you can't trust a beautiful woman, who can you trust?"

"Your dog. Not those little barky ones; the big ones, like a St. Bernard."

He was probably right, except that, unless I was marooned on an iceberg, I would rather spend moonlight nights with an untrustworthy, gorgeous woman than with the most trustworthy St. Bernard in the world.

Jack licked a trace of chili off his lower lip. Then his eyes turned away from looking at me, and I had the impression he was going to ask a question but didn't want to hear the answer, so I helped him out by saying, "What?"

He hesitated before asking, "What about Sharon?"

I stared at him. "What about her?"

"You think she was in on it, too?"

I felt my face sag. For some reason that thought had not crossed my mind, most likely because my mind had closed it out like an unwanted fever. Could she have laughed and joked with me during dinner if she expected me to be dead by the next morning? I grasped at the only straw I could think of. "Not if it was about Jorge. Sharon had nothing to do with that."

"Let's hope not."

We sat for a moment. I'm not sure what was going through his mind, but, for me, I was wondering how I would react the next time I saw Carmelita—or Sharon.

The question was answered when we got back to the airport. I'd planned on doing some maintenance on my Mustang with Jack, but I knew I wouldn't be able to concentrate on much of anything until I'd talked to Sharon.

Her big hanger doors were open and her Mustang was just inside. She was on a step ladder working with a mechanic changing the big 12-cylinder Merlin's spark plugs. For a moment I stood watching. She was wearing an old pair of coveralls and had almost as much oil on her face as she had under her fingernails. She did not appear annoyed by either the dirty job or the oil smears. Rather, she looked almost blissful as she concentrated on her task.

She saw me when she lifted her head to reach for a new plug. She paused long enough to grin down at me. To my intense joy there was no sign of surprise that I was still alive. "Hi. Be with you in a minute," she said.

"Take your time," I said. "I was thinking about doing some work on mine this afternoon."

"Better hold off. Harlen called. He's on his way over."

"Darn," I said. "I really looked forward to changing the oil filter."

She laughed, and it was like sunlight streaming through big, puffy clouds on a beautiful day.

I went out to the flight line. Jack had already brought the ladders and tools to work on my Mustang, but when I told him I wouldn't be able to help him for a while, he took the news very well. He hid his disappointment by waving me away and saying, "Take your time."

I started to turn away, then turned back. "Incidentally. I talked to Sharon. She couldn't have been in on it."

He kind of nodded as though he knew it all the time, but I knew that inside he felt better.

I saw Harlen's big Lexis pull up and stop in front of Sharon's hanger and Harlen got out. A pair of spike-heeled pumps attached to a pair of long legs stepped out of the passenger's side followed by

Carmelita's incredible body clad in a short-skirted flowery dress. As she strode beside Harlen into Sharon's hanger, sunlight glistening on her long silky hair made it appear to undulated down her back in shimmering waves.

Following them gave me time to prepare for Carmelita. As long as she refused to admit being involved, and I had no proof, that she—or Harlen---had anything to do with last night, there was no point in bringing up the subject. The best thing I could do was pretend it never happened, but be wary.

I had my happy face in place when I joined Harlen and Carmelita in Sharon's office area. Sharon wasn't there and I assumed she was cleaning up. They both greeted me as though last night had never happened, and when I gave them a big grin and said hello, I thought my acting was as good as theirs.

Carmelita sat in a chair and her short skirt got even shorter and my eyes got even bigger. I sat down where I could watch her, hoping that something in her expression or her body language would give some indication of guilt, but she was totally relaxed, her expression holding its usual haughty disdain. If she harbored any guilt at all, I would never find out by watching her, although I could think of worse ways to spend my time.

Harlen settled on the couch and to my dismay, fired up a cigar, despoiling the air with clouds of carcinogens that, naturally, wafted in my direction. Thank heavens the big hanger doors were still open.

"How's the Mustang running?" Harlen asked. "Any problems coming back from Acapulco?"

"No. No problems. Sharon's either."

"Shouldn't be. They both have rebuilt engines."

He didn't mention the search he'd said he was going to conduct in the canyon for the drop tanks, which was fine with me. If we didn't discuss them I wouldn't let it slip that I knew what they'd contained. "Wait'll you get the gas bill," I said. "You'll wish they'd put in a couple of Volkswagen engines."

I figured that with the loss of the drop tanks and their contents, plus gas and hanger fees for the two planes and per diem for Sharon and me, his little expedition must have cost him more than a million dollars.

Still, he chuckled and waved the thought aside with his cigar. "The cost of business."

"Right. Tax deductible," I said, as though I didn't know that if his tax form listed the loss of what was in those drop tanks, it would trigger an audit that would get him the same treatment tax problems got Al Capone.

"What's this about taxes?" Sharon said as she came to join us. She still wore the old coveralls, but she had washed away the oil on her hands and face. I had to hide a smile of delight when I noticed she hadn't had time to get rid of the smell of kerosene nor all the black under her fingernails. I'd worked enough as a mechanic to know it would take a major manicure to expunge all traces of grease and engine oil from her nails. I sort of hoped she wouldn't; the little imperfection made her almost human.

"No problem," Harlen said. "Have you thought about attending that Canadian air show?"

"Sarnia?" she said. "Why there? Oshkosh is a lot bigger."

"Oshkosh is in Wisconsin. I need the Canadian exposure."

"But Oshkosh is one of the biggest shows in the world. Hundreds of planes. Two hundred thousand attendance."

"You'd get lost in the crowd," Harlen said. "They'll have almost as many Mustangs there as they'll have at the Gathering of Eagles."

He was referring to an air show held from time to time in which Mustang owners were invited to a "gathering" at Omaha's MacLaren Field. There are only about a hundred P-51s in the world in flying condition, but the last 'gathering' had attracted seventy of them. It must have been an awesome sight seeing all those beautiful Mustangs in the air and on the ground.

"But Oshkosh gets the publicity," Sharon reminded him. "Thousands of fans and pictures in just about every paper in the country."

"If it's exposure you want," I said, "we should enter the Reno air races this fall? When I win you'll get your logo all over the world."

"You? Win?" Sharon said. "In your dreams."

"I save my dreams for better things."

She must have seen something sexy in my completely innocent expression because her face flushed, and her teeth sort of bared like a female dog warning away a male in heat.

"Maybe next year," Harlen said. "The warbirds they fly in those races are heavily modified. Your planes are too stock to have a chance."

"Yes, but it's the only air race left any more. Even if we didn't win, we'd get a lot of coverage."

I hoped he would change his mind about Reno. I had images of whipping around the race course at better than 400 miles-an-hour about 50 feet off the ground, shaving the pylons in a near ninety degree bank, using my superior flying skills to make up for the difference in horsepower.

But Harlen shook his head. "I've got something better for you at Sarnia. In a way, what happened to you in Mexico gave me the idea."

What was he referring to? The attack by the F-16? Did he want us to stage a dogfight of some kind?

"What thing was that?" Sharon asked.

"Dropping your tanks. I got permission from the Sarnia air show for you to demonstrate how Mustangs were sometimes used in World War Two to support ground troops."

"They dropped bombs," I said. "Not fuel tanks."

"We can't very well do that. But dropping fuel tanks will be a good simulation."

"Would they be full of gas?" Carmelita's eyes sparkled as though she could picture the mayhem a few hundred gallons of burning gasoline could create if dropped from a couple of Mustangs.

"No, no," Harlen hastily corrected. "Some inert substance. Like flour or water. It'll make all the papers."

He was probably right. Four 150-gallon tanks slamming into

the ground at about 200 miles per hour could create a hell of a spectacular splatter. "Sounds like fun," I said.

"It won't be as easy as it sounds," Harlen said. "To be safe, and to get good coverage, you'd have to hit a pretty small target."

"Piece of cake," Sharon said.

"Yeah, well, just to be sure I've made arrangements for you to get a little practice."

"Where?" I said. "We can't drop a dime around here without getting some environmental nut in an uproar."

"The military has bombing ranges in the Mojave desert," Sharon said.

"Off base for civilians," Harlen countered. "I've got something better worked out."

I leaned forward. I didn't think for even a minute that Harlen's motive for splattering a target with drop tanks was for publicity. But I couldn't get a handle on what he had in mind. "Something better?" I asked.

Harlen took his time answering, drawing on his cigar while the suspense built. But like an accomplished performer, he didn't give it to us all at once. "Crop dusters."

Sharon looked at him as though he'd lost his mind. "Crop dusters?"

"They're always dropping stuff from low altitude. Nobody'll pay any attention to two planes coming in low."

He was right about that. I'd seen a few crop dusters work farms in the San Joaquin Valley and they did come in on the deck. But they were slow, often old WW II biplane trainers that had been converted to crop dusters.

Sharon shook her head. "The FAA'll never give you permission to fly Mustangs that low and fast."

"Not around here. I'm thinking more like Missouri."

"Missouri?" I said. "That'll be a really long mission."

"On your way to Canada. You'll stop at a crop dusting station in Missouri. Friend of mine works there. Name of Tex Butikaufer. Out in the boonies where nobody'll pay attention to a couple more planes. You'll have a week to practice."

I said, "A week? I won't need two days."

Sharon kind of snorted, which I did not take as a note of confidence.

Harlen stood up and adjusted his suit jacket. "I'll have all your paper work ready by tomorrow, including the coordinates of the place. When you file your flight plan, tell them you're stopping to refuel."

Sharon said, "When do we leave?"

Harlen had already started for the door, followed by Carmelita. He stopped and rubbed his hand across his chin. "One day to get to Missouri. One day to get to Sarnia—"

I interrupted him. "Where is this Sarnia?"

"Sarnia. Ontario, Canada. Close to Detroit. Big air show.

"Never heard of it."

"Doesn't sound impressive," Sharon added.

"You'll love it," Harlen said. "Better leave on Monday. That'll give you time to gear up."

He resumed his march to the open hanger door with Carmelita holding his arm and matching him stride for stride, her long hair and short skirt swinging with the same display of arrogance as the sound made by her stiletto heels pinging on the painted concrete floor.

Sharon came around her desk and perched on a corner. She turned her head from watching Harlen and Carmelita. "Well?"

"Well what?" I said, although I knew very well what she meant.

A slight frown of annoyance crossed her face. She knew I was evading the question. "What do you think? Should we do it?"

She had said 'we.' The thought that she considered us to be a team gave me a warm feeling. But I wondered what she would say if I said no.

CHAPTER TWENTY-TWO

I should have been enjoying the long flight across the American west. Soaring over the snowy crags of the Sierras and cruising eleven thousand feet above the forests, farms and deserts of the eastern slopes, playing tag with towering thunderheads, should have been pure joy.

But the seat of a P-51 Mustang was not made for comfort. After hours of sitting on a parachute most pilots decided the cockpit designer was the same one who designed those bed-of-nails that some hard-assed Hindu mystics favored. Even so, the steady purr of the big Merlin engine was soporific. Continuously adjusting the trim tabs, juggling the throttle and playing with the stick and rudder peddles couldn't keep away a desire to sleep. And when you're flying formation with another plane, even a loose formation, you have to pay attention, and that, too, could be tiring.

A brief stop at Albuquerque to refuel helped, but my growing physical discomfort was not helped by nagging doubts about Sharon. Had she really been disappointed in my decision to go along with Harlen's plan? What about her own? Would she have made this flight without me? How tight was Harlen's grip on her? Maybe there was no grip at all. Maybe paying for the Mustang had little or nothing to do with her decision. Maybe she saw nothing wrong with dealing drugs. After she attained ownership of the plane would she continue working for him, buying into the easy drug money? Maybe she had been part of his cartel all along, dealing in dope simply for the money. Maybe, maybe, maybe.

"Bravo twenty-one. This is Alpha twelve. You read me?"

I jerked to attention, triggering my radio. "A-roger, Alpha twelve."

"We're about an hour out. How's your fuel?"

I checked my tanks. I'd emptied my drop tanks and my behind-the-seat tank and had been flying on the two ninety gallon wing tanks, switching back and forth between the two to optimize the plane's center of gravity. The fuel gauges indicated about thirty gallons in each, enough for another hour at cruise speed. "No problem," I called. "Drop tanks and back tank empty. Just switched to mains."

"I'm the same. I'll try to pick up McGinnis."

She clicked off, and I knew she was changing her radio to the frequency Harlen had given us for the crop duster's small airport. McGinnis was the name of the airstrip's owner, the man Harlen's friend Tex Butikaufer worked for. McGinnis should have his ears on; Harlen had telephoned him when we left and told him our ETA. I checked my watch. 3:23 Right on schedule.

I edged in closer to Sharon's wing so I could see her better. Her lips were moving so she had to be talking to McGinnis.

She turned her head and looked over at me, and tapped her helmet. "He's expecting us in about ten minutes," she said without preamble. "The airstrip is paved but rough so watch yourself."

"How long is it?" I asked.

"Should be plenty of room. It's an old World War Two training base. We're going down. Keep your eyes open for a line of power lines. They'll lead us right to the field. "

I said, "Ah-roger." and clicked off.

We began a shallow descent, and I turned my attention to the earth below. We were passing over huge tracts of farm land, some fields stretching for miles. Most appeared to be growing cotton. Sometimes sunlight glinted from irrigation water in the fields or from rows of low growing plants that could be potatoes or sugar beets or something.

The sight of the long fields brought a bitter taste to my mouth. One summer when I was fourteen I'd been sent to a foster family that owned a big ranch in the San Joaquin Valley. There were five other boys there. The family didn't give a hoot about being foster parents; they were looking for cheap labor. The six of us spent up to twelve hours a day in the fields hoeing weeds or working with the irrigation system. The burning sun had been so hot we sweated right through

176

our leather gloves. When school started in the fall, and they couldn't get a full day's work out of us, they sent us back. You can believe we didn't do any complaining about living conditions at the orphanage. The experience had made our bodies as tough as shoe leather, and it had also convinced me that I wasn't cut out to be a farmer.

We had dropped down to 2,500 feet when I spotted railroad tracks and next to them the towers of a power line. I wiggled my wings, and when I caught Sharon's attention I pointed to the power line. She nodded that she had seen them, and corrected our course to follow the lines.

In five minutes we spotted a couple of old Quonset huts that looked big enough to be hangers. They were facing the head end of a long airstrip. It had been paved with black tarmac, but the black had aged to an earth-colored grey that was full of cracks, ridges and dust. Three ancient mobile homes were sitting on blocks in the shade of a line of cottonwood and poplar trees. Two Stearman biplanes whose yellow and blue paint had seriously faded, sat in front of the Quonset huts. Near them was a newer plane that looked as though it had been developed specifically for crop dusting.

One of the Quonset huts had a wind sock on top that drooped like a pricked balloon in the hot breathless air.

We roared down the length of the runway at about a hundred feet. Two men stood in the hot sun near the Quonset huts. One of them waved as we swept past.

The airstrip looked to be nearly three-quarters of a mile long as though the student pilots who had used it originally had required lots of landing room. It might have been ample room for landing a light trainer at 50 mile per hour, but it was going to take a lot of concentration to bring in a 6,000 pound Mustang at 125 mile per hour.

Finishing our pass over the airstrip, Sharon pulled up and to the left. I followed as she swept up and around in a landing pattern. In the windless air, it didn't make any difference which way we landed so we flew a pattern that would bring us in at the far end of the runway so that when we stopped we'd be in front of the Quonset huts.

I gave Sharon plenty of lead. In the breathless air I didn't want to be so close behind her when I landed that I'd be caught in her propwash and botch the landing in front of Sharon and the two spectators.

Actually, I made a pretty good landing. I even remembered to get the flaps down, and compensate for the drag of the two drop tanks by easing in at a conservative 130 knots. I was glad I'd given Sharon plenty of room for another reason: her prop had kicked up so much dust I had trouble seeing the runway.

On the ground I closed the door to the oil filter and followed her trail of dust to the end of the runway where one of the men directed me to pull off the tarmac. I stopped next to Sharon, our props billowing dust. When we cut our engines the dust settled, coating the planes like they were cotton plants after a dusting.

Climbing out of the cockpit my feet left prints on the Mustang's dusty wing. I hated to think what the dust had done to our filters.

The man who had directed us to our parking places looked to be in his 60s. He was small, wiry, with a stubble of gray whiskers. He wore brown flight overalls that had been washed so many times the collar and the sleeve ends were frayed. On his feet were a pair of worn basketball shoes that had once been decorated with some kind of a red pattern. He stuck a hand out to Sharon that was so knarled it looked as though it could have belonged to a Navaho medicine man.

"Sam McGinnis," he said. "Welcome to Missoura."

"Sharon Daadian," she answered. "This is Ben Roan."

I shook his hand. He had a good firm grip that didn't match his thin body.

He indicated the man who had walked over to join us. He was tall, well set up, wearing a tight T-shirt that showed off muscles that indicated he'd done a good deal of body building. He wore a cowboy hat with the sides curled up and the front and back curled down. Two inch heels on his cowboy boots added to his more than six foot height. I made a shrewd guess that his name was Tex. It was hard to believe he had some connection with Harlen, not in this remote place.

When Sharon slipped off her helmet and shook out her hair the bodybuilder's eyes went smoky like he'd swallowed a hot chili pepper.

178

"Hey, hey," he said. "Not only a lady pilot, but a beautiful lady pilot." He stuck out his hand. "I'm Tex Butikaufer." He pronounced it 'Beautykaufer.'"

Sharon started to shake his hand, but he grabbed her hand and brought it to his lips.

When she got her hand back, he showed her his unbelievably white teeth. "Do you believe in love at first sight?"

She said, "Not any more."

His smile hung on while he tried to figure out whether her answer was positive or negative.

Before he'd made up his mind, McGinnis introduced him to me. He didn't kiss my hand. Instead he squeezed so hard I winced. I should have let my hand go limp, giving him a hollow victory, but I couldn't do it, not in front of Sharon. I squeezed back. We stood like that, each one grinning like an idiot while trying not to show pain. Sharon rolled her eyes and I heard her mutter, "Jesus."

Tex finally gave up and let go. "Nice to meet you," he said.

"Same here."

Sharon turned to McGinnis. "Is there room in those hangers for our planes?"

"Yeah. I've got most of my dustin' gear in there, but I can move a few things."

While McGinnis and Tex cleared space inside the hangers, Sharon and I hooked up hoses and washed the dust off our planes. Then McGinnis used ropes on his pickup truck to tow them inside the hangers.

I took a few minutes to walk over and look at the two Stearman biplanes parked near the hanger. I'd had a love affair with the open cockpit Stearmans since I'd learned to fly. These two had been considerably modified so they could be used for crop dusting.

Sharon saw me looking at the planes and walked over to join me.

"Amazing airplane," she said. "They'll be flying in a hundred years."

179

"Looks to me like these two won't last another one."

"Don't let their looks fool you. They're workhorses." She pointed at one of the planes' rotary engine. "Looks like the original two-twenty horsepower Continental has been replaced with a four-fifty Pratt & Whitney. They need the extra horsepower to get in and out of small fields with trees or power lines." She walked around the plane, pointing out modifications. "The seats in the front cockpit were removed so a hopper could be installed. Holds about a thousand pounds of insecticide." She pointed to a pipe fitted with nozzles under the fuselage behind the wheels that stretched from wingtip to wingtip. "The insecticide is sprayed out by this dispenser."

I'd been listening to her with mounting amazement. "How do you know so much about it?"

"My dad. Before he opened the flying school, he did a little crop dusting."

"I take it you did your share."

"Some. My dad said it was too dangerous. That's why he opened the school."

"Like flying with some crazy student isn't dangerous."

She ran her hand over the fabric of the wing, leaving a trail through the dust. "But not near as much fun."

"I can imagine."

The two open-cockpit biplanes might show their age, but I guess they would always be beautiful to anyone who loved flying by the seat of their pants with the wind and, occasionally, rain in their face. I was kind of hoping McGinnis would allow me to take a short hop in one of them for old times sake.

It was growing dark, and McGinnis said we could either ride the five miles into Griggs Landing and eat at a restaurant or we could have barbeque here.

I assumed one of the mobile homes was for McGinnis and another for Tex. The third was probably a spare if they needed other workers. If their exteriors were any indication of sanitary conditions on the inside, I would have opted for driving into any town within two hundred miles. Sharon, however, said she would just as soon stay for

180

dinner.

I experienced a mild shock when I saw the inside of McGinnis's mobile. For one thing it was more spacious than it looked from the outside. And spotlessly clean. Every thing in order. Not a speck of dust. The floor, partially made of hardwood and partially tiled, shown like a mirror. Even the small kitchen, which surprisingly, had room for a dining booth, looked as though it would have no trouble passing a stringent Food and Drug Administration inspection.

McGinnis showed us the bedroom. He said to me, "You and me'll take the spare." He turned to Sharon. "You take this one."

"I don't want to take yours," she said.

"Don't even think about it. I don't clean up every day, but it's in pretty good shape. I don't get many visitors."

"It's fine," she said. "Better than a motel."

"Well, my wife liked it. When she passed on, I tried to keep it like she'd want it."

"She'd be very proud," Sharon said.

He had a barbeque behind the mobile and a table set up under and awning. I've never tasted better barbequed short ribs with cold slaw, baked potatoes, and garlic bread. We wanted to help him wash up afterward, but he'd have none of it. I was kind of glad he wouldn't let us help. I wasn't sure I would measure up to his antisepsis standards.

It was dark by the time McGinnis suggested we sit down at the outside table. The night was balmy if a little humid, touched with the lingering aroma of barbeque smoke. The sound from an electric bug zapper frying insects with gleeful abandon seemed like the perfect backdrop to a discussion of Harlen's project. Sharon and I sat at the picnic table with McGinnis while Tex slouched in a lawn chair, smoking a cigarette and staring at Sharon.

I thought that Tex, as Harlen's contact, would be versed on the project. But I wasn't sure where McGinnis fit into the puzzle so I didn't bring up the project immediately. If both McGinnis and Tex were part of Harlen's cabal, they might be unhappy talking to strangers about their connection.

It was Sharon who said, "How do you happen to know Harlen?"

McGinnis answered immediately. "Never met the man. Tex knows him. Told me Harlen was looking for a place for a couple of his friends to do a little flying. Said he'd pay. I said hell yes quicker'n you could swat a horse fly. Didn't expect no Mustangs though."

Sharon glanced at me. The glance told me that, like me, she was wondering how much he knew about Harlen. "I hope it's not too much of an imposition," she said.

"No sweat. Besides I could use the money."

"Why is that?" I said. "I'd think dusting in this area would be profitable."

"It ain't the dustin'. That's holding its own. But competition is eating me up. When I started here——twenty-five, thirty years ago——I was the only one in the business. Worked out great, up to now. Now they've got five companies dustin' in this area. Had to get me that Storch Air Tractor to keep up. But I still miss out on the big contracts."

"You've got the two Stearman."

"Stearmans don't cut it any more. They're okay for the small fields. But not with the big fields used by them conglomerates. You need turbine power like my Air Tractor. I've got to get me another one."

"Are they expensive?" Sharon asked.

"Hell yes. More'n half a million with GPS and all the other gadgets you need today. About half of what one'a them Mustangs cost. That's a hell of a lot for me.

"So you don't actually work for Harlen?"

"Never heard of him 'til Tex told me about him."

At the mention of his name, Tex sat up straighter. "You on Harlen's payroll?"

Sharon gave me a quick glance that asked how much we should tell Tex. My feeling was that I had to know more about him before I would trust him, and I doubted if I would even then. "Off

182

and on," I said. "Usually when he wants to do some advertising at an air show."

"Not much of a show," he said, "dropping a couple'a tanks full of water."

So Harlen had at least told him why we were coming.

Sharon's voice was flat, noncommittal when she said, "There's more to it than that. We put on a good show."

"Yeah? That don't sound much like Harlen. What does he get out of it?"

"Publicity," Sharon continued. "Promotion for his company."

Tex stared at us, his eyebrows pulled down in concentration, as he tried to decide how much we might know about Harlen.

"I understand you used to work for Harlen," I said.

His eyes narrowed to slits like a snake sensing approaching danger. "Used to do a little flying for him."

I could imagine what kind of flying a man like Tex would do for Harlen. Harlen probably got rid of him when he sensed that Tex would betray him in an instant if the money was right.

"What's this about droppin' tanks?" McGinnis said.

I looked at Tex. "You didn't tell him?"

Tex wiped at his stubble of beard. He jerked his head at McGinnis. "No big deal. They want'a play soldier. Drop a couple'a drop tanks. You know, World War Two stuff."

"Drop tanks? Full'a gas?"

"Shit no. Full'a water."

McGinnis looked at Sharon and me. "That right?"

There was no point in trying to hide something he would have to know about sooner or later. I grinned at him. "That's us. Two aces from the big war."

McGinnis gave me a look that said I was out of my mind. Here he was risking his life every day, flying at 140 miles an hour about eight feet off the ground despite cross-winds and bad weather, dodging trees, power lines and gophers, trying to save enough money to buy a half-million dollar airplane that could save his business, and Sharon and I were two rich dilettantes flying million dollar toys looking for a few thrills by dropping tanks full of water.

"You ain't plannin' on dropping them on any buildings?" he said.

"No, no," I assured him. "Just some clear place where they won't hurt anyone."

He sort of sighed. "Well, it's clear at the end of the runway. You need some kind of target?"

"If it isn't too much trouble," Sharon said. "Just some black paint on the ground."

"How about avgas? What do you use?"

"L.L. hundred octane."

He nodded. "Close to what I use in the Storch. Should work if you need it."

"Include it in your bill to Harlen," Sharon said.

His laugh bordered on rude. "Bet your sweet ass." His face colored when he realized what he'd said. "Just an expression," he said quickly to Sharon. "Didn't mean..uh...you know."

Sharon's roughish smile let him know she wasn't offended. "A girl is always glad to know she's appreciated."

McGinnis's color deepened. He cleared his throat. "I guess I could make some kind of target out there. Nothing around to hurt."

"How much water'll you need?" Tex asked.

Sharon answered. "A hundred fifty gallons in each tank. Will that be a problem?"

McGinnis shook his head. "Not this time'a the year. Should make a hell of a splash."

"I don't know," Tex said. "Them tanks are made of steel. They might just split open."

"Not these," I said. "They're rubberized cardboard."

184

"Cardboard," Tex said. "You've got to be kidding."

"No. He's right," Sharon said. "They're World War Two surplus. Harlen got them someplace."

"Yeah, but cardboard?"

"What happened," I said, "was that the original tanks were steel. But when they dropped their tanks over Germany they were making the Germans a present of a lot of good steel. So somebody figured a way of making the tanks out of heavy cardboard and lining them with rubber so they'd hold fuel. Harlen got hold of some. They should pretty much explode when they hit."

"We'll come in over the target at about..." She looked at me. "What do you think? A hundred feet?"

"Sounds about right. If we come in too low, they might just hit and skid. We'll need a good impact."

"Okay. We come in side by side. Drop on my signal."

"Your signal?" My pride wouldn't allow me to think she might make a more accurate drop than I could. "Why not mine?"

Sharon stared at me, her mouth tight. "I'm the senior pilot. We drop on my signal."

"Oh, that's great here," I countered. "But if you miss the target at the show, we could drown a couple of hundred people."

"And if you screw up, we could drown a couple of thousand."

McGinnis threw up his hands. "Whoa! Whoa! Tell you what. Each of you make a separate drop. The one who hits closest to the target gets to be leader."

Sharon and I looked at each other's tense face. Then she nodded. "Fine with me."

"Okay," I was confident I'd win, so it was easy to concede.

McGinnis sat back with an expression of his face like he was glad he didn't have any kids. "You bust up your tanks, how are you gonna fly all the way back to California?"

I hesitated before answering. Should I tell him we were heading for Canada? That might cause him to ask questions I didn't want to answer.

While I was thinking, Sharon said, "Internal tanks. They have a range of more than a thousand miles. We can make it with one stop even if we hit bad weather."

"And Harlen'll have replacement tanks we can use in a show when we need 'em." I added.

Tex grinned at Sharon. "Those power lines might give you some trouble. Might be a good idea if I showed them to you."

Sharon glanced at me and I didn't like the twinkle in her eyes before she turned back to Tex. "That's a good idea. When do you want to show me?"

I knew she was toying with him. Wasn't she? After all, how well did I know her? Maybe she went for the pseudo-macho type, although I doubted that Tex's Rambo image would hold up well if push came to shove. But maybe she didn't recognize bull doodoo when she heard it? Maybe she though he was the real deal: a Wild Bill Hickok right out of Texas packing a forty-five.

"How about now?" he said, showing her some of his perfect teeth in a crooked smile.

I couldn't believe it when she said, "Fine."

Tex stood up, standing as tall as possible, his chest out, his smile radiating triumph. Sharon got up and I started to get up too. "Good," I said. "I'll go with you."

Tex lost his smile and his eyes blinked as he searched for an excuse to leave me behind. But it was Sharon who said, "It might be a better idea if you checked on the water supply with Sam."

I froze, dumbfounded. She actually wanted to be alone with Tex. I sat watching them walk away, my mouth dry, my brain numb with shock. What had happened here? And why should it bother me that as they walked away Sharon seemed to be looking at Tex and laughing with delight? Why did I hate Tex? He was only being the predator God had made him. And why was I so disappointed in Sharon? How could she be attracted to that egotistical jerk? Maybe she wasn't as smart as I'd thought. Okay. So my pride was damaged. I would live. She meant nothing to me.

186

It was a lie, and I knew it. The realization hit me hard that during the short time I'd known her I had been subconsciously trying to impress her. Well, maybe not entirely subconsciously. After all, she was a woman, and beautiful. And I liked her, even though she'd never given me a second look. Obviously, she only saw me as a friend, and maybe not even that.

McGinnis seemed to share my thoughts because he sucked in air like he'd been holding his breath. "I'll be damned," he said. "That girl ain't got a lick'a sense."

I could have added one more thing to his observation: neither did I.

CHAPTER TWENTY-THREE

I didn't sleep well, listening for Sharon's footsteps walking to McGinnis's mobile. I never did hear them.

The next morning when I saw Sharon at breakfast in McGinnis's mobile, I surreptitiously searched her face for signs of fatigue...or something. I hadn't slept much, and I was sure I had deep dark circles under my bloodshot eyes, but she was her usual lovely, perky self, smiling at McGinnis and me as though it were just another happy, happy day.

I had too much pride to ask where Tex was, but my unspoken question was answered when he heard the engine on one of the Stearmans cough into life.

"That's Tex," McGinnis said. "Getting an early start," He looked at me with something in his eyes I hoped wasn't pity.

I asked, "He usually skip breakfast?"

He stared at my haggard face, and I decided the look in his eyes wasn't pity. It was amusement. "Maybe he didn't sleep too well," he said.

I couldn't help myself. I glanced at Sharon who was putting bread in McGinnis's toaster. She was humming away with a satisfied look on her face like a cat that had been out all night and could hardly wait for the sun to go down.

During breakfast she and McGinnis chattered away, but my throat was so constricted it was all I could do to force down a few mouthfuls of whatever it was she shoved in front of me.

Our conversation was strictly business as we filled the drop tanks with water from McGinnis's big storage tank. McGinnis had found an old roll of black tar paper and used it to fashion a big X about a hundred feet from the far end of the runway. That way we could make our run down the length of the runway without having to dodge trees.

McGinnis pointed to a row of power line towers beyond the end of the runway. "Watch those power lines. You shouldn't have any trouble with them. You'll in the air long before you get close. But you'll be coming in at about...what?...a hundred ten?"

"To get a good splash," Sharon said. "More like a hundred fifty."

"So after you make your drop, you'll have to pull up pretty sharp."

"We'll be light with the tanks jettisoned," I pointed out. "Shouldn't be a problem."

"Right. Just watch out for birds, especially crows. They like to sit on the power lines. Helps you see the lines as long as they stay put."

"We won't get close," Sharon said. She looked at me. "Who goes first?"

I shrugged. "You decide."

She turned to McGinnis. "You got a coin?"

McGinnis dug a quarter out of his baggy jeans. "Call it," he said to me and flipped the coin in the air.

"Heads," I said. Then I remembered the last time I'd been involved in a coin toss I'd called 'heads' and lost. "No, ta—"

"Too late." McGinnis snatched the coin out of the air and slapped it on the back of his other hand. He removed his hand and looked at the coin. "Tails." He looked at Sharon. "Your call. First or second."

"Second," she said.

I knew she was going to say that. If I'd won, I would have picked second. That way she could watch my release point and see how far off target I hit. All she had to do was adjust her release point a little closer.

Then I realized it wouldn't be that easy. At 150 miles per hour, I would cover the length of the runway in about three seconds. Holy smokes. At that speed and altitude, what would be my release point? I couldn't just rely on instinct. I was going to have to do some mathematics.

"What about a dry run?" I asked.

McGinnis nodded. "Good idea. One pass. Drop on the second pass."

"Okay," I said. "Let's go."

McGinnis pointed to a small rise of ground off to the side of the end of the runway. "I'll be standing over there. Don't drop them damned things on my head."

"If you get wet," I said, "it won't be me."

"You hope," Sharon said.

Miffed, I stomped away. I would let my flying do the talking. I'd only taken a few steps when Sharon called me. She walked over and pointed toward the power lines beyond the runway.

"Watch those power lines on your take off and dry run. Those tanks'll slow your rate of climb. Don't get your shorts in a knot and hit the throttle too hard."

I fought back a tinge of resentment. What made her think I had to be warned like a rookie? I was about to get off a snotty reply when I saw the look of concern in her eyes, and I let it go with a brief, "Right. Thanks."

I wasn't quit so confident when I started thinking about my release point as I made my preflight check. The Air Force would have tables all worked out for speeds and altitudes, but I'd have to do my own arithmetic. Mathematics was not my long suit, but I got out my pocket calculator and gave it my best shot. First I changed knots per hour to feet per second so I could work out how long it would take me to run the length of the three-quarter-mile-long runway. The hard part came when I tried to figure how long it would take an approximately 1000 pound tank to fall 100 feet. I had a general idea of a falling body's terminal velocity, but the tanks would be tumbling which would increase their wind resistance. In the end, I assumed it would take about three seconds for the tanks to hit. That meant I'd have to jettison about 850 feet from the target. Allowing another 50 feet for physical, mental and mechanical lag, I estimated that hitting the handle about two thirds down the runway should put the tanks close to the target.

Still, it was only an estimate, and a poor one at that, and I'd lost a good chunk of bravado when I lifted off. With the two heavy tanks it required the entire runway, and I had a couple of anxious seconds before I cleared the power lines. It scared the devil out of about a hundred crows perched on the lines when I blasted past. By the time they flew off in a panic I was long gone, but looking back I thought a couple of them had turned snow white.

I climbed to two thousand feet and made a slow orbit. I watched Sharon take off and climb to my altitude. She pulled in off my wing and when I was ready to make my dry run I gave her a thumbs up and peeled off.

I made a standard landing approach, lined up with the runway and leveled off at an indicated 100 feet. Even at 150 KIAS and full flaps the runway sneaked up on me surprisingly fast. It took all my concentration to hold the speed and altitude while trying to gauge when I was two-thirds down the runway.

I could see the X marker just beyond the end of the runway. It looked awfully small and was charging toward me incredibly fast.

Two thirds of the way down the airstrip, I mentally hit the release lever, but I knew I was little late. I'd have to do better on my hot run

But right now I had to concentrate on clearing the power lines. The crows were gone. Cowards.

Climbing, it occurred to me that crop dusters had to carry out similar operations many times a day. They had to dodge power lines, trees and posts while getting into and out of small fields. They had to streak down the field, holding a specific altitude (usually 8 to 10 feet) and speed, then pull up at the end of the run into a near stall, whip their plane around in a suicidal dive and do it all again, time after time, day in and day out. Some dusters even did it in the dark so they wouldn't kill any honey bees working the fields in the daytime.

That took guts.

I leveled off searching for Sharon. No sign of her anywhere.

Then I looked behind me and she was right there, sitting on my tail, a couple of hundred yards back. She must have followed me through my dry run. When she peeled off for her test run, I thought: Hey. That wasn't fair. By following me, she had given herself an extra pass.

But nothing I could do about it now except try to think of all the names I would call her when we were back on the ground.

I'd gone through 'cheater,' 'double-crosser,' and 'sore loser' when I suddenly realized I was already on my hot run, and I'd better focus on what the devil I was doing, or I'd not only miss the target I'd probably hang myself on those power lines.

Maybe that was her plan: destroy my concentration. Forget her. Concentrate.

It was easier this time. Lining up with the runway, I was better able to hold my speed and altitude. When I reached what I estimated was the release point, I hit the jettison handle and felt the plane lurch as the tanks let go. I would have felt more confident they would hit the target if I hadn't glimpsed McGinnis running like a mad man with his hands covering his head.

Without the weight of the tanks I was able to pull up in a fast climbing turn so I could look back at where the tanks hit. I missed seeing the their actual impact, but I saw two long gouts of water shoot up about a hundred feet beyond the target and a little off to the right. From the ground they must have been an impressive sight, but I was disappointed. I thought I should have been closer. Still, it wasn't too bad. I hadn't hit McGinnis.

I climbed up and perched off the left side of the runway where I could watch Sharon make her dry run. She came in smoothly, moving down the runway like she was on a rail. From my vantage point 150 knots didn't look that fast, and I wondered if she might be cheating a little.

I dismissed the thought. She wouldn't cheat just to make me look bad.

I sort of changed my mind when she dropped her tanks and they hit almost on top of the target. I knew she'd done it on purpose just so she could gloat. Well, I was sure I could have done just as well if I'd gone second.

CHAPTER TWENTY-FOUR

After we landed Sharon and I walked over to see how we'd done. I thought it looked pretty impressive. Sharon's drop had hit a little short, and its spill had merged with my overshoot so they had formed a huge splotch of mud and water with the target pretty much in the middle. It was a good thing we wouldn't need the tanks anymore. They looked like they'd been run through a cement mixer.

Standing with her hands on her hips looking at the water's muddy footprint, Sharon said, "If we had bigger tanks we could do even better at Sarnia."

"Yeah," I agreed. "If we come in side by side it should make a hell of a splash."

"On my signal."

"Yeah, well, actually you were a little under. I figure—"

"On my signal," she repeated without looking at me.

I capitulated, thinking that some day she was going to make some lucky kid a darn good mother. "Yeah, okay," I said. After all, it didn't make that much difference who gave the drop signal, and I kind of hoped she'd think she owed me one. One what?

I glanced at her standing with the sun shining on her hair, and with her flight coveralls failing to conceal her impressive figure, and I smiled. I liked the idea of her owing me one of just about anything.

We spent the rest of the day washing and servicing our planes while Tex and McGinnis went about their business of crop dusting with Tex flying one of the Stearmans and McGinnis flying the Storch. I couldn't believe the number of takeoffs and landing they had to make to gas up and load insecticides—or whatever it was they were dusting. I offered to help and was kind of relieved when they both waved me aside. I probably would have screwed something up and infected myself with boll weevil fever or something worse.

I made it a point to stay away from Sharon. Even when we brushed elbows while getting wash water, I couldn't bring myself to talk. I knew I'd ask some stupid question that would let her know how upset and disappointed I was about last night.

She also made no attempt at conversation. I assumed it was because there wasn't anything to say. I was almost sure she was playing a game and had gone off with Tex to make me jealous, but I certainly wasn't going let her think her little ploy was working.

So the day kind of wore away. By the time Tex and McGinnis called it quits, they both looked beat. Sharon told them to wash up and she and I would fix supper. She obviously had never tasted any of my cooking, but she knew her way around a kitchen and quickly ginned up a banquet of fried pork chops, fried potatoes, corn on the cob, and string beans. She even heated up a couple of frozen apple pies for dessert.

I was impressed and McGinnis offered to hire her for twice whatever Harlen was paying. When he said it, I watched her face. I'd kind of like to know if Harlen was paying her anything at all. But she just laughed and said that if she ever needed a job she'd look him up.

Tex didn't have a job to offer her, but he sort of figured he had something better to offer. And she wouldn't have to wait until she needed a job to take advantage of his offer. He slid into a place at the picnic table directly opposite Sharon so she could get a good look at what he had to offer, although I assumed she'd found out all she needed to know last night.

I had to admit he looked good. With his curly black hair, dark blue eyes, bronze skin, and big white teeth he could have been playing the lead in a movie. He'd even written the script.

"I understand you've got a flying school," he said to Sharon.

"That's right," she said.

"If I come out to California, could you use another instructor?"

"Maybe. I don't need a Stearman instructor."

"I'm talking about a Mustang. Gonna have one myself some

194

day."

It occurred to me that maybe that was how Harlen had roped Tex in on the deal, by dangling a P-51 in front of him the way he had with Sharon and me.

"You ever fly one?" Sharon asked.

"Hell, yes," he said. "I've flown everything from a Piper Cub to an F-fifteen,"

Behind him McGinnis pulled his lips down and shook his head.

"Well, good luck," Sharon said.

"It's been a while," Tex said. "Maybe I could use a couple'a lessons to brush up." His crooked smile looked as though he had practiced in front of a mirror. "How about it? You wanna give me some lessons?"

Sharon leaned forward across the table so that the front of her shirt gapped open. "Maybe," she said. "Can you afford me?"

Tex's smile turned into a vampire's grin when he senses virgin blood. "Maybe we can work out a swap."

"A swap? What have you got to swap?"

"Lessons. You give me lessons and I give you a few."

Her smile was sickenly provocative. "And just what can you teach me?"

I knew she was toying with him. On the other hand, maybe not.

"I could teach you to fly"

"I know how to fly."

He actually winked at her. "Without a plane"

Good Lord. How juvenile. With a faint chill of surprise, I heard myself say, "You couldn't teach a fish to swim."

Tex slowly turned his head to look at me, and I realized with a sinking feeling I had given him the chance to prove his manhood, and he expected the proof to come at the expense of mine.

"I could teach you a few things, hotshot."

I felt my body wilt. Stupid. Stupid. A fight just now was the last thing I wanted. I tried to think of some way to get out of the situation without appearing to back down. But I couldn't. Not in front of Sharon. When I saw the look of contemptuous anticipation on Tex's face, a quote flitted across my mind: 'Stupidly might get you into trouble, but it's pride that keeps you there.' The quote certainly fit this situation. If I were smart I would swallow my pride and back out ignominiously. But staring at Tex's smirking face, his eyes glaring, his lips curling with the joy of challenging me in front of Sharon, burned away what few sensibilities I had.

"Any time," I snarled.

McGinnis said, "Oh, Christ."

Tex started to get up. "How about right now?"

Sharon reached over and put her hand on his shoulder. "No. This is dumb. You'll both end up in the hospital, or worse."

The thought that flashed through my brain for about a millisecond was that she was right. It wasn't that I was afraid of Tex. During the hours I'd spent with Jack Blucher in hand to hand combat, he had taught me a dozen different ways to disable an opponent, even if he was taller and stronger. I knew I could   put Tex in the hospital. But did I really want that? And suppose he got lucky and broke some of my bones. Could I afford that just now?

From the corner of my eye, I saw Sharon's face, and her expression of disgust and fear yanked me at least partially back to reality.

I forced myself to relax, telling her, "You've got a point."

Tex straightened, his big teeth exposed in a sneer. "Chicken. I figured."

McGinnis said, "Damn it, Tex. Let it drop."

But Tex wasn't about to let it drop. He was winning. "Cut, cut, cut, cadakit," he cackled.

I should have simply turned away, let him have his stupid macho satisfaction. But my blood was still running too hot for that.

196

"Tell you what, Tex," I said, trying to control the harsh anger in my voice.. "You think you're a pretty fair pilot—"

"Better'n you, hot shot."

"Okay. Let's you and me take the two Stearmans up in the morning. Loser leaves town." I was proud of myself. My voice was steady, cool, my toes clinched in my shoes. Just like a real fighter pilot.

Tex grinned. He'd been flying those Stearmans on the thin edge of their capabilities for months. He had no way of knowing that I'd spent hours practicing acrobatics in a Stearman. "Yeah, okay," he agreed. "Loser gets carried out in a sack."

"Hey, now," McGinnis yelped. "I don't want my planes wrecked."

"If I wreck yours," I said. "You can have my Mustang."

Sharon started to say something, probably that, technically, I didn't really own my Mustang. But I raised my eyebrows and gave her a little shrug. She kind of shook her head like a mother giving up on a pair of stupid kids and didn't say anything.

McGinnis said, "What if he wrecks his? He ain't got a cryin' dime."

"I ain't gonna wreck it," Tex snapped. "You're gonna get yourself a Mustang."

McGinnis's eyes sort of drifted over to look at my Mustang sitting in front of his ramble shack hanger. The sun glistened from its sleek skin and bubble canopy. It looked incredible beautiful: fast, deadly, longing for the blue sky.

He considered the odds. He knew that Tex had to be an exceptional pilot to horse a Stearman in and out of small fields day after day without piling it up on a line of trees or decapitating himself on a power line. And all he knew about me was that I could fly a Mustang. And flying a 6,000 pound, 450 mile per hour Mustang was a far cry from flying a 150 mile per hour, highly maneuverable biplane. The experience edge seemed to be with Tex.

McGinnis nodded. "Okay. But you pay for your own gas."

Tex could hardly wait to agree," Yeah, yeah. I won't need

much."

The cold chill of doubt had begun to set in and my formerly boiling blood was now a sluggish trickle. Maybe Tex was as good as he thought he was. He had been flying a Stearman day in and day out under the most dangerous flying conditions in the world, while I'd only had two or three hours a week of flitting around the sky way up where I had plenty of room to recover if I made a mistake. Maybe Tex was right. Maybe he'd drive me into the ground in a matter of minutes.

The look on Sharon's face told me she had much the same thoughts.

That night we made a last check of our Mustangs before we went to bed. It was full dark when we finished. The moon had not yet appeared and the humid air lay heavily on the warm earth. In the darkening sky, one by one, stars began to appear, pin pricks of light in a vast, black ocean. Orion, Cassiopeia, the Big Dipper, Polaris, the incredible beauty of the Milky Way stretching from horizon to horizon until the heavens were a magnificent field of stars. You wouldn't see anything like that in Los Angeles where the carpet of man-made lights on the ground overpowered the heavenly lights in the sky.

Walking back to the mobile homes the only sounds were our muffled step in the dusty earth. Our shoulders almost touched as we walked, and I had to fight an impulse to take hold of her hand.

My hope that the beauty of the night was having the same effect on her as it did on me was shattered when she suddenly said, "I think Tex is so macho he won't even care if he kills himself."

It took me a second to realize she had been thinking about my coming aerial combat with Tex. So much for the warm, romantic night.

"I'll try to help him along."

"I'm not kidding. This might be a stupid game to you, but he wants to kill you."

"If he does, Harlen'll give him hell."

She stopped and pulled me around to face her. "Stop fooling around. This is serious. He's a damn good pilot. Probably better than you. He could do it."

198

I wished I knew whether the worry and pain in her voice was because my untimely demise would ruin our mission, or whether it was because she was only thinking of me. It came as something of a shock how much I wanted it to be the latter. It was a hopeless wish. Her actions last night with Tex proved that.

"Would it matter if he did?"

Instead of answering directly, she said, "If this is because of last night," she said, "you can forget it."

Her words brought a surge of hope. "Last night? That's your business."

"It was a stupid thing to do. I left him as soon as we were out of sight."

I wanted to be angry, but I couldn't stop smiling. "Why did you do it?"

He voice was so low I could hardly hear it. "I guess I wanted to make you jealous."

I was so overwhelmed with joy I almost failed to take advantage of my suddenly superior position. "Me? Jealous?" I said. "Now if you'd gone off with McGinnis..."

She punched my arm. "Liar. I saw your face."

I gave up easily. I couldn't play injured when I felt so good. "You owe me a sleepless night."

"I'm sorry."

It was the perfect time to take her in my arms, but I was too slow. She began walking, at the same time saying "It's only ten o'clock. You can call off this stupid fight, and we can get on with our job."

I hurried to catch up. "It's not that simple," I said. "If I could get him to call it off, I'd—"

Again she grabbed my arm and pulled me around to face her. "Don't be an idiot. He flies those Stearmans every day. You won't have a chance."

She was right, of course. And if she hadn't put it quite like that I would have swallowed my pride and backed out. But instead of making it easier, she had made it impossible.

"I can handle him," I said. "I—"

"All right," she snapped. "Go ahead. Get yourself killed."

She stomped away, her boots sending up puffs of dust.

I instantly regretted my impulsive outburst. Her words echoed ominously because she was right. Tex wouldn't simply try to humiliate me; he would try to kill me. By this time tomorrow, I could very well be dead. How would I explain that to Bremm? What I should do was swallow my pride, go to Tex's mobile and tell him the fight was off. It was a vision of his gloating face that made me hesitate. He didn't know Sharon had told me about last night, so there was no reason for me to fight him. He'd think I was backing out because I was a coward.

Walking to the mobile, alone, I knew that Tex had already shot me down with Sharon. Tomorrow he might finish the job.

CHAPTER TWENTY-FIVE

My dark mood had not lifted by the next morning when I sat in the familiar cockpit of one of the Stearmans. The two planes were supposed to be identical, but Tex knew both planes intimately. If one was more agile than the other or had a few more horsepower, Tex would know it. But McGinnis had made sure he wouldn't be able to arbitrarily pick the best by again using his coin for a coin toss.

Crop dusters worked at altitudes too low to bail out in an emergency so the pilot rarely wore a parachute. But the hell with macho. I wore one, and wished it were bigger. I was glad to see that when Tex climbed into his Stearman, he also wore a chute, which meant that he, too, harbored a few doubts.

I'd hoped that Sharon would come over and give me at least a hug for luck, but she hadn't even come out of her bedroom to join us for breakfast. In a way I was glad she hadn't. It saved me from trying to pretend I wasn't apprehensive. I was somewhat heartened by Tex's sullen silence during breakfast, leading me to believe that he wasn't confident it was going to be an easy victory. But at least he could eat, hunching over his plate and shoveling down everything put in front of him; it was all I could do to force down a piece of toast and a cup of coffee.

Even McGinnis was not his usual jovial self. "Are you two idiots sure you want to go through with this?" he said.

I pasted on a smile, thinking this might be a face-saving way out. "Well, if you think—"

Tex shot me down again, grunting, "Damn right."

McGinnis shrugged and quickly said to me, "And I get your Mustang when you wreck my Stearman."

I winced at the way he said 'when.' "That's right. As much of it as I own."

He grinned and shoved away from the table. "Okay. Let's go. I'll do the dishes later."

At least someone was happy.

I wished Sharon had come out to see us off. McGinnis had loaned me a leather helmet and goggles and I thought I looked rather jaunty sitting in the Stearman's open cockpit.

We lifted off side by side so one wouldn't have an altitude advantage over the other. The additional horsepower that had been added to the Stearman's engine for crop dusting made the plane practically jump in the air, and I had to stay on top of the controls for a few minutes until I got used to the feel of the aircraft.

Tex eased off to the right and I made a climbing turn to the left, giving full throttle to the straining engine, trying to get above him. I kept an eye on Tex off to my right and saw that he had the same idea.

Lying in bed during the night, unable to sleep I'd tried to form some kind of battle plan. The idea was to force him to land, and the only way to do that was either to damage his plane by taking a chunk out of it with my propeller, or to attain a position so close above him he'd have to lose altitude to keep my wheels or the metal spray bar from either damaging him or his plane. Either maneuver seemed next to impossible.

Maybe we'd just horse around until we ran out of gas. I wondered if it would count if he ran out of gas and had to land before I did.

I felt the first touch of alarm when I noticed Tex was climbing a little faster than I was. I tried to shove the throttle through the instrument panel, but he still out-climbed me. I couldn't help but wonder if the two Stearmans were not really twins and McGinnis had cheated on the coin toss so that Tex was flying the Stearman with a few more horsepower.

We'd reached a little over a thousand feet, and he had the altitude advantage by a couple of hundred feet when he abruptly made a sharp bank to the left, trying to dive in behind me.

If I turned left, he'd be on my tail, so I turned hard right, inside his diving turn. He tried to tighten his turn to pull in behind me, but he was going too fast and shot past me on my left. I reversed my bank and pulled in behind him. But he was at least a hundred yards ahead of me and pulling away. If I'd been armed with .50 caliber machine guns I could have blown him away. Instead, he pulled up in a steep climbing turn to the right, a maneuver he performed dozens of times a day when crop dusting. I tried to stay with him, but the speed he'd built up in his dive was too much for me and I couldn't catch him. At the peak of his climb, he made a steep bank in a diving turn that would bring him around on my tail.

I tried turning inside him again, but this time he was ready and he tightened his turn, sweeping in behind me in a pursuit curve like a Messerschmitt-109 coming in on the tail of a B-17 bomber. I dived, turned, twisted, but he clung to my tail like he was tied with a cable, his superior horsepower allowing him to slowly close the distance.

Then he was about a hundred feet behind me, and closing, with that big prop looking more like a buzz saw than a propeller. By this time we were only a couple a hundred feet above the ground, too close for me to even dive away or even use my parachute. But unless I came up with something, and fast, his prop would chew off my entire tail.

Okay. I couldn't shake him off. But I could give his prop something to chew on that would give it acute indigestion.

I eased back on the throttle, flying straight and level, allowing him to close the gap, giving him some bait. Looking back over my shoulder I could see him in his cockpit, his goggles like huge bug eyes, his big teeth bared in a predatory grimace.

Just as his propeller was about to chew up my tail like a giant weedeater, I snap rolled the agile Stearman over on its back, holding the up-side-down position, presenting him my belly. But now, instead of the Stearman's fragile vertical stabilizer to chew on, the big prop was about to break its teeth on my plane's steel tail wheel. And if it missed the tail wheel, it would be chewing on the crop dusting dispenser bar or the Stearman's big wheels.

Tex had the reflexes of a cat, and he pulled his plane up just enough to keep the prop clear of my plane's undercarriage, and hung there waiting for me to make a move.

Stearman's are not designed for prolonged upside down flight, and it was either roll back upright or lose my engine. But as soon as I was upright, I'd be chewed up by the buzz-saw propeller.

Worse, we'd worked our way over the landscape until we were almost over McGinnis's runway, and over my shoulder I saw McGinnis and Sharon outside their mobile homes watching us, their hands shading their eyes.

The runway! What was there about the runway that gave me sudden hope?

Then it hit me. Hope?! Good Lord! Unless I gained a few feet of altitude I was going to be joining the blackbirds perched on the power lines.

No, no. Don't gain altitude. Just the opposite!

Half way down the runway, I rolled the Stearman upright. Tex must have shouted with glee as he bore in, his maniacal propeller inching up on my vulnerable vertical stabilizer. And I had nowhere to go. I was only a few feet off the ground and to clear the power lines I'd have to come up, right into his killer prop!

Except I didn't come up.

The knuckles of my hand on the throttle were white with pressure, and all the horses in the radial engine were trying mightily to kick a few more rpm out of the straining pistons. I had to concentrate on the power lines, which seemed to be lunging toward me. I was sure I had to be rocketing at better than 150 mph about ten feet above the hard ground. The crows clustered on the power lines saw me coming, and they just had time to flee in terror as I shot under their perches on the lines with a couple of feet to spare.

Charging along about ten feet above and behind me, Tex was headed directly for the power lines. He had two choices: either be hung out to dry on the steel lines or go over them. He went over. Bad news for the crows. Worse news for Tex. In their desperate effort to escape from me, the entire flock, as I anticipated, had sprung upward, directly in the path of Tex's propeller. The result was mayhem. Pieces of shattered propeller, wing fabric, and fricasseed crow filled the air. I'm sure black feathers were still floating over the landscape two months later.

But not Tex.

With a shattered prop and battered wings, it took all his skill to bring the Stearman down in a corn field where he cut a swath through startled stalks of corn who avenged themselves by flailing away at Tex and his invading charger.

I eased back on the throttle and circled, coming in low. I was relieved to see Tex climb out of the cockpit, apparently unhurt. He was too busy pulling crow parts and shredded corn stalks out of his helmet and goggles to give me a salute of victory.

It wasn't the classic perfection I'd hoped for, but sometimes close enough is good enough.

When I landed gracefully and cut the engine in front of the hanger and climbed out of the cockpit, McGinnis and Sharon trotted over. McGinnis didn't look too happy, but Sharon was wiping away tears of laughter.

"Oh, my God," she said. She wrapped her arms around me, and I puckered up for a victory kiss. Instead, she said, "When I saw you heading for those power lines I was sure you were dead."

"You did that on purpose." McGinnis snapped. "You're gonna pay for that Stearman."

Sharon let go of me and turned on McGinnis. "Bull! That wasn't the deal. First one down loses. That was Tex."

I unpuckered my lips. The enchanted moment had passed-- again. "Yeah," I said. "Loser pays." Actually, I don't know if Tex ever paid for the damages to the Stearman. When Sharon and I took off in our Mustangs the next morning, he still hadn't come back.

I didn't mind. McGinnis had cheated by putting Tex in the better plane. And I was sure he would get his money from Harlen. Besides, my thoughts had no room for gloating. They would be occupied for days remembering how it had felt with Sharon's arms around me and her lithe body pressed against mine, her hair and her breath caressing my cheek and her perfume imprinting my brain with erotic images of Persian dancing girls.

The one little nagging thought that crept into my dream was that I still didn't know why Harlen wanted us to drop those tanks, nor who had killed Carmelita's brother and was trying to kill me.

CHAPTER TWENTY-SIX

The weather held and we made good time heading north-north-east over the towns and farmlands of Iowa and Illinois. Afternoon heat had piled up miles of cumulus clouds, and to my delight Sharon began flying between towering cloud valleys then climbing to scatter mist from the tops of white mountains. It's a real thrill to hedgehop from cloud top to cloud top, and when you don't quit clear a cloud, to smash into its white mass, inwardly bracing for the shattering crash, only to plunge into the diaphanous mist, your propeller ripping its way through to the crisp clear air on the far side, only to soar up to skim the top of the next towering white giant. If I were an eagle, I'd spend hours of each day up here on the edge of the blue, dancing my way from cloud to cloud, dipping and soaring through the canyons and valleys, ending with a heart-stopping dive toward the cloud-shadowed earth far below.

When we sighted Lake Erie it was time to start our descent. I waited for Sharon to nose over into a mile-long plunge to 5,000 feet. She had other ideas and the plunge turned out to be more of a gentle glide. As we descended, slowly and safely, Sharon got in touch with Detroit's airport to make sure their radar would help us keep clear of commercial aircraft during our 200 mile stretch across Lake Erie into Canada and over the huge Ontario peninsula.

Sarnia is a relatively small town at the western tip of the peninsula where it juts into Lake Huron. Sarnia is separated from the U.S. state of Michigan by the St. Clair River, which connects Lake Huron to Lake Erie.

Streaking above the forests and farms of the Ontario peninsula we called Sarnia tower and they vectored us in to the single runway of Sarnia's Chris Hadfield Airport. I considered giving the folks on the ground a thrill by making a low level flyby, but Sharon's voice on my earphones said, "You want to kill somebody? Don't even think about it."

How did she know?

But she was right. We did, however, received clearance to make a formation landing, and during our approach I saw that the parking areas on both sides of the runway were packed with planes and people there for the air show. One little mistake while showing off what a hot shot I am, and I could wipe out a couple of hundred people.

Even while concentrating on landing wing tip to wing tip with Sharon's plane, I could see that everyone had turned to watch our two warbirds land, with, I was sure, envy stark in every eye. I understood their fascination. The P-51 Mustang has to be one of the most beautiful airplanes every built. Even the deep throated sound of its big Merlin engine sends chills up the spine of anyone who loves to fly. You don't get that sound from a rotary engine. I don't think there isn't a pilot in the world who doesn't dream of one day flying one of the forever-young warbirds. It is not unusual for all flight-line work to stop, all spectators to stare, and all customers at the tent-topped shops and boutiques to halt all activity to watch warbirds take off or land, especially two P-51s landing in formation, their wings almost touching, their wheels kissing the earth at exactly the same instant (well, close to the same instant) and their pilots with their canopies open waving to the adoring crowds (actually, one idiot pilot waving to the adoring crowds).

Following tower directions we taxied off the runway. I parked next to Sharon's Mustang, sandwiched between a blue-painted, bent-winged Corvair F4U and a blunt-nosed P-47.

Running through the shut-down check I had trouble keeping my mind on the familiar procedures. Except for Mexico, I had never attended an air show and even though I knew the Sarnia show was small compared to the Ottawa International and the big ones in the States, its scope left me slightly dumbfounded. Crowds of people were milling around an amazing variety of aircraft that were haphazardly parked on a huge green meadow near the main runway. The planes ranged from homebuilt experimental aircraft to glistening new private jets and propeller aircraft. There were dozens of privately owned, meticulously restored vintage fighters and bombers going all the way back to World War I. There was even a bright red Fokker Triplane with German markings like that flown by the famous Red Baron,

Manfred von Richthofen. Next to it was a WWI Spade bearing the hat-in-a-ring squadron marking of Eddie Rickenbacker, the American ace. World War II was well represented with what seemed like dozens of vintage warbird aircraft. A British Spitfire, looking sleek and deadly, sat next to a Hawker Hurricane, which, although not as beautiful as the Spitfire, was even more deadly. Near them was an array of American warbirds: several Mustangs, a couple of powerful-looking P-47 Thunderbolts, a P-40 sporting a Flying Tiger snarl, a Navy F4B Bearcat, half a dozen A-6 'Texan' trainers, a couple of Stearman PT-17 biplanes, a Ryan monoplane trainer, even a Japanese Zero fighter,--the only one remaining that was flyable--and what seemed to be the hit of the show, a B-17G flying-fortress bomber.

Colorful tents and canopies housed book stalls, miniature restaurants, hot dog, hamburger and soft-drink stands, and ubiquitous T-shirt and aircraft-related paraphernalia concessions.

On the opposite side of the runway, temporary grandstands had been erected. Deserted now, they would be full tomorrow when the flying part of the show would take place, featuring parachute jumping, parasailing, and aerobatic flying. During the next few days there would be performances by the famous Snow Birds of the Canadian Air Force and the U.S. Air Force's Thunderbirds. Sharon and I were scheduled to perform our tank drop tomorrow at 1:00 P.M.

Before we even had time to wash up or hit the restroom after our long flight, Sharon and I were surrounded by people asking questions about our planes. They all seemed to be slightly in awe of anyone who actually flew one of the famous Mustangs. They especially clustered around Sharon, as though unable to believe a woman was capable of flying a complex machine with such a deadly reputation. Looking at the expressions of wonder and rapture in their faces, especially those of the children and teenagers, as they reverently ran their hands over the gleaming aluminum skin of the Mustang and asked questions about its flight, I began to understand how a movie star or sports hero could become addicted to such adulation. But after more than an hour of answering questions, my voice began to grow harsh with fatigue. I finally excused myself, retrieved my flight bag from the cockpit, and went to rescue Sharon. She looked grateful when I explained to her fans that we had to go for a post-flight briefing.

Walking away, she said, "Wow. I had no idea people were so crazy about Mustangs."

"Not just Mustangs. I understand air shows attract more people every year than any sport in the world."

"Really? I thought it was soccer. The world championships."

"Not from what I've read. There are more than fifty shows in the U.S. alone. People are fascinated by airplanes."

"Yeah, well, me too. If I wasn't so darn tired I'd be right out there with them. I'd love to take a look at that Spitfire."

I kind of laughed. "I know. I'd sure like to climb in that B-17 myself."

"Tell you what," she said. "We're not scheduled until 1:00 tomorrow. How about making a tour in the morning?"

"Sounds good. Even better,"--I checked my watch—"how about a nap, then dinner?"

"Dinner sounds great." The way she smiled and gave me a mischievous glance made me a little dizzy, especially as she added, "As for the nap, you're on your own."

"Thank God," I said. "I'm too tired and hungry for any serious napping."

"Oh?" Her mischievous glance turned sultry. "Which would you rather do: lie around in bed or eat?"

"Uh?" Startled, I lost a step, stumbling embarrassingly.

"That's what I thought," she said. "You men are all alike."

She walked away, but I was pretty sure she was smiling. I called after her, "Not me. I'm looking forward to dinner."

"Call me," she said without turning.

I stood there, pondering. When she said, "You men are all alike," did she mean we thought more of eating than, uh, napping? Or was it the other way around? I wondered what her answer would have been if I'd been smart enough and quick enough to choose lying around in bed.

Harlen had made arrangements for us to stay in a nearby motel that had its own shuttle bus to the airport. I'd hoped Sharon and I would be on the same bus, but she completed checking in with the air show registry and Canadian customs——who had set up a temporary desk--before I did, so I missed her.

After a hot shower I hit the sack for a two hour nap. I had always been able to awaken at any time I wanted, so I didn't bother to set the alarm. To my disgust, I overslept almost a half hour and I grabbed the phone.

The motel operator connected me to Sharon's room, and while the phone was ringing I gave my subconscious a good talking to for missing its wakeup call. I hoped I hadn't missed Sharon. With my bad luck, she was probably already having dinner with those British guys who had flown in the Spitfire and the Hurricane.

But she answered the phone. Her 'hello' sounded sleepy.

"What about it?" I asked. "You feel like dinner?"

"As apposed to what?" Funny. The drowsiness had disappeared from her voice incredibly fast.

"Lying around in bed," I suggested, and held my breath.

"Meet you in the lobby in a half hour," she answered and hung up.

I carefully placed the phone back on its cradle. 'Lying around in bed?' I was forced to reevaluate an opinion of myself. I'd kind of thought I was capable to clever repartee, but twice now she had left me floundering for a clever reply. Well, that was going to end. From now on, I was going to be ready no matter how much she surprised me.

It was a great plan. A terrific plan. During dinner at a really nice restaurant the hotel concierge had suggested, I sat on the edge of my seat, ready for a fast and clever riposte of her most startling innuendo. Except that there were none. No matter how I tried to steer the conversation in the direction of intrigue, she hauled it back to business.

I'm not sure how well my plan would have worked anyway. I was hypnotized by her mane of dark hair, her velvet eyes, and the lustrous skin of her arms and shoulders. Besides, her cocktail gown's décolletage was so low that every time she took a deep breath, I lost mine.

"They're going to put our target in front of the grandstand," she was saying. "We'll make the run from north to south..."

"Down wind?"

"There's not supposed to be much wind tomorrow."

"From what I understand, there's always wind off the lake."

"True. But only about five miles per hour tomorrow. It shouldn't be a factor."

"Those stands are pretty close to the runway. Wouldn't dropping in trail be safer than side-by-side?"

"I was thinking about that. But side-by-side will be more spectacular? We'll just have to be right on target."

"On target. Right."

"The grandstands will be on our right. You take the left side. I'll come in down the middle of the runway. That way most of the drop will be on the far side of the runway, away from the crowd. Drop on my signal."

I didn't protest. She'd proven that she was more accurate than I was, and I sure didn't want to look like a doofus in front of the crowd.

"Harlen's supposed to have those drop tanks waiting. Have you heard anything?"

"I haven't checked yet. But I'm sure they'll be here. Harlen doesn't screw up."

I hoped my face wouldn't give away my thoughts because her mention of Harlen made me wonder again how well she really knew Harlen. I also wondered why I should care. But every time she mentioned his name I got a queasy feeling. At first I had attributed the feeling to disappointment that she could be a part of Harlen's ring of dope dealers. Now I think my suspicions were mixed up with a growing jealousy. My speculations seemed to be dwelling more on her personal relationship with Harlen and less on her business dealings.

Had she known Harlen before he started going with Carmelita? If so, had she ever dated him? Was that really how she became involved with his operations? Would she go back to him if he dumped Carmelita?

"Did I hear my name mentioned?"

Harlen walked toward our booth, Carmelita at his side.

Harlen was dressed for the occasion with twill Docker pants and jodhpur boots. A pilot's leather jacket--that looked very expensive--was worn over an open-neck shirt,

As usual, Carmelita caused everyone in the restaurant to watch her passage. Her light summer minidress flowed and shimmered with her erect, striding, runway walk. The bangs of her straight dark hair highlighted her eyebrows. She carried her head slightly tilted downward so that her eyes seemed hooded, lethal, like a hawk zeroing in on its prey. One hand rested easily on Harlen's arm, the other clutched a small, beaded purse that probably cost more than Harlen's leather jacket.

I edged around in the booth to make room for them. Carmelita sat down first and slid over so close I could smell her perfume and feel her body heat. Or was it my own rising temperature? With Carmelita close by on one side and Sharon equally close on the other, my blood began to percolate all on its own.

Harlen sat down and broke out one of his famous grins. "So, all set for tomorrow?"

"If you are," Sharon answered. "What about the tanks?"

"They'll be installed in the morning. I'm having them add red dye to the water. Make a hell of a splash."

"I wouldn't want to be sitting in the front row," I said.

Harlen lost his grin. "Is that a problem? How did it go when you did it in Missouri?"

"He's joking," Sharon said. "The momentum keeps the splash pretty much straight ahead."

Carmelita said, "But you did hit the target?"

I felt Sharon tense, and she kind of glanced at me before she said, "Bulls eye."

Carmelita looked slightly disconcerted. "Bulls eye?"

It was the first time I'd seen any expression on her exotic face other than a look of imperious contempt, leading me to believe that under that hauteur there might be a real human.

"She means they hit the target," Harlen told her. He turned his attention back to Sharon. "That's great. You're going to need real precision for the next drop."

I edged a little forward. This was what I'd been waiting for: the real purpose behind the water drops. I'd never believed Harlen had us coming all this way and spending so much money just for some rather ambiguous publicity.

"Another show?" Sharon said. "Where?"

Her question surprised me. If she were part of Harlen's dope dealing, she did not seem the type to be left out of the loop and should already know—or at least have an idea--about what Harlen had in mind. Maybe she was putting on a show for me.

Harlen kind of hesitated, and Carmelita said, "If they're not ready after tomorrow, we don't have much time."

"Right," Harlen agreed.

Time? It wouldn't take much time to get ready for another air show. So if time were short, she had to be referring to something else.

Harlen looked at me for a second as though speculating about how much he should trust me. Then he reached inside his leather jacket, and I tensed ready to upend the table and run. To my relief, when his hand reappeared it held a folded paper. He cleared a place on the table and unfolded a map. There wasn't much illumination in the upscale restaurant, but I saw that it was a map of the eastern Canadian/US border area.

Harlen moved the table candle closer and in its flickering light, pointed to the Sarnia area on the tip of the Ontario peninsula. "Tomorrow after you make your drop, you make a pass to keep the air show people happy, then you head east."

"Without landing?" I said. "We don't hang around 'til the end of the show?"

"We're a little short of time. You fly straight to my lodge. Here."

He pointed to a location in Canada that looked about 100 miles north-west of Quebec. I didn't see a town or city anywhere near the indicated place.

"Lodge?" Sharon said. "In Canada?"

"Hunting lodge. That's right."

"The area looks like it's all wilderness," I said. "Where do we land?"

"I had a radio beacon and a five thousand foot runway put in. The SPC coordinates and the radio frequency are on the map. You won't have any trouble."

He folded the map and handed it to Sharon. She seemed as surprised as I was that Harlen had a hunting lodge, so obviously, she'd never been there. I was glad to see she didn't look any too thrilled when she took the map.

"Okay," she said. "Looks like we can make it on our internal tanks. I'll lay in a course."

"Stay low. Keep clear of the airports."

He didn't give a reason for his command, but I was sure he had something planned that he would prefer be kept secret. I wondered what the Canadian FAA would think when two Mustangs disappeared from their radar. They would probably think we had landed at the air show after our act. Besides, there were so many performer and flying aircraft at the show, they wouldn't miss us for days. I had to hand it to Harlen. He'd worked out a fool-proof plan: two Mustangs cleared to cross the border to appear in the air show, then three or four days later, after the show, they fly back to the U.S. carrying a couple of drop tanks that the FAA would assume were filled with fuel instead of almost two tons of dope every trip. Mexico has two or three air shows every year. Canada has around eight. We were going to be busy.

Sharon didn't ask him for an explanation. Why should she? She knew what was going on.

Harlen slid out of the booth. "We're flying out in the morning.

214

We'll be waiting for you at the lodge. Don't screw up."

I kind of wished he hadn't said that, at least not while looking at me.

"Don't worry," I assured him. "We'll be there."

I was very grateful to Carmelita when she slid out of the booth. Watching the way her hips and shoulders moved made me forget even Harlen and what he could do if I did screw up.

Carmelita must have sensed my admiration because just before she turned to follow Harlen, she smiled at me. It wasn't a big smile. Just sort of..uh..winsome. By the time I'd collected my senses and grinned back, her back was turned and the part of her I focused on hurrying to catch up with Harlen made me forget everything.

I might have been grinning the rest of my life if Sharon hadn't accidentally spilled a glass of water in my lap.

CHAPTER TWENTY-SEVEN

A little later I came out of the restaurant's men's room where I'd gone to use their paper towels to sop up as much of the water as possible. Fortunately, I was wearing dark pants so the water stain wasn't too obvious. I'd just walked around a partition that shielded the restrooms from the dining area, when I noticed a man approach the table where Sharon sat sipping a postprandial cup of coffee while studying Harlen's map. I wasn't certain why seeing the man caused me to stop unless it was because there was something oddly familiar in his movements. Also he wore a dark suit and necktie in a restaurant where no one wore a suit, let alone a necktie. He probably would walk past her on his way to another table, but for some reason, the thought jumped in my head that he meant to talk to Sharon.

I stood near the partition, partially concealed by people at other tables, and watched him stop in front of our booth. I think he said Sharon's name because she looked up at him, startled. Without waiting for an invitation, he sat down in the booth beside her.

She hastily folded the map, clutching it in her hand, edging away from the man. Judging from the look of surprise and alarm on her face she didn't know the man, and I started to move toward them.

Then he said something that caused her to stop her exit from the booth. She appeared to be surprised at what he had said, but lost her look of fear and apprehension, so I stopped and moved back.

The man, without waiting for her reply to what he'd said, stood up and walked toward the door.

His path to the restaurant door brought him near me, and I edged back out of his sight. As he passed, looking straight ahead, I was sure I'd seen him before. When it struck me, I sucked in my breath. He was now clean shaven, but I knew he was one of the two men who had killed Carmelita's brother. Or if he wasn't, he certainly looked like them. He was medium height, olive complexioned, with straight black hair, thin face, aquiline nose, heavy dark eyebrows, eyes half concealed by dropping eyelids, and with a grim mouth that looked as though it had never smiled in its life.

I was glad I stayed out of sight because, as he reached the door, the man glanced toward the restrooms as though to make sure I hadn't come out.

After he left the restaurant I returned to the booth and slid in beside Sharon, expecting her to tell me about her strange visitor. But she said nothing, sitting quietly, not even drinking her coffee, as though in shock.

"Would you like more coffee," I said to remind her I had returned.

She swiveled her eyes toward me, and sort of gasped like a person who had been holding their breath. She forced her lips into a smile and shook her head. "No, no thanks." She glanced at her wrist watch, her movement so jerky and her glance so swift I doubt that she read the time. "I have to go. Let me know my half of the check."

Clutching Harlen's map, she slid out of the booth. As she walked away I just had time to tell her, "Don't lose that map."

She gave the map a little wave to show she heard me. I watched her leave the restaurant, moving fast. Before the door closed behind her, I saw her turn right toward the restaurant's parking lot, which was odd since we had arrived in a taxi. I was certain she was going to meet the man. I hoped she knew he had a partner.

I tried to get the attention of a waiter to pay the check, but, as usual, they all had tunnel vision. I couldn't wait. I'd have to pay later.

I hurried to the door, my heart pounding with pent up anxiety. If the man had a car waiting in the parking lot they could be gone before I could get there. And I desperately wanted to keep them in sight, as much as to protect her as to find out why she didn't want me to see her talking to the man. I was almost certain it had something to do with Jorge or Harlen. But what? It had to be something Sharon didn't want me to know. Or, maybe, something the man didn't want me to know. Was he a part of Harlen's dope cartel? Had he been acting on orders from Harlen when he and his partner killed Carmelita's brother? Could he be telling her something about me? Had my cover been blown? Were they discussing a way to eliminate me the way they had eliminated Jorge? The thought gave me a chill despite the warm, humid night.

The restaurant's parking attendant stepped forward to intercept me, assuming I would be asking for a car. I brushed past him saying, "Forgot something. Be right back."

He stood looking at me as I hurried away, probably wondering why so many people where rushing toward the rear of the parking lot.

The lot was dimly illuminated by fluorescent lights on tall metal poles. Crouching between the cars and keeping to the shadows as much as possible, I searched for Sharon. There were thirty or forty cars in the lot, and if she were sitting in one of them with the man, I'd have a tough time locating them.

A sound brought me up short. A short, coughing sound. I couldn't immediately identify it, although I knew I'd heard the sound before. Then it hit me. A shot. From a gun with a silencer.

Oh, God. Sharon.

I straightened and ran toward the sound, my fear for Sharon overcoming all sense of caution.

There she was. Standing between cars near the far edge of the lot. There was no sign of the man, but there was something peculiar in the way she was standing by the driver's side of the car, partially bent over, her arms hanging. Had she been shot? Why didn't she fall? She just stood there, silently looking downward. For an instant, I thought the man might be seated in the car, and she was bending down to hear him talking. Then who had fired the shot? Her?

I slowed. Moving cautiously, I crept toward the car, trying to get close enough to hear any conversation. I managed to move close behind the car, listening, but there was no sound. The car was a new Lexis with tinted windows so I could not see inside. I was considering creeping up on the passenger side when Sharon straightened and walked toward me. Her move was so abrupt it startled me. But I wasn't nearly as surprised as she was when she almost ran into me.

I opened my mouth to say, "Hi," but before I could get one syllable out she grabbed my arm, kicked my legs from under me and slammed me to the ground.

218

My hours of training with Jack Blutcher kicked in, and I twisted away. Coming up I grabbed a handful of her hair, yanked her head back and just managed to stop my ridged knuckles from crushing her exposed throat.

I pushed her away, against the trunk of the Lexis, and moved back so she couldn't reach me. "What's going—" I stopped. Just beyond where she was regaining her balance, and despite the dim light, I could see the body of a man. He lay on his side between the parked cars, his arms and legs sprawled as though he had been unconscious before he hit the ground. His black hair glistened with what I thought was blood. He wore a black suit and while I couldn't make out his face, I was sure it was the same man I'd seen talking to Sharon in the restaurant.

Sharon straightened her clothing, her movements without a hint of panic. "Sorry," she said. "I didn't know it was you."

I stood, looking at the man, "Is he dead?"

"I think so.

Watching where I put my feet in case there was blood, I knelt beside the man and checked his wrist for a pulse. "No pulse," I said. "Who shot him?"

"I don't know. I saw him. I heard a shot. He went down. When I got here, he was like this."

I was about to straighten when I noticed that the man's right hand, partially concealed under the car, was clinched on what appeared to be a short length of rope. I didn't touch it, but looking closely I saw that each end of the rope had been tied into a knot. The rope was a garrote. The man had meant to kill someone. Was it Sharon...or me?

"I heard the shot," I said. "I--"

I was interrupted by the sound of angry voices from the restaurant entrance. The voice belong to one of the waiters who was waving his arms and shouting at the parking attendant. I knew why: he was looking for the guy who had run out on his check.

I didn't think it would be a good idea to go back and let him get a good look at us, not with a dead man hanging around. "Let's get out of here," I suggested.

Sharon didn't argue. She started to move away, then went back and bent over the body of the man. Taking care not to touch the blood on his shirt, she quickly searched his jacket pockets, then the back pockets of his pants. If she was looking for identification, it had to be because she didn't know who he was.

The waiter and the parking attendant were walking toward us, the waiter still shouting, and I pulled Sharon away. "Come on," I said in a hoarse whisper.

She started to stand up and I pulled her down into a crouch. "Keep down."

Moving fast between the cars we headed for the back of the lot. There was no fence around the lot, and we stepped out onto the narrow sidewalk of a tree-lined side street. Keeping to the deepest shadows, we moved away, half walking and half trotting.

"Head for the boulevard," I said. "Look for a bus."

"A taxi'd be faster."

"The driver might remember us. Better to take a bus."

"Okay. He voice sounded odd, hollow, as though she were on the edge of shock.

We rounded the next corner and headed for the boulevard in front of the restaurant. At the boulevard we turned away from the restaurant and walked two blocks before we stopped at a corner where there were bus signs.

While waiting for a bus, any bus, I asked, "Who was he?"

As I expected, she said, "I have no idea." She did not volunteer more information, and I assumed she was trying to decide how much to tell me. She could hardly say she had left the restaurant to take a stroll through the parking lot and came across the body.

I didn't think she'd done it. He had been shot, and although today deadly automatic pistols could be very small, I doubted that she could conceal even a small gun with a silencer in her clutch purse. And there certainly was no way she could conceal it under her dress. But if she hadn't killed him, who had? And why? I hadn't seen anyone else, which meant nothing. In the dark it would be easy to hide among the parked cars. Sharon had been near him when he fell, but she said she

220

hadn't seen anyone. Why was she even out here? If he was a stranger, what had he said inside the restaurant that was important enough for her to follow him into a dark parking lot? What was he going to tell her? Something about Harlen? Something about me? Had he already told her something about me inside the restaurant? Was there a leak in Bremm's office? Did she know I was working with the DEA?

I was burning with curiosity so I prompted her to talk by saying, "I saw him say something to you, then you followed him out."

She chewed at her lower lip while she decided how much to tell me. "He came in while you were in the restroom. All he said was: Come to the parking lot. It's important. I wasn't about to do such a stupid thing. Then he said it was about Harlen. I thought I'd better go."

"Why didn't you wait for me?"

"He was nervous. He might not wait. I thought I'd better find out what he wanted."

"But you didn't actually talk to him?"

"No. He was shot just as I got there."

I suppressed a sigh of relief. I didn't know whether to be happy because he hadn't told her anything about me, or sad because he hadn't said anything about Harlen.

"I wonder what he was going to tell you."

"Yeah," she answered. "Me too."

"You're lucky whoever shot him didn't shoot you, too."

"Yes. I wonder why."

"If you'd had time to talk to him, they might have done it."

She gave a little shiver. "I thought of that. I guess I really was lucky."

I heard the sound of approaching sirens just as a bus driver saw us waiting and pulled over. We climbed aboard, not caring where it was headed. After a few blocks we got off and located a taxi. During the ride to the hotel, I said, "They might tie us to the guy, but there's no way they can ID us."

"That's right. We might have left fingerprints on the table ware or the glasses. I hope they'll be cleared and washed by the time they think of it."

"Let's hope so," I said with no real conviction. "Harlen wouldn't like it if we messed up his plan."

The thought that crossed my mind was that Bremm wouldn't be very happy either. I considered telling her that the man looked suspiciously like one of those who had killed Jorge, but decided against it. What good would it do? And the knowledge that there might be other killers out there would just upset her.

Suddenly, I felt a disturbing koan. "Oh, oh. Your purse. We forgot your purse."

She lifted her left hand. It was holding her purse. I couldn't believe she still had a death grip on it. I should have known; a woman's purse is like another limb to her. In fact, she would probably rather lose an arm or a leg than her purse. I was certainly glad she hadn't forgotten hers. She had money to pay the taxi.

222

CHAPTER TWENTY-EIGHT

At the hotel I left Sharon outside her room, but before going to my own room, I went looking for a pay phone. In this age of digital phones, it isn't easy to find a land-line pay phone, but right now I was so paranoid I didn't trust the security of my cell phone nor the phone in my room. When I found one in a corner of the hotel's lobby. I called Bremm at his home. It would be about seven o'clock in California, and he probably wouldn't be in his office. And I sure didn't want to leave a message.

I breathed a sigh of relief when he answered. I told him about Harlen's plan for us to fly to his lodge and pick up the drop tanks there, probably loaded with dope, then fly back to the U.S. Bremm told me to keep my eyes open; there were rumors that something else was going on, but he couldn't find out what it was.

I said he may be right, and I told him in about the dead guy at the restaurant.

"I think he was one of the same guys who killed Jorge."

"Why would he be in Sarnia?"

"He had a garrote. I think he wanted to kill either Sharon or me."

"Or both."

That startled me. "Both? What for?"

"Jorge was training to fly for Harlen. So are you and Daadian."

"You think they're trying to stop Harlen by killing his pilots? Why don't they just kill him?"

"I don't know. Just a guess. Maybe it's easier to kill his pilots."

Oh, great. Talk about occupational hazards.

Bremm said, "If he didn't intend to kill Daadian, what do you think he was going to tell her?"

"I have no idea. I just hope it wasn't about me working for the DEA."

I heard him take a deep breath. "Not likely. There's no way he could have found out about that."

The way he said it made me think he was holding something back. Probably something like: "Unless you screwed up."

But I didn't think I had. I said it might be a good idea if he could find out the identity of the dead guy.

He hesitated, and I knew he was debating about how much to tell me—or the Canadian authorities. I made a calculated guess about why. "You already know who he is." He didn't answer, and I added, "What's the big secret?"

Still, he said nothing, and I gave him time to make up his mind. Finally, he cleared his throat and said, "If it was the same men who killed Jorge, we think we know who they are." He paused again.

"And..." I prompted.

"Iranians, in this country illegally. We think they were members of Savak, the Iranian secret police."

"Secret police? I thought they were closed down when the Shah was thrown out by that Mullah: Khomeini."

"About all they did was change the name. They're still active."

"But...here?" There was another long pause from Bremm before I said, "What could they possibly have to do with Harlen?"

Instead of answering the question, he said, "Keep after Daadian. It's possible she's working with them."

I sucked in my breath. What he suggested was impossible. "Then why would they want to kill her?"

"Maybe it was you they were after."

My mind refused to accept it. Sharon working for the Savak? Those brutal killers? Still, she was Iranian. An image of Mendez's body lying on the locker room floor flashed through my mind. But why

224

would Savak be interested in Harlen, in drug dealing? "I doubt it," I said. "They're the same ones who killed Jorge. She wouldn't get mixed up in that."

"She might if he wasn't Latino," Bremm said. "His real name was Hussein Abjuba Madevia. We think he was Syrian."

Thoughts of the 9/11 World Trade Center disaster flashed through my mind. "If he wasn't interested in Harlen's operation, why would he be taking flying lessons?"

"That's what we'd like to know."

Possibilities were spinning by in such a jumble I needed time to sort them out. On the other hand, maybe we were making mountains out of mole hills. "Suppose," I said, "Harlen had nothing to do with it. Maybe the Savak had a bone to pick with Jorge. I'll bet Harlen deals with a lot of pilots. He just picked the wrong one."

"So you're saying Harlen---and Daadian---are just what they seem to be: friggin' dope dealers."

It seemed like the lesser of two evils, so I answered, "That'd be my guess."

He made a sound in his throat that expressed his disbelief. "Well, keep your eyes open. I still think this is something bigger."

I didn't answer immediately. I would like to tell him I didn't want the job. He would, of course, think I was quitting because I was afraid I might end up like Jorge. I couldn't say the thought didn't give me nightmares, but the real reason I considered quitting was that I didn't want the responsibility. I didn't want the fate of the nation in my hands. So why didn't I tell him? Maybe it was because I wanted to do my part to stop the drug dealing. Maybe it was because I wanted to find out who killed Jorge and why. On the other hand, maybe I wasn't so quixotic. More likely the real reason was because I wanted the Mustang.

There was another part of the mystery that might have had a bearing on my decision to continue the deception. Well, two reasons actually: Sharon and Carmelita.

"What about Jorge's sister? Carmelita," I asked. "How is she involved?"

"She's a real piece of work. Not much on her, but for one thing, she's not his sister." His words brought a sense of shock and at the same time, a pleasant relief. Whatever Jorge's motives were, maybe Carmelita wasn't part of the deal. On the other hand...

"Why would she say she was?"

I could almost see Bremm shaking his head. "Maybe she had a thing going with him and wanted to get him in with Harlen."

"So why change his name?

"If you were in Harlen's line of work, would you want an illegal Syrian named Hussein working for you?"

"I guess not."

We both digested the information. Or rather, our lack of information.

"But then...why would she want me dead? If I was taking Jorge's place--"

Bremm interrupted: "What makes you think she wants you dead?"

"She made that call that set me up at the motel."

There was a pause, and I wondered if I'd said something that he didn't want to believe. "Are you certain it was her?" he asked.

I tried to remember her call, not so much what she'd said but how she sounded when I'd called her. Frightened. She'd certainly sounded like Carmelita. But I hadn't listened that closely. I'd been more interested in what she was saying than the quality of her voice. So it was possible, even probable, that Carmelita hadn't been involved, just like she said.

Well, that was good news.

I told that to Bremm and he said, "Keep in touch. If you find out anything, let me know."

"Right. You too."

"Yeah, will do."

He broke the connection. I was slow hanging up the phone.

There hadn't been much conviction in his voice when he promised to keep me informed about what they found out. I had the distinct impression that I was pretty much on my own. Why was that not a big surprise?

I was dead tired when I finally crawled into bed. Tired as I was, I knew I wouldn't get a wink of sleep, not with all the questions I had that demanded answers. But there were no answers. Only more questions on top of questions, questions about Harlen's operations. I couldn't believe Sharon would sell her soul for a Mustang. And what about being tied in to Jorge's murder? I refused to believe that, too. But if she had sold her soul, would she stop working for Harlen once she obtain full ownership of the P-51? Maybe she was working with the Iranian secret police. But that didn't make sense. Those guys were terrorists; what would they want with Harlen? Maybe they were dealing drugs and Harlen was muscling in on their territory.

And Carmelita. Did she really want me dead? What would be the point of that? If she had wanted Jorge kept alive to carry out Harlen's mission—whatever that was—why would she want me dead if I were filling in for him? More likely she would try to keep me alive.

And what about Hussein, also known as Jorge? What was his reason for taking pilot training? Was it simply to fly dope into the U.S. for Harlen. Bremm didn't think so. And what had been his relationship with Carmelita? And with Sharon?

My head was reeling with all the implications. One thing was certain: the best thing I could do was keep my mouth shut and my derriere covered.

CHAPTER TWENTY-NINE

I couldn't believe it when I woke up and it was morning. I had been certain I wouldn't ever get to sleep. I did, however, wake up wanting more sleep and with the taste of nightmares in my throat. I was glad I hadn't made a date to meet Sharon for breakfast. I had no desire to talk to her, or anyone else for that matter.

After a tasteless breakfast and two cups of coffee, I discovered another disturbing thing about myself: I'm not good at depression. I keep forgetting I'm depressed and catch myself smiling and chuckling for some unknown reason. Then I suddenly remember I'm supposed to be depressed and that makes me even more depressed.

The weather didn't help my dark mood. The sun was bright, painting the earth with brilliant colors, its healthful rays suffusing my body with vitamin D. Every leaf and flower in sight was working hard to saturate the air with perfume.

The air show had started and the sight and sound of cavorting aerobatic fliers, streaking the cobalt sky with generated smoke to mark their tumultuous shenanigans, brought joy to hundreds of watching people while other people milled around the planes on exhibition, with everyone wishing he or she was a pilot. On my way to the flight line, wearing my flying coveralls and carrying my helmet, it seemed that every person I passed was smiling and laughing, giving me so many cheery 'good mornings' that I eventually just had to give up on depression and started feeling pretty good.

That is until I talked to Sharon.

Our planes had been moved away from the crowds and a swarm of technicians struggled to attach 150 gallon drop tanks under the wings. Sharon stood talking to a guy wearing a baseball hat who appeared to be the crew chief. When she saw me sauntering toward them, she came to meet me. She was wearing her white, eye-popping coveralls with her long hair pulled back and secured in a French braid.

Her frosty eyes and first words—"You're late."—clued me in that the lovely day and friendly people hadn't improved her opinion of me and my ties with Harlen, although it seemed to me like the pot calling the kettle black.

"No problem," I assured her. "Plenty of time. How they coming with the drop tanks?"

"On schedule. They added red dye to the water."

"Yeah? If we miss there's gonna be a lot of screaming mad people."

"We won't miss, unless you screw up."

"Me," I said. "You're the lead bombardier. I'm just a togglier. I drop when you do."

"And don't forget it. Stay close off my left wing. We take off in formation,--"

"I know the drill," I reminded her. "We take off. Climb to two thousand. Make a low level pass. Dry run. Back to two thousand. Make the hot run. I drop on your command: ready, go! Climb out. On your command, you roll right, I roll left. Form up and head for Harlen's lodge. Simple."

"Yeah, simple," she agreed. "Like I said, don't screw up."

I reassure her with my most sincere grin. "Never fear. Just like the Red Baron."

"Don't you wish." She started to turn away, then stopped. "Anything new?"

"New?"

"About last night."

I wished she hadn't brought that up. Visions of the man's body on the ground brought back my depression. And I certainly wasn't going to tell her anything I'd learned from Bremm. "No," I said. "If they'd tied us to it, we'd know it by now."

"Unless they're still working on it."

Remembering how she had lied to me before going to meet the guy in the parking lot brought back my depression. Why did she go alone? Could the guy had been going to tell her about my being a stooge for the DEA. And who had shot him before he could talk? Whoever did might have saved my life. Had David Bremm assigned me a guardian angel? It didn't seem likely. On the one hand I doubted that he'd do so without telling me. Besides, the DEA didn't go around killing people. On the other hand, if the dead guy was really a good guy trying to warn us about something, what was it? And who had killed him?

There was also that ugly possibility that he had lured Sharon way from me to kill her, but she had killed him first.

Damn. There were too many 'whys?' and 'ifs' for me to form any reasonable opinion. I would have to live about a thousand years to get the answer to so many questions. I half expected a squad of Canadian mounted police to gallop up and haul me off in handcuffs. I could only hope that Bremm could establish a rapport with the Canadian authorities that would keep Sharon and me in the clear. By this time the Canadian police might even know who the guy was. I'd have to call Bremm again. But when? We were due to take off in a few minutes, and I still had to run through my preflight. And we wouldn't be on the ground again until we got to Harlen's lodge. I doubted that Harlen would let me use his house phone to call the DEA.

But I didn't like going into Harlen's lair blind, not knowing whether my cover had been blown, or was about to be blown. But short of simply bugging out, there was nothing I could do. I would just have to play it by ear.

I concentrated with special care during my preflight. Not only because an incident in front of the crowds of people would be embarrassing, but because if someone knew I was working with the DEA they might try to sabotage my plane.

I also examined the drop tanks. I didn't want any more surprises about their content like in Mexico. Instead of steel, the tanks were made from the same rubberized fabric we'd used on the practice drop in Missouri. I wondered where Harlen had picked them up.

I thumped each one. They felt and sounded like they were filled with liquid. I'd have to make sure the auxiliary fuel switches were off. I certainly didn't want to try running the big Merlin on water, even if it was colored red.

With Sharon handling communications to the tower, we taxied out for takeoff. We had our cockpit canopies open so we could hear the public address system as the announcer introduced us and told the crowd what to expect. I have to admit, waving to the crowd gave me quit a thrill. Being a star was something I could get used to real easy.

I was brought down from my silver cloud with a jolt when we swung our planes into position for a side-by-side take off, and before we closed our canopies, Sharon looked over at me—well, more like glared over at me—and jerked her thumbs up in a gesture that was more like a warning not to screw up than a sign of encouragement.

I heard the tower give us permission to take off, then Sharon's voice in my earphones said, "Let's go," and I turned my concentration to staying inches off her left wing as we charged down the runway. She talked us into lift off, gear up and climbing with me working hard to stay in sync.

Even though she made her turns wide and easy, staying glued to her left wing took every neuron of my concentration. I knew it looked easy from the ground, but air is never perfectly still or perfectly homogenous in density, and an airplane moving through the ether is never perfectly steady. They are constantly undulating, their speed minutely varying. When you're flying alone you tend to ignore the small variations, instinctively correcting those that require correction, but generally allowing the plane to seek its own stability. But trying to synchronize to the flight variations of another aircraft requires constant adjustments of trim tabs, throttle, stick and rudder. As our speed increased, the perturbations tended to decreased and it was easier to hold the tight formation, but even before we began our descent for the initial dry-run flyby, sweat was running from under my helmet and making my hands slippery.

It was worth the effort. When we charged the length of the runway at more than three hundred mile an hour the crowd in the stands came to their feet. I could guess how they felt. The sound of more than 3,000 horses from the combined Merlin engines, and the sight of two of the most beautiful planes ever built charging out of history would bring tears to the eyes of everyone imbued with the love of flight. Jets couldn't do it. They could be beautiful, majestic even, but they would never have the deep-throated sound nor the sheer panache of propeller-driven machines.

A large bulls eye had been painted in the center of the runway, in front of the grandstands. Sweeping over it at about fifty feet, it looked ridiculously small, and it shot past us in a fraction of a second. Even at a reduced speed, Sharon would really have to know what she was doing for us to hit it.

Then we were up and sweeping around for our hot run. "Here we go," she said. I sort of expected her to give me her mantra of "Don't screw up," but she didn't say it. I guess she was impressed by how well I was holding formation.

Sharon told the tower we were coming in and we swept in for the kill, a hundred feet higher than we'd been on the dry run, and about two hundred miles per hour slower, with me straining to catch every syllable of her voice.

Sharon split the runway, right down the center, keeping her distance from the grandstand. Perfect. "Get ready," she said. My hand on the tank release was trembling with tension. I saw the target charging toward us incredibly fast.

"Go!" I hit the lever. The Mustang lurched as the tanks fell away. I wanted to look back to see them hit, but I had to concentrate on holding formation. I knew the tanks, tumbling at more than a hundred miles per hour, would literally explode when they hit the hard tarmac, spewing huge geysers of red-dyed water high in the air. It had to be a fantastic sight.

We were only another hundred feet off the ground and about fifty miles per hour faster when Sharon gave the signal to make our rolls, and I snap-rolled left as she rolled right. She straightened, but I threw in an extra roll. It put me some distance behind her and I had to hurry to slide into formation off her wing. She looked over at me and shook her head, but I swear I caught a glimpse of a smile.

Harlen had filed our flight plan so it didn't come as a surprise to the tower when Sharon cleared out course with them and we headed northeast. The tower guy said, "Hell of a show, guys. Cheerio," so I guess we hadn't splatter too many of the crowd.

CHAPTER THIRTY

With the introduction of the Global Positioning System it's easy to navigate even when you're far enough north to screw up a magnetic compass and where there are few geographic features for visual pilotage. I eased to a position where I wouldn't have to work so hard to stay in formation, and with Sharon leading we streaked across eastern Canada at 1,000 feet and 325 mph. In less than half an hour we had left behind most of the towns and farms that dotted the Ontario peninsula and were gliding over vast green forests, dotted with small lakes and stitched with silver rivers and streams. I hoped Harlen's radio beacon was operating. Even with a GPS it would be difficult to spot a small airport buried amidst the thick forest.

A little more an hour later we switched to the radio frequency Harlen had given us and picked up the beacon. It only required a course correction of three degrees to bring us in over a paved runway that had been carved out of the forest in front of a large building that looked like a hunting lodge. Two large Quonset-type hangers were at the opposite side of the runway. The runway looked long enough to land a 747. A high-winged Beech craft was parked near one of he hangers. I assumed it was the one that had brought Harlen and Carmelita from the air show.

Harlen himself came on the radio and gave us landing instructions, although there wasn't much to give except the altimeter setting and direction of a three-mile-per hour wind. I followed Sharon in. After we landed, the runway was wide enough to make turning around easy, and we taxied back to the hangers. Two men shoved the doors open to one of the hangers and another directed us to park just outside.

Climbing out of the cockpit I looked around. Everything looked new. The tarmac on the runway had the dark color and glassy smoothness of not having to survive even one Canadian winter. The corrugated metal of the Quonset hut hangers gleamed in the afternoon sun. The peeled logs used to construct the hunting lodge that could be seen through the forest of tall fir and spruce trees, still glistened with a new coating of lacquer. The air itself smelled fresh, scented with the crisp, clean odor of evergreens as though we'd landed in the middle of a Christmas tree lot.

Sharon and I had no sooner finished our post flight check than the three men, without a word, began pushing the planes inside the hanger. The men all had the same look, with close-cropped black, curly hair, thick, black eyebrows, black five-o'clock shadows, and dark, mean looking eyes. Each one looked strong enough to have pushed the planes into the hanger by himself.

I noticed Sharon studying the men and I said, "Must be part of Harlen's dope cartel. Probably from Mexico."

She continued to study the men. "I don't think so. I'll bet they're not even Latinos." She called to the men pushing my Mustang into the hanger. "*Donde esta Señor* Harlen?"

The men didn't even bother to look at her. Without a word they continued pushing the Mustang. Sharon looked at me and raised an eyebrow.

"Doesn't mean anything," I said. "They could be Canadian Indians. Algonquin or Seminoles."

"Seminoles are from Florida."

"I knew that. I was testing you."

She hoisted her overnight bag to her shoulder. "Harlen must be in the lodge."

I picked up my bag and followed her across the runway. Her bag looked a lot lighter than mine. It was probably filled with shoes.

We weren't half way across the tarmac when we saw Harlen coming from the lodge to meet us, following a path through the forest.

We met him on the far side of the runway. He said, "How did it go?"

"No problem," Sharon said. "We dropped the tanks on target, and came straight here."

He grabbed the bag from her shoulder and led the way back

toward the lodge. "Good. You can relax here a couple of days. You'll love it."

He could be right. The lodge was massive, Swiss chalet style, with two stories. The upstairs rooms had balconies with pots of flowers on the railings just like pictures I'd seen of those in Switzerland. White smoke drifted lazily from a big stone chimney. I noticed a large swimming pool near the lodge and a tennis court back in the trees. It wouldn't have surprised me to discover an eighteen hole golf course. The place looked as though it could easily accommodate ten or fifteen guests.

On the far side of the lodge, separated by a thick stand of trees, was a long, low log building that I assumed housed the help. Although mostly obscured by trees, it looked big enough to provide lodgings for eight or ten people.

A garage near the building had doors for six cars. A big Cadillac SUV and a Ford pickup truck were parked in front. Next to them was a van with Harlen's company logo on the side.

All in all it gave the impression that Harlen expected to be around for a considerable time. He probably planned to bring dope into Canada by boat or plane from South America or Asia, fly or truck it to this staging area where Sharon or I could fly it into the States every time there was an air show. I'd have to pass this along to Bremm when I could find a safe place to use my cell phone.

We entered the lodge through a small foyer designed to trap cold weather. When we walked into the main room, I stopped to stare. The place was huge like the main room of a ski lodge. The wooden floor was strewn with large Moroccan carpets that must have cost a fortune. A huge rustic table with matching chairs occupied the center of the room. A scattering of leather-and plush-covered couches, recliners and deep arm-chairs invited any one who didn't plan to get up for a while. A curved couch faced a fireplace big enough to burn a California redwood tree, although at the moment there was only a small fire, more of a concession to décor than to the weather. A stairway made of the ubiquitous peeled logs led to a balcony across the rear of the big room. The balcony railing was draped with Native American blankets and rugs. A cozy-looking bar occupied one corner. The stools in front of the bar were upholstered with hairy animal hides. Where the hides had come from was explained by a couple of deer or elk heads with impressive antlers that decorated another wall. I suspected that a close inspection of the heads would show bullet holes where Harlen had shot them between the eyes.

A Neanderthal stirred the fire with an iron poker that, in his hands, looked like a lethal weapon. The waiters white jacket he wore was totally out of character. It was way too small. He should have been wearing the animal hides off a couple of bar stools.

"Take your stuff up stairs," Harlen said. "Take any room. The place is empty right now. When you're ready, come back here. Tell Pierre what you want to drink. He'll have it ready."

Pierre went behind the bar and looked at us expectantly. At least, that was what I assumed his look to mean. I was glad he only planned to fix us a drink.

Sharon gave a little shiver before she asked Pierre to make her a Margarita so I knew she was also impressed by his personality.

I said I'd have the same and followed Sharon up the stairs. The stairs were wide enough so I could have walked beside her, but I sort of hung back so I'd have a better view of her climbing the stairs ahead of me. When we reached the top she turned and said, "Enjoy the view."

How did she know? Her back had been to me. Even so, I didn't think my slight leer warranted quite so much sarcasm, and I defended myself with a quick witted, "I like the deer head best."

"Watch yourself," she said. "You might join him."

She was jesting, of course.

She waited for me to catch up with her, and we walked in formation along a wide, colorfully carpeted hall. There were five doors on each side and Sharon stopped at the first on the right.

"I'll take this one," she said.

Thinking the two rooms might have adjoining doors like some hotel rooms, and ever the optimist, I indicated the next door. "I'll take that one."

She was no dummy. She pointed to the last door on the

opposite side of the hall. "That's yours. Don't get lost."

She went in her room and closed the door. To show my independence I ignored the one she'd pointed out and instead went into the room directly across the hall from hers.

It was beautiful, rustic, smelling of pine. Like the walls and floor, all the furniture was made of pine. I pulled aside thick drapes from large windows and allowed the late afternoon sun to pour in. There was a balcony outside a sliding glass door, and I went out to draw in deep breaths of the crisp, pine-scented air.

As I shaved and showered in a spacious bathroom, I wondered if after two days I would have soaked up so much of the pine scent that I would smell like a Christmas tree the rest of my life. But, I reasoned, it could be worse. Harlen could have chosen a eucalyptus grove for his headquarters.

I took my time, but I was in the big room down stairs, sipping my Margarita and staring out one of the big windows, when I noticed Sharon descending the staircase. I froze, watching her, wishing I were a painter, although I didn't think she would take her clothes off even for Duchamp.

Actually, she didn't have to be nude to keep me mesmerized. Her long legs were clad in tight blue jeans that were practically molded to her buns. Unfortunately, her white, long-sleeved sweater was not tight, but it held vast promise. On her feet were white tennis shoes with light blue decorations that matched her jeans. She had unbraided her hair and it framed her face in dark curls. She moved down the stairs with the delicate grace of a ballet dancer, chin up, eyes focused on infinity, one hand resting lightly on the banister, each step making perfect contact with the riser. Even Pierre stood motionless behind the bar, staring until she reached the bottom of the stairs, and I heard him let his breath out in a deep sigh.

I got up and clumped over to meet her, but Harlen appeared out of nowhere and beat me to it. He even brought her Margarita.

He led her to the curved couch in front of the fire. I hadn't noticed but Carmelita was already seated on the couch, looking exotically woodsy in corduroy pants and a beige sweater with tailored camouflage jacket. Her hair hung over her impressive chest in two long braids.

237

Pierre came over and handed her a martini glass containing some kind of greenish liquid and a white cube that I suppose was sugar. He also brought a glass of beer for Harlen. For a man of his bulk, Pierre moved with surprising agility, and his eyes were never still, flicking from person to person and probing the shadows of the room. I'd worked with enough security personnel to know that he was a trained body guard. It seemed odd that Harlen would have a bodyguard here in this isolated wilderness, but I hadn't seen the man anywhere else.

Instead of sitting down, Harlen raised his glass. "Here's to the future. It should be very...uh...rewarding."

We sealed the toast by sipping our drinks.

Harlen moved to stand with his back to the fire. I tried to think of something to say if this turned out to be a cocktail party where everybody engaged in small talk. Somehow baseball didn't seem like the right topic for this group, and politics held too many pitfalls. Health. That was it. Everybody either had health problems of their own or knew someone who did. I didn't know if any of them would be interest in the time I had my adenoids removed, but I was willing to give it a shot.

To my relief, Harlen wasn't interested in small talk. "Unless you're really stupid, by this time you know why I've had you participate in those air shows."

I glanced at Sharon, kind of hoping I'd see a puzzled look on her face. But she just stared at Harlen, not at all surprised.

Harlen continued. "You've proved that we can use drop tanks to bring the merchandise over the borders without raising questions. The problem is that there are not many air shows in Mexico and Canada. But the U.S. has about thirty major air shows every year. That could solve our problem. You know how?"

I was trying to figure out how going from air show to air show inside the U.S. was going to benefit Harlen when Sharon said, "Register the planes in Mexico or Canada. That way we could enter the U.S. to attend every show."

My disappointment wasn't so much because she knew what Harlen had in mind, but because she had more or less proved that she

238

was a member of Harlen's cabal.

"Right," Harlen said. "Canada would be the least obvious site. I've got my eye on a P-47 and a Corsair we can also run out of here. There's no telling how many we can run eventually."

"Wouldn't they get suspicious after a while," Carmelita said.

"Not if you didn't register all of them in Mexico or Canada," I said, trying to sound like a solid member of the group. "Run some of them out of the U.S. whenever there's a Canadian or Mexican show. Keep them all registered to individuals. Change up the shows so we're not all doing the same tank dropping act."

"Good," Harlen agreed. "In a couple of years we'll all be drinking Margaritas in Rio."

"I'll drink to that," I said.

"Okay," Harlen said. "Come over here. I want to show you where you'll make your next drop."

We got up and followed him to the big table. He carried a folded map that he spread out on the table. The map featured Canada and the United States. A red line was drawn from our location to a location south and east of Chicago.

Harlen pointed to the end of the red line. "Here. Just south of Chicago. I'll give you the exact coordinates just before you leave."

Apparently Harlen didn't trust us—or anyone—enough to give the precise coordinates until the last minute. I glanced at Sharon. We both knew what would be in the tanks when we dropped them. But her face was impassive as she stared at the map. But what did I expect? A protest?

"After you make the drop, you continue on to California."

"That's a long trip without drop tanks," Sharon said. "We'll have to refuel at least twice."

"You'll have enough internal fuel to make Kansas City's Fairfax Municipal airport," Harlen said. "You spend the night there. Then Albuquerque. I'll have you set up for fuel."

I asked, "What about flight plans?"

"I'll take care of that. They'll call for a direct flight from here to Kansas City. Nobody'll notice a slight detour."

"Somebody might wonder why we left Canada with drop tanks and landed in Kansas City without them."

"I doubt it. We won't advertising you were carrying them when you left here. Nobody'll even think about it."

He was probably right. And crossing the border into the U.S. nobody would think anything about two planes supposedly flying back from the Sarnia air show with drop tanks, heading for California. A neat plan I had to admit.

"When do we leave?" Sharon asked.

"In two days. No flying tomorrow. Tonight you can party as late as you want."

The way he smiled at Sharon when he mentioned a party set my teeth on edge. It also brought a couple of scowl lines to Carmelita's lovely face. I'd be willing to bet she wouldn't be leaving any party without Harlen.

Harlen folded the map. "Any questions?"

I had one. "Your ground crew guys. They know anything about servicing Mustangs?"

"They're experienced. I pay for the best."

He probably did. Money didn't seem to be a problem in the waste disposal business.

Carmelita glanced at her wrist watch. "We have dinner at seven. A half hour."

Only a half hour until 7:00? The time surprised me. I'd forgotten that at the higher latitudes the sun stayed up longer in the summer and, conversely, set sooner in the winter. Although we weren't exactly in the 'land of the midnight sun,' at our location in Canada it probably didn't get dark at this time of the year until ten o'clock.

My guess at the time of sunset missed by about half an hour. Well, actually, the sun set right on schedule, but there was a long twilight, as though the earth remembered the short, dark days of winter and didn't want to let go of the light.

240

It was still light when we finished a really great dinner. I wasn't sure what to expect from Canadian cooks—probably a lot of French dishes with soups and sauces. Instead, there were several strange dishes I'd never seen before. I knew they weren't Mexican or Spanish. In California you learn your Mexican dishes early. I passed on a couple of dishes that offended my vision. (I didn't like to eat anything I couldn't identify.) There was a lot of lamb and beef wrapped in leaves, so I figured Harlen had a Greek cook.

During dinner Harlen concentrated on Sharon, pretty much ignoring Carmelita and me, which didn't make the two waiters happy because Carmelita took out her displeasure on them, barking suggestions, and at one point, she got up and went back to the kitchen. The strange thing was that she didn't speak to them in English or Spanish. It was a language I'd never heard before, but judging by its cadence and use of diphthongs, it could have been Greek, or Latvian, or Chinese. Whatever it was, my opinion of her went up a few notches. I'm not much of a linguist myself and I have a profound respect for anyone who could speak more than one language.

It was still light outside when we settled on the big couch in front of the fireplace, and Pierre brought us some really good Burgundy wine. Harlen sat between Carmelita and Sharon, but he talked to Sharon.

Mostly, he talked about travel. He had been to a lot of places, but he concentrated on Europe. Sharon—like me—hadn't done much traveling to foreign countries, and she seemed to be enthralled by Harlen and his stories. I noticed he gradually worked the stories around to places she said she'd like to visit sometime, and he let her know that seeing those exotic places might be one of the perks for being part of his team. In fact, he himself might even take her to Paris or Monaco or anywhere else she liked. I noticed Sharon didn't discourage the idea.

About eleven o'clock I started doing a lot of yawning and stretching my arms in subtle hints that it was beddibye time. Nobody took the hint, and although I was apprehensive about leaving Sharon with Harlen, I convinced myself that she was a big girl and could handle him.

Carmelita didn't seem to share my optimism, because when I

finally got up and said I was going to hit the sack, she moved in close to Harlen and even looped one arm around his neck. Judging by the malevolent gleam in her eyes, she wished her arm was looped around Sharon's neck.

I was half way to the stairs when I heard Sharon give a yelp, and I quickly turned, ready to whack Harlen in the back of the head. But it wasn't Harlen who'd caused Sharon to yelp. It was Pierre. Apparently, he'd spilled a drink on her.

She leaped to her feet and began brushing away whatever he'd spilled on her sweater and jeans. Harlen tried to help, all the while laying some choice words on Pierre. Carmelita made a show of helping, but her heart wasn't in it.

Pierre scurried to the bar. When he hurried back with a fist full of napkins I was sure that, for an instant, his face bore a trace of smile before it froze to its customary ugly.

I had to hide a smile of my own, especially when Sharon stormed past me and bound up the stairs two at a time, her mouth forming words I couldn't believe she could possibly know.

I heard her door slam, and I said to Harlen and Carmelita. "Well, pleasant dreams." At least, I knew that Carmelita's dreams would be pleasant. And I was pretty sure Pierre's would be ecstatic.

Climbing the stairs I thought about Pierre. No doubt he had spilled the drink on purpose. Was it because he wanted to please Carmelita, or because he hated Harlen?

Whatever his reason I was pleased with the results. Sharon had been rescued from Harlen's charisma, and I knew I would sleep better. A lot better.

CHAPER THIRTY-ONE

One of mankind's greatest joys is to awaken without unwelcome help from an alarm clock.

It was the deep throated sound of a jet engine that woke me,-- thankfully, after eight o'clock. The source of the sound was close, seemingly just outside my window. Even then the only reason I forced myself out of bed was curiosity. What was a jet doing here?

I got dressed in a hurry and without even washing my face, hurried to the flight line. The sound was being produced by a gorgeous F-86 that looked as though it had just come off the North American Aviation production line back in the 1950s. I stared at it, feeling as though I were looking at a ghost. I'd read somewhere that there was only one of the magnificent jets in existence. Obviously, someone was wrong.

The vintage jet had been pushed out of the second hanger where it sat in the brilliant morning sun, the engine throbbing, a plume of exhaust gases stabbing the chill morning air. The barrels of four .50 caliber Browning machine guns jutted from the wings making the Korean War veteran seem anxious to begin the day's hunt in Mig Alley.

One of the guys I'd seen yesterday stood by with a fire extinguisher. Another stood next to a wheeled generator.

They didn't try to stop me when I walked over and climbed a cockpit ladder to the open cockpit. A young man with a swarthy face and eyes as dark as his curly hair was studying the instrument panel. He looked up at me and smiled. Tobacco-stained teeth was the only flaw in his handsome face.

"Good morning," he said. Even in just the two words I detected a trace of accent.

"What's going on?" We had to shout to be heard over the

sound of the engine.

"Engine check," he said. "Hope we didn't wake you up."

"No problem. I didn't know there were any of these F-86's left."

"Only a couple. We're restoring this one."

"Looks like you've done a terrific job. Will it fly?"

"It will now. You should have seen it a year ago. Scrap heap."

I gestured toward the ugly barrels of the .50 calibers. "Are those real?"

He ginned. "Yes. Mr. Harlen believes in authenticity."

"This is Harlen's?"

"That's right."

It seemed like Harlen was planning on expanding his operation "I suppose he's going to show it in air shows," I said.

He nodded. "That's the plan. We've got our eye on an F-100."

"Who flies this one?"

"Usually I do."

He began engine shutdown and I watched him go through the operation without referring to a checklist. The guy knew what he was doing.

"You fly one of those Mustangs?" he asked.

"Yeah. I'd sure like to fly this some day.

"Maybe you can. Talk to Mr. Harlen."

"I'll do that."

I climbed down off the ladder. It seemed that Harlen had everything worked out. Every air show in the world would welcome even one of the rare jets. It was too bad that with his organizational skills he had elected to go over to the dark side. All his talent, all his efforts would soon be wasted by a long prison term.

When I returned to the house, Sharon was seated at the big table having breakfast. She wore the same blue jeans she'd worn last

244

night—dry now---but a with a T-shirt and a light sweater with opened buttons. She had pulled her hair back and fastened it in a long pony tail. If she wore any makeup it was so subtle I couldn't detect it. Not that she needed makeup. He face had the natural glow of good health and a positive attitude.

She said 'hi' when she saw me, but there was no happiness in her voice despite beams of sunlight dancing in through the windows and a plate of bacon and eggs in front of her. Could she be one of those morose people who saw the world as a sorry place where even a bright morning did not warrant the effort of a cheery smile?

I'd no sooner pulled up a chair to join her than one of the waiters from last night put a plate of bacon and straight-up eggs in front of me. He'd either seen me coming or was psychic.

"Coffee or milk?" he asked.

"Coffee with milk," I instructed.

"Cappuccino?"

"No, no. Just coffee with a little milk?"

"Not cream?"

"No, just milk."

The waiter headed for the kitchen, and Sharon said with a nod of her head. "What's going on out there?"

"A pilot, checking out a North American F-86."

"A Saber?"

"Yeah. Harlen's having it restored. He's also trying to pick up a Super Saber. Gonna display them at air shows."

"They have drop tanks?"

"Not yet, but I'll bet a million they will have."

She thought for a second before she said, "Maybe that's what he meant.

"What who meant?

She turned her head as though she had let something slip out and now didn't want to answer. I was pretty sure who she meant, but I wanted her to tell me. So I repeated, "What who meant?"

She touched her lips with her napkin, then said, "The man who was killed."

I leaned forward. "What did he say? Something about the drop tanks?"

She put the napkin down. The way she looked at me I could tell she didn't want to answer, but she had gone too far to back out. "All he said was...I couldn't really make it out...he had an accent...something about drop tanks."

"That was it?"

"I assumed he was going to tell me what he meant when I met him."

"In the parking lot."

"Yes. But...he never got the chance...to explain."

So I really didn't know anything more than I had before. 'Something about drop tanks' didn't tell me anything. We already knew why Harlen wanted us to carry the tanks. Still, I wondered who the man was. Maybe by this time Bremm had come up with an answer, if I ever got a chance to find out.

"You said he had an accent. Could you tell what it was?"

She make a slight grimace. "Could have been anything. Guttural. Bad diction."

"Spanish?"

"No, no. Eastern Europe maybe. He only said a few words."

"Drop tanks, huh. He probably meant to tell us about Harlen smuggling dope."

"That was my guess."

We ate in silence like a married couple who'd just begun to realize that the person they married turned out to have a few hidden flaws.

"You seen Harlen?" I asked.

She shook her head. "Not yet."

246

"He's got to have an office somewhere. He's probably on the phone working out deals to fry a few more brains."

She looked directly at me, her gaze inquisitive and at the same time disbelieving. "You don't approve?"

I realized our conversation was heading down a path that could blow my fake persona, and I quickly backtracked. "I don't have to approve or disapprove. If some people want to kill themselves that's their problem."

"All we have to do is help them."

"Yeah. Close our eyes and take the money."

"Yeah."

She got up and went up stairs, her breakfast only half eaten. The realization that when I blew the whistle on Harlen I would also be slamming a cell door on her didn't do anything for my appetite either. I went up to my room and lay on the bed staring at the ceiling, watching the shadows of trees outside the window playing tag with the morning sunlight. I heard the cheery cry of a blue jay telling the world it was a lovely day. I breathed the crisp, clean scent of pine and newly sawed wood and wondered for what seemed like the thousandth time how anyone could risk losing all this to deal in dope just so a few people could be blown out of their minds.

Maybe Harlen was a user himself. Unlikely. He'd displayed no signs of being a user. Besides, most dealers knew better than to fool around with drugs. But some did.

Maybe the few minutes of being lifted out of their sorry existence made the downward spiral worth the price. And there usually was a downward spiral. Those who started at the bottom were few. The vast majority of users started with good lives, lives full of promise, lives of accomplishment, lives of good health and good families, and still they chose to risk it all for a selfish high. Could men like Harlen be blamed for taking advantage of fools? Maybe not. But like the Peter Principle, the good had to take care of the fools, had to make sure that neither the beast called dope nor its foolish prey would spin the world out of control.

Except that it was hard to stay out of the trap. Some of the people who preyed on the fools were attractive, smart, fun to be around. Some, like Sharon, under different circumstances, you could even love. I hated to think of Sharon in a prison cell, to never again know the joy of skipping across the clouds, of playing tag with rainbows. I felt like a betrayer, knowing I were going to ruin a lot of lives. It got even worse when I realized that taking out a few dealers would hardly make a ripple in the cesspool.

I got up and went out among the trees, walking away from the lodge, trying to put what it stood for behind me. I hadn't gone far when I heard the sound of a stream, and I remembered when we'd come in for a landing yesterday I'd caught a glimpse of a stream near the lodge.

It turned out to be more river than stream, its waters looking deep and quiet, just easing by with a few swirls and eddies until their brooding silence was shattered by a series of boulders where they leaped and fell, making sounds that could either be expressing ecstasy or agony, until once more they settled into a dark, scarcely-moving serenity.

On a matt of green grass, unmoving, her arms circling her drawn up knees, Sharon sat staring at the river's dark current.

She wasn't startled when I sat beside her, almost as though she expected me. We sat for a moment, then she leaned against me, putting her head on my shoulder. I put my arm around her shoulders and we sat quietly, lost in the solace of the dark water. I tried not to wonder what thoughts were flowing through her mind? Could they be the same as mine: Wondering how I could allow myself to become a part of Harlen's company of monsters, trying to submerge the thought of herself in a prison cell? Or of me in a prison cell.

"When I was a little girl..."—her voice had the same soft flow of the river's current--"I had a gold fish. In a round bowl. I named her Goldie. I'd watch Goldie swim round and round, looking out at the world, but never able to be a part of it. I knew she was lonesome. I thought about getting another goldfish so she wouldn't be lonesome. But then I'd just have two goldfish looking out at a world they could never have. One day I went with my folks to the beach. I took Goldie with me. I carried her out in the ocean and let her go. She swam away without looking back."

Her voice stopped. After a moment I asked, "Did you ever

248

wonder what happened to her?"

"Lots. But I gave her the whole ocean. She had to be happy, don't you think?"

"Sure. That explains the huge golden whale I saw one day."

She moved back and whacked me on the shoulder. "Nut," she said.

Then she put her head back on my shoulder. It really felt good.

I don't know how long we sat there staring at the river before she said, "Do you think it's worth it?"

"What?"

"What we're doing?"

I couldn't answer her question. My reasons were not her reasons. I knew that the narcotics I'd be delivering would never reach any users, would never infect the lives of foolish men, women and children. I knew I was tightening a noose around the necks of dealers like Harlen and, yes,—her. Was it worth it? Putting Harlen and his people in prison surely was. But destroying the life of Sharon. I wasn't so sure.

So I said nothing and after a while we got up and walked back into reality.

CHAPTER THIRTY-TWO

Before we even got to the house, Carmelita came out to meet us. "Where've you been," she said. "I've been—"

It finally registered with her that Sharon and I were coming out of the woods holding hands. Her eyes narrowed and she grimaced. "Shit," she said, and I let go of Sharon's hand. Carmelita's gorgeous lips impersonated a smile. "Okay. What the hell." Her eyes hardened. "Come on. There's been a change of plan. You're leaving in an hour."

She headed for the house, moving fast. Sharon and I sort of hesitated. At least I did. It took a moment for me to make the transition from euphoria to dismay. An hour? That didn't give me much time to talk Sharon into changing her mind about this whole mission.

I certainly couldn't talk to her now. She was already heading for the house. As I hurried to catch up I noticed the hanger doors were open, and the three men were pushing one of the Mustangs out on the runaway.

In the big living room, Carmelita had the map spread out on the table. She was using a red Sharpie to draw a new course, one that arrowed almost straight southeast from our current location to a small red X she had placed on the map. It was in upper New York state in an area that seemed to be in the middle of a forest.

"Here," Carmelita said. "Chamile Chateau. Near Troy, New York. I'll give you the GPS coordinates. You're to make your drop in the courtyard. Side by side, just as you did in the air show."

"A courtyard," Sharon said. "How big?"

"Rectangular," Carmelita answered. "Only thirty meters wide but fifty long. You'll come in the long way, east to west. Drop as close to the main chateau as possible."

"That's damn small," I said. "We might hit the chateau."

The look she gave me said she did not appreciate any questioning of her orders. "Don't worry about it," she said. "It's important to drop close to the chateau. Damage can be repaired."

Sharon and I both stared at her. A couple of thousand pound wrecking balls coming through your roof could cause more than 'damage'; it would be catastrophic.

"Are you sure about this?" I said. "We could drop—"

She interrupted. "No. This is an emergency. It has to be the courtyard."

Sharon said, "Do we have to come in over buildings? How high are they?"

"Altitude is not a concern. Come in as low as you can to hit the courtyard."

"Not a concern?" Sharon's voice echoed my own skepticism. "If we're too high the damn things'll rupture. Your junk'll be all over the place."

Carmelita straightened from bending over the map, and her voice hardened. "The tanks are strong. If they burst, that's not your concern."

"Where's Harlen," I said. "I want to ask him about this."

"Harlen's working on changing your flight plans." She started to fold the map. "Go change your clothes. You don't have much time."

She was right about the time. Through one of the big windows I could see the ground crew pushing the other Mustang out of the hanger.

"Okay," I said. "But if we put a hole in their roof, I hope Harlen has a lot of insurance."

I inferred from the look she gave me that neither she or Harlen cared much about insurance. Any complaints would probably be settled with bullets. The same treatment would probably be used to settle complaints from any recalcitrant member of his team.

I grabbed Sharon's arm and got her started toward the stairs. There seemed little point in arguing, and I wanted to get away so I could call Dave Bremm. Much as I disliked risking a call with my cell phone where it might be intercepted, I'd have to take the chance. If he were going to prevent several hundred pounds of junk from getting on the street, he'd have to know the location, and soon, so he could get some of his DEA people in place before we made the drop.

I left Sharon at her door saying I'd meet her down stairs and ducked into my room. I dragged my bag out of the closet where I'd tossed it and dug down for my phone. But...it wasn't there.

I carried the bag to the bed and dumped its contents on the bed. There wasn't much besides my flight coveralls and a couple of shirts and underwear. My shaving kit was already in the bathroom. But no phone. I rummaged through the bag's side pockets. No phone.

I stood, stunned, staring at the jumble of clothing. Had I forgotten to pack it? No. I remember stowing it in the bottom of the bag. But if I hadn't forgotten it, where was it? Could it have slipped out when I carried the bag in? That didn't seem possible. The bag was closed when I brought it in. Besides, if it had fallen out, I would have heard it hit the ground.

So, there was only one explanation: someone had taken it. Apparently, Harlen didn't trust me.

But I had to make that call. I had to get my hands on a phone. And there was only one chance of that.

I went across the hall to Sharon's room and rapped softly on the door. I felt the faint vibration of her footsteps as she walked to the door. She cracked it open and one eye checked to see who it was.

She opened the door a little wider. "What is it?"

"Uh, can I..uh..borrow your phone?"

"My phone?" Apparently that was the last thing she expected to hear.

"Yeah. Mine is..uh..broken and I've got to check with my office."

I'm not sure she believed me, but she said, "Yeah, okay. Hold on a second."

She closed the door. She must have already started changing into her flight clothes when I'd knocked because when she opened the door a few seconds later she wore her flight coveralls. She went to her bag that was in a chair and unzipped one of the side pockets. She reached in and her hand came out empty. She muttered something like, "What the hell," and begin searching through other pockets. I knew it wouldn't do any good. Harlen not only didn't trust me, he didn't trust her either. The thought gave me a little jolt of pleasure. Maybe she wasn't in as deeply with Harlen as I thought.

She straightened and turned to me. "It's gone. Yours is gone too, isn't it?"

"Yeah. I guess Harlen isn't taking any chances."

"Well, neither am I. There's something damned funny here. I'm going to find Harlen."

I followed her out the door which she didn't bother to close before she strode down the hall toward the stairs.

I had to walk fast to stay with her. "Where do you think he is?"

"He's got an office downstairs. He's probably there."

We hurried down the stairs with me trying not to think about how she might know the location of Harlen's office.

There was a set of doors at the rear of the big room. Sharon pushed both sides open and led the way down a hall that appeared to be the twin of the one above it on the second floor.

"I saw him and Carmelita come in here," she said, lifting a heavy weight off my mind.

She stopped in front of a door where a small version of Harlen's company logo was painted. "This must be it."

I half expected the door to be locked, but she opened it easily and stepped inside with me close behind.

It was an office, a big one, carpeted, with a couple of large windows, the requisite four drawer filing cabinets, a leather couch, two leather arm chairs, a water cooler, a big rustic desk designed to match the lodge decor, and a big directors chair behind the desk with Harlen sitting in it. I should say 'slumped' in it. Someone had hit him in the temple with a blunt weapon that had caved in the side of his head. It was obvious he was dead.

The death blow had come as a surprise. His right hand still clutched a newspaper. His left hand was resting on a desk phone as though he'd been reaching for it when he was struck.

"The killer was left handed," Sharon said.

Her voice snapped me out of my shock. She was standing beside Harlen's body, studying hin without a trace of revulsion or fear.

"What makes you think so," I said. Or I should say, I whispered. There was something about being in the presents of the dead that made me want to keep my voice unobtrusive.

"The killer stood behind him. He was hit on the left temple with a lot of force. Probably with a hammer. Whoever did it was strong."

A picture flashed through my mind of Pierre mixing and serving cocktails. "Pierre is left handed."

"Why doesn't that surprise me."

Something in the newspaper caught her attention and she gently pulled it free of Harlen's grasp.

"Should you be doing that?" I asked. "You're not supposed to touch anything."

As I expected, she ignored my advice. "He was reading this." She pointed to an article with the title "SECRET MIDDLE EAST CONFERENCE."

She held the paper up to light from the window, muttering as she read. "Israel...Saudi Arabia...Syria... Palestine... the U.S. All the envoys are meeting in upstate New York."

"Don't tell me," I said. "Chamile Chateau."

Sharon clinched the paper. "I knew it!" She glanced up. "Did you ever hear her speak Spanish?"

"Carmelita? A little. But now that you mention it, it didn't sound fluid. Like a native. I just thought it was because she was second generation."

"Last night at dinner. All those Middle Eastern dishes. She knew the names of all of them."

"So what is she?"

"Persian." The voice came from the open doorway. I knew before I even turned my head she would have a gun. I was right. Carmelita stood just inside the door. The gun in her hand looked like a 9mm Glock, fitted with a silencer. As though the gun wasn't terrifying enough, Pierre stood behind her, filling the doorway.

"Persian," I said. "That's Iran."

She motioned with the gun. "Move. Away from the desk."

Before we moved away, Sharon edged behind me and, using my body as a shield, dropped the newspaper on the desk. She wanted to make it appear that we hadn't seen it.

Apparently, it didn't matter whether we'd seen it or not. Carmelita nodded to Pierre. "Tie them."

Pierre had come prepared. He had a roll of duct tape and he moved behind us. I considered trying to take him out. I was pretty sure I could do it, but while I was causing him considerable pain, Carmelita would be putting holes in me.

Sharon read my body language and said, "No. They don't want to kill us."

Carmelita pointed the gun at Sharon's head, "Don't count on it."

It was too late anyway. Pierre had already yanked my arms behind my back and wrapped my wrists with duct tape.

He ripped the tape and did the same with Sharon's hands. Then he shoved us to the floor and went to work on our legs.

"What's the point of this?" Sharon said. "You taking over Harlen's operation?"

"Yeah," I said. "We're ready to go. We don't care who we work for."

"Apparently not," Carmelita said. I hadn't noticed before but she carried two cell phones in her left hand. One of them looked like mine. I winced when she dropped them on the desk. She turned her piercing eyes on Sharon. "How is it your phone lists a number for the FBI?"

Sharon simply stared at Carmelita, her mouth a grime line, but I felt such a surge of adrenaline I jerked around to face her. So that was why she was working with Harlen. She wasn't a dope dealer or working for the Iranians. She had to be doing the same thing for the FBI that I was for the DEA.

She must have taken my silly expression for condemnation because she refused to meet my eyes.

I knew how she must feel. She had been torn up about doing her job, which she thought would condemning me to a long term in prison. And now it might cause both of us to end up like Harlen.

I wanted to tell her it was okay, that I understood, but Carmelita didn't give me the chance.

"It doesn't matter," she said. "We don't need you

Whatever she meant by that, it couldn't be good. For some reason I focused on the gun and its silencer, and something that had been gnawing at my mind suddenly made sense. I said, "It was you. You killed him."

Carmelita just stared at me, her eyes hard as though she were rethinking her decision not to kill me. It was Sharon who said, "Who? Jorge?"

"No. That guy in the parking lot."

"Traitor," Carmelita said. "He deserved to die."

"Traitor?" I said. "Traitor of what?"

Carmalita's lips curled in a sneer of disdain. "I saved your lives. He would have killed you."

"Like he killed Jorge?" Sharon said.

Carmalita's laugh was more chilling than her growl. "The fools. They thought killing the pilots would end it."

"It is ended," I said. "I quit. We quit."

She jerked her chin at Pierre. "Come. We don't have much

time."

They left, closing the door.

We were lying on the floor, trussed like mummies, but I had never been so happy in my life. "FBI," I chortled "Why didn't you tell me?"

"I'm not FBI," she snapped. "I don't know what she's talking about."

"Maybe not, but you're working for them. That's why you're into this. I knew it had to be something."

"If we don't get out of here, it won't make any difference who's working for who."

"Whom."

"Stop clowning around. Turn over."

"Why?"

"Do it. We don't have much time."

I was lying on my back. I didn't know what she had in mind, but I turned over. She began tearing at the duct tape on my wrists with her teeth.

"No hurry," I said. "Without us to fly the Mustangs, their operation is busted. They're probably pulling out right now."

As though in answer to my speculation, I heard one of the Mustangs' engine start.

"Hey," I said. "They can't pull this off without us."

"They've got pilots. All they need are our stupid American bodies."

It fell into place like a Chinese puzzle. Why hadn't I seen it sooner? They wanted to kill the conference delegates. After we dropped the tanks—which we were supposed to think were full of dope, but which were probably bombs--on the chateau, we'd be arrested and the entire plot blamed on the Americans.

But now? They could still pull it off. Their pilots would drop the bombs, then bail out at some designated location. Our nice, fresh bodies would be put in our wrecked planes, which would probably be set on fire to hide the fact that we were murdered. Finding the American planes and our bodies would pin the blame for the assassinations of the delegates on the U.S. It wouldn't be as neat as their first plan, but it could work.

"What about Harlen? You think he was in on it?"

"I doubt...it." She tugged hard at the tape and I heard it rip. "He thought...he had a good...deal for bringing...in drugs."

"I'll bet that was Carmelita's idea. Set him up"

"Wouldn't...be sur...prised."

I heard the second Mustang engine start.

"Hurry up," I said. "We've got to stop them."

She spit out a mouthful of tape. "This stuff tastes like shit. Try your hands."

I strained against the tape, my muscles creaking. There was a tearing sound and I was free. I turned and started tearing at the tape on her wrists.

"There are too many of them," she said. "We've got to get the Mustangs."

"We can call the Mounted Police, the FAA. They'll shoot them down before they get to the border."

"You know those drop tanks are bombs."

"I kind of figured that."

"They planed to assassinate those delegates."

"And blame us. Right."

I had my feet loose and I went for the cell phones Carmelita had left on the desk. Both phones had been smashed. I reached across the desk and picked up Harlen's desk phone. Dead. I was sure every phone in the building had been sabotaged.

Sharon almost had her legs free. "You help me on this," she said. "I'll put in a good word for you. You can turn state's evidence."

She still thought I was part of Harlen's dope cartel. But I didn't

258

have time to explain my connection with Bremm and the DEA. I was not sure I wanted to. Not yet. It felt kind of nice to have her worry about me.

"Okay," I said. "One other promise or I won't testify."

"What's that?"

"You've got to spend a weekend with me in Newport."

She stopped working on the tape and stared at me. "No way."

"Okay," I said. "We can always replace a few diplomats."

She made a sound of disgust deep in her throat. "What the hell. We'll probably be dead anyway. Okay."

I was pleasantly surprised at how easily she'd given in. Maybe I could have talked her into the weekend without having to be some kind of hero. On the other hand if I told her I was working for the DEA and would be testifying anyway, she might withdraw her offer. Judging by the set of her jaw as she tore away the last of the tape from her legs, I decided to keep my mouth shut.

She was right about one thing: if we decided to be heroes and try to stop these guys, we stood a good chance of being dead in the next few minutes.

The smart thing for us to do was escape in the surrounding woods. Maybe we could find a town or a house where we could us a phone.

The decision was taken out of my hands when Sharon got to her feet and moved to the door.

"Come on. We've got to hurry."

I was a step behind when we ran down the hall toward the big room. "I've been thinking," I said. "Why don't we head for the woods. Try to find a phone. We could call the FBI—"

She stopped, whirled to face me. "They'll be taking off in a minute. You in this or not?"

If only she'd been a man. I could have told her to forget it. But the way she stood, like a female warrior in a video game, her hair a dark cloud, her eyes blazing, her fists clinched and her chest heaving, it would have taken more courage to back down than to go to my grave, so I said, "What have you got in mind?"

She turned and hurried into the big room, talking as she moved. "We've got to find the pilots. Take them out."

"They're probably already in the planes. We can't—"

"Maybe they're not. They've been warming up longer than a pilot would do it. I think—"

She didn't get a chance to finish her thought. We were half way across the big room when the door opened and Pierre's huge body blocked out the light. He didn't notice us immediately, giving us time to run.

I was already moving fast when Sharon dashed to the big fireplace and snatched up the iron poker. Pierre caught the movement, and took a step into the room, his eyes wide with surprise.

The surprise didn't last long. Sharon charged him, the heavy poker poised for a blow. Instead of retreating, Pierre moved to meet her, moving with the speed and grace of a trained fighter. Sharon swung the poker at his head, and he raised a massive arm to block the blow. But Sharon's move had only been a feint, and she finished the swing with a backhanded slash at his legs. The heavy poker caught him in the thigh, and he grunted. But it didn't stop him. He caught Sharon before she could bring the poker up for another blow and wrapped his arms around her, lifting her off her feet in a crushing grip.

I knew it would be futile to hit him even in his vulnerable kidneys; it would be like pounding a grizzly bear. If we were going to have any chance at all I had to disable him, so I smashed the back of his right knee with a hard karate kick.

There was a 'crack' as the tendons in the knee ruptured. He screamed in pain, and toppled, hitting the wooden floor like a fallen Sequoia. But he kept his crushing grip on Sharon. In a spasm of rage and pain, his grip tightened and her mouth opened in a silent gasp of agony.

Where should I attack? Where was he vulnerable? His body? You can't stop the crushing grip of a python by attacking its body. The head. The vulnerable head.

I reached around and sunk my fingers in his eyes.

It worked.

He let go of Sharon, gripping my hands, wrenching them away from his eyes.

He came up on his good knee, gripping my hands, blinking and shaking his head, trying to see.

He didn't need to see. His grip paralyzed my hands, pain shooting up my arms, exploding in my brain.

No room to kick.

I brought my knee up, smashing his chin, tilting his head.

I butted him, hard.

I felt his nose shatter, and my hands were free.

He fell, writhing in pain, gasping for breath, hands press to his bloody nose.

I grabbed Sharon by one arm, winching at the pain in my bruised hand. "Come on. Hurry."

We staggered out the door, across the wide porch and down the steps with me half dragging Sharon, her with an arm around my neck and me with an arm her waist. Through the trees and across the runway, I could see men attaching drop tanks under the wings of the idling Mustangs. They were working fast. They had to; the engines would overheat if left idling too long, and they had to get the planes in the air soon if they were going to make it to that chateau before dark.

But where were the pilots? No one was in the cockpits. Which meant they were either changing their clothes or being briefed, probably by Carmelita. Either way they would be in the hanger.

"Can you walk?" I asked Sharon.

She pushed away from me, drew in a deep breath that caused her to wince with pain. "Yes," she said. "I'll make it."

"Good. We've got to find those pilots."

We started along the path toward the runway. I still helped

support Sharon with one arm under hers. At the edge of the runway, I pulled us to a stop.

"Hold it."

"Why? We've got to—"

"They'll see us. What we need..." My desperate glance fell upon the cars parked outside the garage. "The cars. They won't pay any attention to a car."

"Yeah."

Moving at a limping run, concealed by the trees, we headed for the garage. I left Sharon leaning against the Cadillac while I checked for keys in a dash. I found them in the Ford pickup. "Here," I called. Without waiting for her, I climbed in and started the engine. She opened the passenger door and dragged herself inside.

I backed up, then straightened and raced toward the road away from the hanger. When we were out of sight of the hanger at the end of the runway, I turned and headed back on the other side, trying to stay out of sight. I came up behind the hanger and pulled in around the side.

I stopped next to the hanger's side door, jumped out and ran to help Sharon, but she was already out of the truck. She was holding her side, her face white, but she was standing straighter.

She led the way to the door where she paused. "The pilots might not know who we are, but if Carmelita is there... What'll we do. She's got that gun."

I tried to picture the interior of the hanger. The big doors were open, so there would be plenty of light. If Carmelita was in the process of giving a last minute briefing to the pilots or if they were watching the crews at work on the Mustangs, they might be standing just inside the doors. Their backs would be to us. If we could get close enough, I should be able to take them out.

"They should be at the front of the hanger," I said. "There's equipment next to the wall. Keep close to me."

I eased the door open, ready to duck back.

Nothing happened.

I slipped inside, followed by Sharon, and pulled the door shut, praying it wouldn't squeak.

I paused, waiting for my eyes to adjust to the gloom. I'd been right. Carmelita and two men wearing flight coveralls and carrying helmets were just inside the open hanger doors watching the ground crews working on the Mustangs. One of the pilots was the young fellow I'd seen in the cockpit of the F-86. Carmelita was doing all the talking. I didn't see the gun.

Hugging the curved side of the hanger, I edged toward the front, followed by Sharon. Most of the equipment in the hanger was parked near the wall and we were able to stay fairly well concealed until we were behind the last piece of equipment: a dolly containing welding tanks of oxygen and acetylene near the open door only a few feet from Carmelita and the two pilots.

Carmelita was telling them that after they made the drop and bailed out at the designated place, to wait for her. It would take her about four hours to drive there with the Americans.

I knew which Americans she meant: us.

Our bodies, wearing flight suits, would be placed in the cockpits unless the planes burned when they crashed. Then they would make it look as though we'd been thrown clear. That's why we hadn't been killed. Modern forensics could tell precisely when a person died.

But now, if she had the gun on her, I didn't think she would hesitate.

I picked up a foot-long wrench used to change the welding tank valves and whispered to Sharon. "Wait here."

I took her silence for accent, and leaving the concealment of the tanks, I crept toward the three. Still no sign of the gun.

They were watching the ground crew when I whacked the first pilot in the head with the wrench. At the sound of the blow and the man's grunt of exploding breath, the F-86 pilot spun with the speed and grace of a ballet dancer. Too late. His hands were coming up in defense when I clubbed him in the side of the head and he grunted and collapsed.

I turned toward Carmelita, expecting to hear the sound of a

shot. She was gone, the sound of her heels pounding toward the back of the hanger where she probably had the Glock.

I plunged after her, knowing I was already too late.

But Sharon wasn't. She lunged from behind the tank and slammed into Carmelita. Both crashed to the floor with Carmelita on the bottom. Her head banged against the concrete with a sickening thud. Her momentum rolled her over on her back where she lay, her beautiful eyes staring at nothing.

I helped Sharon to her feet. "You okay."

"Are you crazy," she said. "I hurt in every bone in my body."

"Can you fly?"

"Fly?"

"We've got to get the Mustangs out of here, before somebody gets another bright idea."

"Yeah, right. We'll need their clothes."

She limped to the downed pilots and began stripping off the coveralls of the smallest one. I did the same with the other.

She jerked her chin toward the Mustangs on the flight line. "Better hurry."

I looked up. The ground crews had finished loading the drop tanks on the planes and were walking toward the hanger.

Helping each other, Sharon and I struggled into the flight coveralls. She bunched her hair up and held it while I helped her pull on one of the helmets. I put on the other and we walked out toward the ground crew.

"Walk like a man," I whispered. "Longer steps."

She increased her stride, her hips swinging.

I said, "Oh, God," and crossed my fingers.

As we walked passed the crew, one of them said something in what I assumed to be Farsi and Sharon growled an answer. I lifted a hand in salute, and they kept on walking.

Once past them we picked up our pace and were practically

running when we reached our planes. Parachutes had been placed on the wing of the planes, and we struggled into them expecting every second to see the crewmen bolt out of the hanger.

I only needed a second to check one of the drop tanks. It was made of heavy steel with no seams except around the nose. I had no doubt that it was packed with explosives.

I climbed in and pulled the canopy closed. Releasing the brakes, I eased the throttle and began taxiing toward the end of the runway, fastening my shoulder straps as I went. With the heavy tanks, we would need every inch of runway.

I swung around, lining up on the runway. Sharon was right beside me. I looked over at her and gave her a thumbs up. She replied in kind, and without any checks we set the trim tabs and opened the throttles. I had to fight to keep from jamming mine to the wall, remembering what would happen if I did. Still, I pushed it to the limit, trying by sheer will to make the speed climb.

When we roared by the hanger, out of the corner of my eye I saw Carmelita standing outside the door, the Glock in her hand, firing.

I didn't have time to worry about being hit. The end of the runway was streaking toward me and my speed was increasing terribly slow. I took my eyes off the indicator to watch the onrushing end of the runway. I shoved the throttle farther, and I felt the left wing trying to come down. More tab. I cranked in another couple of degrees and the wing steadied. I felt the Mustang lighten. I was sure the wheels were off the ground and I hit the retraction lever. For an instant the Mustang seemed to settle back and I gritted my teeth, waiting for the deadly sound of the prop shattering on the hard tarmac. Then the wheels thunked into place and the Mustang seemed to breathe a sigh of relief as it surged ahead, clawing for altitude.

Somehow Sharon had edged ahead of me, and I followed her up, up in a shallow climb, hanging off her left wing. At 1000 feet we made a slow turn to the right and as we came around, passing back toward the runway. I found that I was breathing in short gasps, sweat making my clothing sticky, and I forced myself to relax, sucking in air. We were safe, heading for the wild blue. The radio crackled and I heard Sharon say, "Oh, my God. Look at that."

She had to be referring to the runway, visible to our right. I couldn't understand the note of panic in her voice. We were way out of range of anything short of a .50 caliber...

Then I saw the reason for her fear and my own chest tightened, by breath sucking air. The F-86 jet fighter. The ground crew had pushed it out of the hanger and the young pilot struggled to pull on a pair of pants as he ran toward the jet. Even from more than a 1000 feet in altitude and a distance of almost a quarter of a mile, the jet fighter's machine guns, looked ugly, deadly. I was sure they were loaded. If they weren't why would they send the fighter after us? And if they got it airborne, we were dead ducks. Two unarmed Mustangs wouldn't have a chance. There were no canyons to duck into the way we had with the F-16 in Mexico. We might be able to avoid him for a while, but eventually he would get one of us, then turn on the other.

"Drop the tanks," Sharon yelled. "Make a run—"

"No," I snapped, cutting her off. "We've got to stop him before he gets in the air."

"Oh, sure. How?"

"They said these tanks are full of dope. Let's give it back to them."

"Gotcha!" She said. "Follow me, just like at Sarnia."

Her wing came up in a steep turn, circling back so we could run down the length of the runway, coming up behind the jet.

When we straightened to begin our run I saw that the jet was already moving down the runway, flame spurting from its tailpipe. Could we catch it before it lifted off?

"Light the fire," I said, and jammed the throttle to full military power. The Mustang tried to roll and I fought it level, passing Sharon, picking up speed in a shallow dive, gaining, gaining on the jet."

"Not too low," Sharon yelped. "We don't want to kill ourselves."

I scarcely heard her. My attention was focused on the jet, willing my plane to catch it. Then I was over it and my instincts took cover. I hit the jettison handle and felt the plane lurch as the tanks fell away.

266

I heard them hit with a dull 'whoomp' and the Mustang rocked from a concussion wave. When we swung back around for a look, it appeared that one tank had hit in front of the jet and it had run into the explosion and was now a twisted pile of wreckage. One of the tanks had exploded just in front of the hanger where Carmelita had been firing. Another had made a direct hit on the hanger. I saw pieces of what could have been Carmelita's dress scattered across the ground. The last tank must have bounced before it exploded, sailing off the hard tarmac, making a direct hit on the lodge that was now a pile of burning timbers Poor Pierre.

"What now?" Sharon said.

I pulled up beside her, and showed her a big grin. "First Kansas City," I said, "where Harlen was kind enough to arrange refueling. Then Albuquerque and Newport Beach. Don't forget your promise."

There was a brief silence, and I thought she was going to tell me the promise had been made under duress, and I could put it where the sun didn't shine."

Instead she said, "Maybe they'll throw you in prison, and I won't have to go through with it."

For a second I thought about telling her I had a deal with the DEA like the one she'd made with the FBI. But then she might see no reason to keep her promise. I decided to hold on to my secret for another few days, at least until after the weekend. Then if she killed me, I wouldn't care.

"Maybe they won't," I said. "I feel lucky."

"So do I," she said, "California here we come." Leaving me to wonder what she meant.

She made a slow roll and headed west, toward California. I didn't bother to slow roll. I planned on keeping an eye on her all the way. Maybe she would kill me, but it would be my way...and take a long time.

The End.

ABOUT THE AUTHOR

ROBERT L. HECKER was born in Utah but grew up in Long Beach, CA. He is married with two grown children.

Graduated from the Pasadena Playhouse School of Theater and the Westlake College of Music. Later matriculated at UCLA.

In WWII he was a bombardier and a pilot with the Air Corp.

His writing career began with radio and TV dramas. Then he moved on to writing and producing documentary, educational and marketing films on subjects ranging from the education of Eskimos and Native Americans to astronaut training and nuclear physics.

His first novel, "Rush To Glory," took first place in its category in the Dream Realm Awards. His second, "Whispers In The Night" was an EPPIE finalist and "The Angelic Prophecy," was a Dream Realm Award finalist. His latest novel the mystery/thriller "Murder By Proxy," took first place at the prestigious EPPIEcon.

In addition to writing novels, he is a playwright with several award winning plays produced.

Robert is also a composer, with songs in country, gospel and big-band albums.

He is a member of Mensa, the Writers Guild of America, the Mystery Writers of America, and the Dramatists Guild.

268

Breinigsville, PA USA
24 February 2011
256225BV00002B/4/P